To Julia,
With Much ♡ ♡

A PICTURE OF PRETENSE

If given a chance—
kiss the dolphin !

CHRISTINE NOYES

A PICTURE
OF PRETENSE

a novel

Haley's

Athol, Massachusetts

Haley's
488 South Main Street
Athol, MA 01331
haley.antique@verizon.net • 978.249.9400

Copy edited by Mary-Ann DeVita Palmieri.

Proof read by Richard Bruno.

Cover designed by Amber Robidoux of Doux Wild
douxwild.com

Cover photo by Studio Barcelona.

International Standard Book Numbes
trade paperback, 978-1-948380-42-3
ebook, 978-1-948380-44-7

Library of Congress Cataloging-in-Publication Data pending

For Al,

always . . .

you continue to inspire me every day

CONTENTS

PROLOGUE

FLORIDA

The police siren screamed as the adrenaline-charged officer ran from his vehicle toward the wreckage. A pickup truck embedded itself in the backseat of the sedan. *If there had been any passengers back there*, the officer thought, *they did not survive.* The smell of gasoline permeated the scene.

He caught movement in the passenger seat of the car. Glass had blown onto the street, and the jammed car door would not budge. A blood-soaked man wearing a business suit sat crushed against the door. The unresponsive driver lay in his lap. The officer leaned in to hear what the man tried to say, his voice drowned by the blare of the siren. In obvious pain, the passenger labored to hand him a plain white business card inscribed with the name *James Harrison* and a phone number.

In his last moments of consciousness, the man moaned, "Tell Harrison he will have to make other plans," and passed out.

ARRIVAL

HOLLY

Port Charles bustled as the young woman approached the gangway of the cruise ship *Perth*. Wispy clouds gave way to sun on that mid-May afternoon, and it promised to be smooth sailing.

Ready for an adventure and the opportunity to try out her new personality, she advanced with fresh confidence. She promised herself she would be outgoing, optimistic, and fun. No more worrying about what people thought of her. Nobody here knew her. She deliberated on the improbability that she would ever see any of them after the cruise. The vacation would provide just the kind of anonymity she needed to practice self-assuredness.

Her newfound confidence lasted almost to the top of the nonskid gangway when the carry-on bag she toted slipped out of her hand and its contents rolled down the ramp, unintentionally kicked along by the people in line behind. Weaving between oncoming passengers and making apologies, she scurried down the plank to catch up with her belongings. She slipped on her tube of toothpaste and hit the deck. In that moment, the minty cream oozing onto her buttocks, she realized everyone had stopped moving and focused attention on her, a familiar occurrence conjured up from the worst of her dreams. Her dad ran after her as he picked up her personal items along the way. He reached out his hand to help her up and looked at her with the endearing smile the women in their neighborhood could not resist.

"Just a minor setback, Holly. Nothing to dwell over."

Easy for him to say, she thought. *He doesn't have to walk the rest of the way to their cabin with a Colgate-covered ass.*

CATE

The line had stopped moving, and her arms began to shake. She was not sure how much longer she could hold on to her bags. Her polarized black tortoise Ray-Bans shielded her from the blinding sunbeams bouncing off the fresh white paint of the floating city she waited to board.

"What was I thinking?" she murmured.

Seven days on a cruise ship did not require fifteen days of clothes. *But you never know what you might need*, she rationalized. Besides, she hated packing. She found it far easier to take everything than to make a decision. Her sister would give her hell when she saw her suitcases. *Maybe I can get to the room before her and hide the bags somewhere, like in someone else's room.* Not a chance. She knew her sister would already be in the cabin, unpacked, and looking impeccable, as she always did. She nicknamed her sister Sheila *TP*, as in Triple P, because Sheila portrayed herself as pleasant, prompt, and put together, which annoyed the hell out of Cate. She also prided herself on the double entendre comparison to bathroom tissue. People assumed Sheila was the older sister, but that was not the case.

Everyone called her Late Cate, the nickname she received at eleven years old because of her persistent tardiness for school. Even her teachers used the slight, although not to her face. They never understood how hard she tried to be prompt. She even set her alarm an hour earlier than her sister's. But something always happened to hold her back, usually having to do with making a decision.

The nickname suited her, even at age twenty-seven.

SHEILA

Should I tell her, Sheila worried as she sat on the lower bunk of the cramped room. She contemplated the pros and cons.

Con: Cate loves David, and it would devastate her and ruin her vacation.

Pro: Sheila would be free to openly enjoy some male companionship, without having to hide from her sister.

Con: Cate would try to talk her out of it.

Pro: She didn't care. She and David were through. They just weren't meant to be.

I will tell her as soon as she is settled in. Well, maybe I will wait until they got to a bar. If other people were around, she reasoned,

Cate wouldn't make a scene like she always does when it came to Sheila's husbands.

It's not that Sheila treated men poorly. Her marriages failed for any number of reasons, but only she understood them. At eighteen, she married her first husband, Scott, the stockbroker, who took her to the best restaurants and clubs and doted on her every move until their divorce two years later. When she turned twenty-one, she married Marc, CEO of a major corporation who took her on glamorous vacations and attended balls and banquets at the homes of the area's richest citizens. And then David, her husband of two years, son of wealthy parents who dabbled in the entertainment business as a producer of Hollywood movies. All of them handsome and all treated her like a princess. But she remained unhappy, and she could no longer pretend otherwise. She was not getting any younger. In two days, she would celebrate her twenty-sixth birthday.

HOLLY

After recovering the contents of her bag, Holly and her dad, Mike, walked back up the gangway and onto the teak parquet floor of the main deck. A bellman pointed them in the direction of the elevators where passengers gathered. Mike pushed the up button to signal one of the lifts.

Holly glanced at her father and said, "Dad, our room is below deck. We need to go down, not up."

Mike flashed her the grin and did not say a word. He stepped into the elevator, and Holly followed. The elevator quickly filled, and before the doors closed, every lettered button on its wall glowed bright green.

The cramped space exposed the minty fresh fragrance of Holly's backside. Though no one commented on the unexpected odor, she noticed some puzzled faces.

The elevator stopped on the next deck, letter U for Upper Deck, and Holly prepared to step out onto the light blue short-nap carpet but waited for her Dad's cue, likely a slight nod of the head almost imperceptible to others. They had cultivated a silent language over the twenty-four years of her life. He was up to something, she could tell. But he had practiced keeping things to himself when he wanted to, which didn't happen often.

They did not keep secrets from one another, not meaningful ones anyway. Mike had encouraged her always to say what she meant and mean what she said. They had some very enlightening conversations in her younger years—no question off limits, no subject taboo. If he didn't have the answer, he said so. If he did, he said so.

Six of them remained in the elevator, and it became increasingly more difficult to dismiss the source of the Colgate-infused aroma. At the next stop, Deck E, the Empire Deck, two passengers stepped onto a mint green hallway. Holly knew herself all but exposed, and her stomach tightened. She imagined two sets of strangers' eyes peering at her. She got Mike's nod at the next floor, Deck V for Veranda. She disguised visual evidence of the odor by holding her carry-on behind her as she followed her father out of the lift and down the hallway to the right, noticing the soft rose-colored carpet beneath her feet.

He stopped in front of the seventh door on the left, room number V7.

"What are you up to, Dad? This isn't the room we booked."

"Well, this is the room you get!" He opened the door with one of two key cards he pulled from his pocket.

Mike stepped aside so Holly could enter the cabin first. The size of a double-wide truck container, the room hosted twice the space as the one they had agreed on. It provided a decent-sized bathroom on the immediate right as you entered with one twin and one queen bed after that, each with its own night table. A partially pulled folding panel extended from the wall to separate the sleeping areas. On the left side of the room, a two-door closet awaited the addition of the few items of formal wear they had packed. A dresser sat next to the closet and a desk with chair beyond that. In each far corner of the room sat a pale-yellow padded chair, its color matching the paint on the walls.

But Holly didn't notice most of it. Her eyes went to the far side of the room where a sliding glass door led to a balcony. She strode through the room and opened the door to a view of the river and ocean beyond. Two blue-and-white lounge chairs flanked a small round white metal table on the veranda. Holly already pictured sipping morning coffee while lounging in one of the chairs.

She turned to her father and twisted her expression into a quizzical look. "How can we afford this? I thought we agreed to get the small cabin with bunks. This is way too much."

Mike looked at his feet, adjusted his stance as if readying himself for battle, took a deep breath, and in a delicate tone uttered the words he prepared to say.

"Holly, you need to start living. I know it's scary. I know it's hard for you. When your Mom died, I did the best I could, but circumstances forced you to grow up too fast. You missed out on your childhood, and I don't want you to miss out on life, love, and a family of your own. It's time to start living your life. It's time to give yourself a chance."

He had rehearsed the speech over and over in his head. He managed to remember most of it, but he forgot the part about the turtle in the shell, probably for the best. It reminded him too much of one of Holly's favorite childhood books. He had read it to her almost every night, and he didn't want to ruin that memory for either of them.

Mike had planned many times before to deliver that same speech, but he always found a reason to wait, possibly his own selfish need to hang on to his only child, the child who reminded him so much of the woman he loved. Prompting him to finally follow through with his intention, the realization filled him with guilt.

Numbed by her father's words, Holly stood between the glass pane sliders. The lighthearted mood had shifted, twisting her stomach into knots. The sun's heat showered her back, and a tear began to form in the corner of her eye.

Not wanting to show the fear his words provoked, she held it back. She didn't want to disappoint him. And then, the rumbling began. She felt it first in her upper abdomen, then it moved quickly as it traveled south through her digestive tract, increasing in volume as it rounded each turn to build momentum with the ferocity of a caged lion.

Mike, seeing familiar panic in her tear-filled eyes said, "Breathe, Holly, just breathe. Deep breaths, in . . . out . . ."

But it was too late. Holly darted into the bathroom just as the enormous buildup of gas demanded an escape route, the roar like a lioness protecting her cubs seemed to echo off the walls of the small room. Embarrassed and ashamed, she sat on the toilet, sobbing.

Her dad knocked on the door. "It's all right, Holly. It's not a big deal."

Not a big deal? He reiterated the sentiment ever since the unveiling of her awkward reaction at her sixth-grade dance. Tommy DePoula unexpectedly asked her to dance and before she could say yes, the lion made its debut. She never forgot the look on Tommy's face and the laughter that followed. She ran then, too, out of the room and hid in the hallway until her father arrived at the prearranged time to pick her up. She never attended another school function. She was twelve years old.

She could not bring herself to tell her father what happened, but he soon learned of her condition when they bumped into Tommy and his mom while shopping in the local grocery store.

Soon after her thirteenth birthday, Mike arranged for Holly to see a therapist. Her anxiety limited her interaction with anyone her own age whether boys or girls. She talked with a couple of the girls at school but never accepted invitations to birthday parties or sleepovers. She just didn't trust herself.

The therapist was a bust. The doctor only wanted to talk about Holly's mother, and Holly had nothing to tell her. She didn't remember her mother. She was just a baby when she died. An aggressive cancer took only four months to alter her and her dad's life forever. So, she had no identifiable hidden guilt nor repressed memories to attribute to the gas invasion Holly experienced when she got overly anxious.

When the doctor deviated from questions about her mom, Holly faced probing questions such as, *Does your father ever get angry? Have you ever had a broken bone?* and *Does your dad ever come into your bedroom?* When Holly finally had enough, she answered *yes* to the bedroom question. She lowered her head in a shameful guise and, leaning close to the doctor's ear, whispered how he came into her bedroom late at night when she was supposed to be sleeping. With the light off and trying not to make a sound, he walked slowly toward the bed. When he reached the bed, he bent down and . . . Holly paused for effect . . . picked up the pile of dirty clothes that lay on the floor by her slippers. Then he kissed her on the forehead and left the room.

Holly did not visit a therapist again.

Holly got good at recognizing her anxiety warnings, so could avoid a repeat of the devastating sixth-grade incident. Her father talked to her teachers without divulging all the details but enough to cut her some slack if Holly had to leave the room quickly. Luckily, Tommy DePoula's family moved to Detroit the following year. She found it easier to walk down the hallways in school not having to worry about bumping into him.

CATE

Cate had appropriated a deck hand to help her with her bags. He followed behind on the sand-hued rug to the room she would share with her sister on Deck P, the Promenade Deck.

Not ready to face Sheila, Cate hesitated before she entered, but the deck hand mistakenly thought she waited for him to open the door. He set down one bag, stuffed the other under his armpit, and reached for the door handle. As he did, Cate panicked and lunged for his arm. Her foot caught on the makeup case he had placed on the floor, and she propelled into his chest. The bags hurtled to the floor followed by the deck hand and finally Cate topping off the pile. For an instant, as she lay on top of the startled man, Cate could focus only on his intensely deep auburn eyes peering back at her. She lay mesmerized until the door opened to redirect her attention.

"What's going on out here?" Sheila spouted as she opened the door. Then seeing her sister in an obvious mishap, she teased, "Cate! You didn't waste any time. Who have you got there?"

Cate rolled off to the side to allow the handsome deck hand to rise. He held out his hand to help her up. A little wobbly in her heels, she accepted his hand as he seemed effortlessly to pull her upright. *Even though he is short in stature, it seems he is long on strength*, Cate thought, remembering the line from the most recent romance novel she read.

"Well?" Sheila asked again.

"Oh, hi, Sheila. This is . . ." Cate paused. She hadn't asked his name nor noticed a nametag if he had one.

"Eduardo, Miss," he replied with a slight bow towards Cate, then Sheila.

"Eduardo," repeated Sheila as if trying out the name as she would a new dress.

Cate cast her sister a quick forbidding glance then returned a smile to Eduardo.

"I'm so sorry, Eduardo, I hope you're not hurt," Cate purred.

"Not at all, Miss. Where would you like me to put your bags?"

In your room, she thought, amused.

"Under the bottom bunk please, Eduardo."

Cate enjoyed saying his name. He wasn't really her type, but she enjoyed the momentary fantasy that played out in her head.

Eduardo quickly stacked the bags under the bunk and moved back to the door.

"May I be of any further service, Miss?" He emphasized the word service.

Cate let out an involuntary giggle. She smiled and handed Eduardo a ten-dollar bill.

"Not just yet, Eduardo." She returned the innocent flirtation. "Thank you."

After another slight bow Eduardo returned to the hallway, closing the door behind him.

"What the hell was that?" Sheila laughed. "Did someone give you a flirt pill instead of a Dramamine?"

Cate gave her sister a big hug and flung her arms up in the air.

"I'm on vacation. And what's up with you? Don't think I didn't notice you trying his name on for size. You've been doing that since you were ten years old. Try this name . . . David."

Cate felt a twinge of satisfaction in her retort. She did not often get to play the big sister role with conviction.

"He's not your type, you know. But it might be fun to remind yourself of that." Sheila raised an eyebrow at Cate.

That's all it took for them to erupt as only sisters can do, the music of laughter, a harmonious melody.

While Cate unpacked, they caught up on family news. Sheila had already organized her own belongings, so she helped her sister by moving some of her own clothes to accommodate Cate's expansive wardrobe. The tiny room bloated with female baggage. Sheila wished she had fought harder with Cate about booking a larger cabin. But Cate's proud nature would not yield, and Sheila admired that trait in her sister, however inconvenient for her.

SHEILA

As Sheila refolded Cate's clothes and put them in the small overstuffed dresser, she thought of David. Cate always had a way of making Sheila second-guess herself, but she tried not to let Cate know it. At times it yielded educational improvement, as with high school homework or her one-and-only job as a cashier before she got married. Cate's goading propelled her to push herself more than she normally would.

When it came to men, though, Cate just didn't understand her. In fact, Sheila began to think she didn't understand herself. She was in unfamiliar territory. She had always been confident she knew what men wanted, but David was different. He never asked anything of her. Both of her previous husbands had great ambitions in their work, and their achievements became her goal in life. Scott, a stockbroker with a thoughtless tendency to insult people, was exceedingly good to her. However, Sheila found herself making excuses to avoid parties and banquets with Scott because they made her too anxious as she wondered whom he would offend next and if she would feel the need to make an apology tour for him. And as fun as the rich and indulgent life may have seemed to her, Marc made it unbearable. He needed constant attention and it became a full-time job just to stroke his ego. But David wasn't defined by his work, and he didn't have grand ambition. *He is comfortable with himself and the Hollywood lifestyle,* Sheila thought. *He doesn't need me.*

"... do you think?" Sheila heard Cate through her thoughts.

"I'm sorry. What?"

"I said, do you want to go to the pool first or hit the air-conditioned bar?" Cate repeated.

"The bar, definitely the bar. Let me just change my shoes to flats."

Sheila decided to tell Cate once they perched themselves on a barstool. She would tell her everything. *Everything ... Cate will understand*, she told herself.

HOLLY

The ships's itinerary called for a six o'clock departure. Holly looked forward to seeing the sunset from an ocean liner, but first she needed to finish cleaning the toothpaste from her slacks. She had packed minimally, and if her packing plan had a chance of success, she would need to wear the slacks one more day during the trip.

She came out of the bathroom a little after five and didn't see her dad in the room. She felt slightly relieved. She did not wish to continue the conversation that propelled her to retreat to the tiny refuge.

The cabin felt cozy and warm. The beds, both draped in white spreads with beautifully drawn yellow daffodils and lush green stalks, gave the room an early spring feel.

She reached for her camera and a complimentary bottle of water on her way to the balcony. Outside, the sounds of the city became more noticeable. But her view was of the other side of the city, beyond the river to the immense world of oceanic governance, where her journey would begin. She somehow felt the need to leave the shore behind, to break the connection between soil and self-consciousness. She imagined it as her sink-or-swim crossroads. Or crosswaves. She silently giggled at her own turn of phrase.

"Okay," Mike called as he burst into the room. When he saw Holly on the balcony, he claimed the other bottle of water and joined her.

"I've got the activity schedule for tomorrow," he told her. "The only thing going on tonight is the special welcome dinner in the dining room at nine o'clock."

"That's good, because I want to get pictures of the sunset. It should be beautiful tonight. Since when are you an activities guy?"

"Who, me?"

"Yes, you!"

"I guess I never told you about my beer pong champion status in my dorm at college."

"For winning or for drinking the most beer?"

"Yup!"

"I always pictured you as kind of a dork in college—you know, studying all the time."

"Hey, now. I was the most fun guy in the library," he chuckled.

She knew of only one reason he picked up the activities schedule, and she determined not to disappoint him. *Maybe she could find a good beer pong tournament onboard.*

"Okay, hit me. What's on the docket for tomorrow?" she tried to sound enthusiastic.

Mike scanned the list of events before committing to sharing any. Knowing that every one of them would be a tough sell, he wanted to present the best options.

"The day begins with breakfast—they call it M&M, meet and mingle. It says, *A gathering of guests, crew members, and ship's captain combined with an artful breakfast buffet provides the perfect opportunity to meet your fellow travelers and begin the vacation of a lifetime.* That sounds easy enough."

"Mmmm."

Mike lifted his left eyebrow slightly and moved on. "At ten o'clock they're offering free surfing lessons at the SeaSurf on the Aquarius deck."

"Uh huh."

"Zipline at noon?"

"Ahhh."

"Treasure hunt?"

"Ugh."

"Okay, I'll sign us up for karaoke."

"Don't you dare!"

"Come on, Holly. There's got to be something that interests you."

She whisked the paper out of his hands and quickly perused the activities. *Well, at least he skipped over bingo,* she noted.

"I like the outdoor movie night," Holly offered.

"Of course, you do. You won't have to talk to anyone there. I'll tell you what. We'll do outdoor movie night if you commit to . . . he glanced at the sheet she held, " . . . Murder on the High Seas escape room."

Her stomach contracted, as if someone punched down freshly risen bread dough and released all the air.

"All right," she agreed. "But you're doing it with me. I'm betting it's going to be as lame as the name suggests." A grin occupied her untanned face. And just like that her stomach perked up just as bread dough tends to.

CATE

It took Cate twenty minutes to decide which sandals to wear. She had brought three pair, whittled down from the five she wanted to bring. She chose light blue to accent the flowers decorating her sleeveless lilac cotton top rather than the white sandals to compliment her white denim shorts. It posed a difficult decision that still hadn't settled in her brain as the sisters reached the Shell-Shuck Bar on the Empire Deck.

Decorated in unimaginative teal, peach, and pearl white, the bar looked like something out of the *Golden Girls* television series. It did, however, have an extensive selection of bourbon, Cate noticed as she browsed the offerings. Most of the tables already taken, she chose two seats at the bar. She preferred the bar—much less formal and the best way to endear herself to the bartender who could greatly influence her cruise experience. If Cate had learned one thing in her twenty-seven years, it was to always take care of the bartender, server, and chef.

Sheila took the seat to Cate's right, and they both fixed eyes on the considerably tanned and attractive bartender.

They watched as he muddled lime wedges with sugar for what looked like the beginnings of a tangy Caipirinha, a Brazilian favorite. The muscles on his forearm danced with each crush of the stainless-steel muddler. He offered a welcome smile their way as he mixed in the Cachaça and began to shake the concoction. Neither of them could take their eyes from his perfectly proportioned biceps.

Cate began to rethink her drink choice. She would not mind watching him muddle again. The could-be model made his way over to Cate and Sheila and, with an unidentifiable accent, asked what he could make for them. Sheila wasted no time before ordering her signature cocktail, champagne with a Luxardo cherry. Cate always thought the addition of the cherry showed off that she knew what they were, although Cate had to admit that, once she found out about the specialty cherries, she never went back to ordinary maraschinos. Thinking it best to start with something familiar rather than a tropical cocktail, Cate ordered an Old Fashioned. The bartender, whose name perfectly matched his body style, asked Cate which bourbon she would prefer.

"Well, Maximus," she read from his tag, "why don't you just make me the best old fashioned you possibly can."

Challenge thrown.

Maximus quickly went to work reaching for W. L. Weller twelve-year bourbon. Challenge accepted.

Cate knew she was in good hands.

SHEILA

"To a carefree vacation." Sheila raised her glass and toasted.

"Absolutely." Cate happily touched her glass to the champagne flute.

Sheila took a sip of champagne to help work up the nerve to broach the subject of David. *Maybe,* she thought, *I can ease into it.*

"I don't remember the last time I felt this good." Sheila glanced at Cate. "You know. No troubles. No complications."

Cate rolled her eyes. "Says the woman who employs a maid and cook. How is this different from every other day for you, except the location?"

Sheila felt the barb. Cate had reached into her chest and hooked it there. Sheila held her retort, but she could not hold back involuntary tears. *Cate really does not know me at all.* She sat on her barstool and stared straight ahead.

Cautiously, she began again, "Cate, I need to tell you . . ."

"And let's not forget the chauffeur, gardener, and pool boy. Hell, we could have just stayed at your house and saved all this money." Cate snickered as she looked over at Sheila for a response. She noticed droplets on Sheila's cheek, and the wounded eyes they trickled from.

"Sheila, what's wrong? What's the matter?"

"You, Cate. You're the matter. You think I've got it all?" Sheila stepped down from the stool, "You just don't know anything! You don't know what it's like!" Sheila turned and stormed out of the bar.

Wide-eyed and frozen in place, Cate whispered, "What the hell was that?" to no one in particular.

HOLLY

"The muster drill is at six thirty, Holly. Our station is just down the hall through these doors and down the elevator." Mike showed her on the map affixed to the inside of the cabin door. "We still have a little over half an hour. Do you want to see what else is on this deck?"

"Sure." Holly was curious about the layout. She relished being on a cruise ship. It crossed off a bucket list item for her. She never thought she would actually have the courage to do it.

To familiarize themselves with the area, they took a right in the hall outside their room and headed through the designated doors to follow their muster station route. From the port side, they could hear the activity of the crew readying the ship to sail.

The air soon permeated with the unmistakable smell of fresh roasted coffee beans from the small café decorated with a wooden sign carved with the name Aweigh from the Grind. The menu consisted of regular and specialty coffees, teas, juices, assorted smoothies, and bakery favorites. You could also buy a book, magazine, or newspaper to, as the menu suggested, "complement your morning or afternoon café experience." Outdoor seating provided an unobstructed view of the journey ahead if you had not buried your head in a book.

Holly had thought she would have her morning coffee on the balcony in their stateroom, but Aweigh from the Grind presented an inviting setting, and the only books she had brought to read were manuscripts from the publishing office.

It might be nice, after all, to sit in the café and read a book fresh out of the wringer.

Mike and Holly decided to sit and have a cup of coffee while they waited for the muster drill. Since most people were still getting settled into their rooms and others began their travel with an alcoholic beverage, the café was quiet. Only a half dozen chose to begin the cruise with coffee at the café on the Veranda Deck.

CATE

Sitting somberly on her stool, Cate tried to recall the conversation that led to Sheila's outburst. *We ordered our drinks, we toasted, she said she was happy about this week, and I made a joke about staying at her place. What the hell made me say that?* She thought about it and remembered Sheila had been about to say something. *What was it?*

She said she had to tell me something. Then she said I thought she had it all, but she was happy to be away from her troubles.

And then it hit her like a June bug to the forehead at sixty miles an hour. *Money—it's got to be money. Sheila never seems troubled when she has money.* Cate imagined it possible that David blew it all in Hollywood. Even though she loved David, Cate didn't think much of his business acumen. And it had been Cate's idea to take the cruise. She had begged Sheila to come with her since none of Cate's friends could join her. *Oh, poor Sheila,* Cate thought. *No wonder she seemed so tentative and out of sorts.*

Cate felt like a heel, horrible and selfish. It's no wonder Sheila felt obligated. *I am a rotten person*, Cate thought. *I've got to go find her.*

SHEILA

Sheila had no idea what deck she was on. To her, they all looked alike. She didn't notice that the herringbone wood floor lay differently than the parquet she arrived on, nor how the pillars changed from yellow to blue from one floor to the next. She had no awareness that each level of the ship depicted a different culture, from Grecian to Parisienne, Middle Eastern to Middle American. Details had always eluded her except when they concerned her personal appearance. Then she paid flawless attention. She found a chair on the right side of the ship; she could never remember which was port and which starboard. She watched the crew at work, each having a purpose, working in unison to release the large ship from its tether to the dock. She wondered if they enjoyed their lives. *Do they have families somewhere, wives or husbands and children who wait for them to come home? Are they happy?*

"Stupid," she whispered to herself. "How could I be so stupid?" She had never been that thin skinned. Why had Cate's remarks hit her so hard? She answered the question before the synapses of her brain had a chance to counter. *Because what Cate said is true*, she thought. She had been thinking about it for a few months. She was the wife of a handsome, rich young man and living in a large estate in Hollywood Hills. She had staff to take care of her every need, enough money and freedom to jet off to Monaco if she felt the urge. Every woman's dream . . . except for hers. It was true: once in her life, she wanted exactly that and strived for it. But she never imagined how shallow and superficial it could all be. She was expendable. *If I go away, there will be another just as beautiful and just as willing, ready to take my place,* she imagined.

I have no purpose, and neither does David.

She imagined the two of them on the decks below, towing in the ropes and doing whatever else it took to make it all work smoothly. Would they be happy then?

Unencumbered from the dock, the ship began to glide across the rippling water of the river pouring into the ocean ahead. Passengers gathered on deck and waved to those on shore.

Sheila decided she had to apologize to Cate.

CATE AND SHEILA

The International Convention of Safety of Life at Sea requires and regulates muster on a cruise ship. Safety officers instruct passengers what to do in the case of an emergency at sea. Every passenger on board must attend the drill.

The muster alarm cut through the Florida air as the ship sailed toward open water. Dutiful passengers had already made their way to their respective muster stations, as all had been previously informed when to expect the impending notification and positioned themselves nearby before the alarm sounded. All except one. Cate had lost track of time and searched for Sheila on Deck SP, the sports deck on the bow of the ship. *Why didn't I just wait until the muster call to see Sheila,* she thought, *instead of running all over the ship looking for a flea in a poppy field.*

Seven floors down and across the floating city the Main Deck at the stern of the ship hosted their muster. Had she been thinking clearly, not her strong suit in such situations, she would first have headed to the stern of the ship and then made her way down to Deck M, the main deck. But all she could think about was getting to her designated station as quickly as possible. She headed to the elevator, pushed the button, and waited and waited and waited.

Finally, the empty elevator arrived. She imagined everyone on the ship already at their assigned positions. She pushed the button and rode down seven floors to the main deck till the elevator doors opened. It was then she realized her mistake. People crowded the parquet from bow to stern. She weaved her way through hoards as safety instructors delivered their rehearsed speech. *Sheila will be furious,* she thought. She knew everyone must be in attendance before the instructor could commence. She kept a lot of people waiting. Out of breath and completely embarrassed, Cate finally joined her muster group.

"Are you Catherine Wayland?" the displeased but professional safety officer asked.

"Yes, I am. I'm so sorry I'm late." All eyes fell on her. Angry eyes. Rumblings circulated in the small crowd.

"Okay. Let's begin," the officer said.

She saw her sister on the other side of the group. As the officials began passing out bright orange life vests, Cate noticed Sheila trying to make her way through the crowd to join her. She braced herself for the inevitable lecture about being on time and respecting other people when Sheila broke through the last of the human shield.

Sheila reached Cate and, without a word, threw her arms around her, embracing her firmly and dearly.

It jolted Cate. She hadn't expected it.

"Sheila, I'm so sorry. I'm an idiot."

"No, Cate. I'm sorry. I didn't mean it. You're my favorite person in the entire world."

"Ahhemmm." Clearly annoyed at the lack of attention from the two young women, the officer cleared his throat.

Cate and Sheila obediently donned their life jackets and turned their attention to the instructor.

The muster lasted another twenty minutes as they learned which lifeboat to get into when the shit hit the iceberg.

Cate and Sheila proceeded to the nearest outdoor bar, ordered a couple of rum-based fruit punches each with swizzle sticks decorated with fresh fruit and a paper parrot. They found two deck chairs and settled in to watch the sunset.

They laughed about their scolding from the safety officer, made fun of the older ladies with their disapproving glances, and compared notes on which guys at the muster were really single and which pretended to be single.

After a few moments of silence Sheila began, "I'm so sorry Cate, I didn't mean to snap at you like that. It's just that . . . there's something I have to tell you."

Cate stopped her. "I know, Sheila. It's okay. I already know."

Surprised, Sheila braced herself for a rebuke with Cate listing David's merits and how she would be crazy to let him go.

But it didn't happen.

Instead, sweet and caring, Cate said, "It was pretty obvious from your reaction when I said we should have stayed at your house, you know, with the maid and pool boy and all. I'm so sorry. Is there anything I can do?"

Tears filled Sheila's eyes. She set down her cherry-red drink, got up from her chair, and gave Cate a hug.

"Oh, Cate, thank you. I've been so worried. I was going to tell you as soon as you came on board, but I chickened out. Thank you for understanding."

"Of course, Sheila. We're sisters. Now, no more negative talk. Let's just relax and have a wonderful week away from it all. Cheers!"

Cate and Sheila clinked their glasses together allowing two paper parrots to kiss.

The sun lingered briefly before yielding to the moon-filled sky.

HOLLY

With the muster behind her and feeling only slightly concerned about the vacation vessel she chose, Holly meandered to the bow of the main deck. She raised her Nikon camera multiple times along the way. The bow, however, held the prize. The western sky supplied the perfect sunset canvas. Her camera captured the essence of her feelings, the transition of life streaked in hues of bold, bright, and invigorating colors.

The soil that nurtured her inhibitions fell further behind as the sun put itself to bed.

A new day. A new way.

Holly checked her cellphone for the time, eight ten. Time to go. She wished she could bottle the feeling inside her, carry it with her, and pour it out when it was most needed. She closed her eyes, imprinting the moment to memory. This will have to do, she thought.

Had she opened her eyes before she turned to walk away, she may have noticed the approaching wheelchair behind her. Not until the heavy wheel of the chair rolled over her right foot did her eyes fly open—as well as her mouth.

The involuntary "Owwww" escaped her lungs before she could help it.

"Oh, I'm so sorry. Are you okay?" The tiny woman pushing the chair winced, her faced contorted as if it were her foot under the wheel.

Holly took stock of her foot, bent it, rotated it, wiggled her toes, and ultimately realized she had suffered no long-term damage.

"Totally my fault," Holly replied. "I wasn't paying attention to where I was going. I'm fine. See?" She made a show of stomping her sneaker-clad foot to prove her point.

The petite woman looked relieved and a bit worn. She smiled and extended her hand. "Hi, I'm Lynn," and then, pointing to the occupant of the wheelchair, she said, "and this young man is Bradley".

"Hi", said Bradley, looking her squarely in the eyes. "Sorry about your foot. My mom isn't the best driver, at least that's what my dad says." He looked back at his mom with an engaging smile as a chuckle escaped through his perfectly lined pearl-white teeth.

Holly laughed. "Hi, I'm Holly." She extended her hand first to Bradley and then to his mother, "It's very nice to meet you."

"Is this your first cruise?" Bradley asked. "This is my first time. I've been wanting to do this all my life."

"That's true." Lynn spoke to her son. "All these long years." Lynn tousled Bradley's light brown hair.

"Yes, this is my first cruise, too. But I don't think I am as excited about it as you are," Holly professed. "I'm a little nervous. I don't like crowds much".

"Well, you picked a good ship then. Even though this vessel has about three thousand people on board, including the crew, it has a passenger-to-space ratio of almost forty, thirty-nine point three to be exact," Bradley cited. "I ran the numbers myself just to make sure. The cruise line fact sheet was off by point three points."

Bradley was used to seeing a dumbfounded look like the one Holly displayed. It mimicked the look he saw when he spoke to most adults.

"I'm a fact geek," he explained, "and I like to read."

"I love to read too," Holly said, "but I've never heard of the passenger-to-whatever-you-said thing. What is that?"

"It's the passenger-to-space ratio. The higher the number, the more feeling of open space a passenger will perceive. Perception is the key. The builders can create the illusion of open space without having open space, like using mirrors on a wall to make things look bigger."

"How old *are* you?"

He rolled his eyes slightly and answered, "I'm twelve. I'll be thirteen next January."

After watching the familiar scene play out, Lynn spoke up. "He's a research fanatic. He can remember all these facts, but he still can't remember to make his bed in the morning." Mother and son shared a look and a laugh, both understanding that the remark was payback for the dig about driving.

"Well, I hope the ship isn't so big that I won't run into you both again," Holly said, "but I'm afraid I have to go get ready for dinner. It was great to meet you." Holly gave them a quick wave and, trying hard not to limp or show any sign of foot discomfort, walked toward the elevator.

As they had planned, Mike had finished dressing for dinner. He told Holly he would wait for her on deck. The dining room dress code for the night called for semicasual, so Holly wore her white sundress showered in bright yellow flowers outlined with black paint-like brush strokes. Her golden-brown hair, drawn up slightly by a yellow headband, tickled her shoulders. Holly was not one to wear makeup daily, but she gave herself a light touch for the occasion. She felt happy, but better yet, she felt confident.

She thought of Bradley, and that made her smile.

CATE AND SHEILA

As Cate and Sheila passed fashionably late into the dining room through two carved wooden doors with *Perth* etched in glass oval windows, it was as if a cue card dropped from the ceiling that said to everyone present, *Turn your head and look at the two women who just walked in.*

They made a stunning pair: Sheila, tall with flowing blonde hair and modeling a royal blue sleeveless sundress printed with varying sizes of colorful butterflies and black high heels followed by Cate, a wavy-haired brunette wearing a tea-length dress with a solid black bodice, the white skirt splashed with vivid purple flowers and green leaf stems. The piping on her black, open-toed pumps coordinated with the purple flowers on her dress.

The maître d' showed them to their assigned table covered with a deep-rose cloth and eight assorted place settings. Lavender spider-spray chrysanthemums flanked by white baby's breath filled the center vase. Sheila showed delight in the décor, as it perfectly complemented her evening wear. The sisters were surprised to find they were the first to arrive at their table. Once seated, they each ordered a white wine, scanned the large dining room, and saw most tables filled. They thought it even more curious that their dinner companions remained absent. Just as their wine arrived, so did their tablemates. A handsome youngster with light brown hair rolled his wheelchair over to the table. He wore a blue Oxford shirt and black slacks.

"Hi, I'm Bradley." He smiled and stuck out his hand to greet the two beautiful women allocated as his dining companions for the duration of the trip. "This is my mother, Lynn, and my father, Doug." He pointed to his parents who stood behind him.

Cate and Sheila stood to shake hands first with the engaging boy with eyes the color of Sheila's dress and then with his parents.

"Sorry we're late," Lynn said. "I was having trouble deciding what to wear. It's been so long since I had to think about such a thing," she confessed.

"Well, you look stunning," Sheila replied. "I just love your shoes." Cate nodded in agreement.

"See, Honey? I told you the shoes would make all the difference," said Lynn to her husband.

"I see we are going to be outnumbered this week, Bradley. I'll be counting on you for backup," Doug grinned.

"Don't count too much, Dad. I think I might like it on their side." The five of them fell into a comfortable laughter.

The three other seats at the table remained unclaimed, but no one seemed to mind. Bradley had completely endeared himself to the sisters by the time the waiter whisked away the appetizer plates.

"Those were the best frog legs I ever had," Bradley remarked, "and thanks for letting me try your snails, Sheila. They were wicked good."

"Escargots," Lynn corrected him. "If you're going to have expensive taste, you'd better get the lingo down pat, young man. And they were the only frog legs you've ever had." She flashed him a smile.

"Did you say, wicked good?" Cate looked confused as she asked.

"Yeah" Bradley replied. "Oh, that's right, it's just a New England thing. I keep forgetting. It means really good." He thought about it a little more and added, " . . . exceptional. We're from New Hampshire. That's how we all talk up there."

"Well, we're from California," Sheila chimed in. "We say *exceptional*." The five laughed as the waiter brought their dinners.

"Thank you, Oscar," Doug said to the waiter. "This looks delicious. Could you bring us another bottle of white wine when you have a moment, please?" Doug enjoyed the conversation. He had been a little worried they would be seated with people Bradley could not connect with, but the charming sisters didn't talk down to his son. He thought that called for another bottle of wine.

HOLLY AND MIKE

By Holly's quick calculation, the stately dining room appeared to hold close to two hundred round tables. Tablecloths of varying cheerful colors distinguished them. Unique fresh floral arrangements sat centered on each, the flowers surrounded by place settings dissimilar from those nearby.

Holly sat to the left of her dad at a table swathed in royal blue decorated with white and blue hydrangeas. She imagined her place setting suitable for a banquet befitting British royalty. Someone occupied each of the eight places. To her left sat a couple in their late seventies, a retired bank president and retired psychology professor from Santa Fe. A couple who seemed in their late sixties had places across from Holly. The gentleman talked about his multimillion-dollar water filtration business, and his wife spoke about the multiple charity organizations she chaired. Seated on Mike's right, the third couple each practiced law. The husband said he worked in business law, his wife as a prosecuting attorney.

The conversation had gone around the table and sat in Mike's lap. Mike explained he worked as a civil engineer for a firm in Massachusetts that specialized in industrial parks. He made no mention of the loss of his wife, Abby.

"And this is my daughter, Holly. Your turn, Honey." Mike knew the fear Holly faced at that moment. Speaking with strangers filled Holly with anxiety.

"Um . . . I work at, um, a book company. I mean a, ah, a publishing company. I read books." Holly stopped there.

Mike stepped in to save her. "She's a reader for Parrot Publishing. She's being modest. She decides which manuscripts warrant publishing. Two of the manuscripts she recommended for publication received movie contracts. Holly has a knack for knowing what works."

Mike exhibited the look of a proud dad, but their dinner companions met Holly's accomplishments with little enthusiasm. Conversation during the rest of the meal consisted of the three couples talking to each other about their investments and vacation properties as they largely ignored Mike and Holly, who had neither and ate in near silence.

"Hey, Oscar," the water filtration guy shouted to the nearby waiter. "Get me another martini."

Holly and Mike rolled their eyes at his brashness. They decided to skip dessert and excused themselves as the dinner plates disappeared. The three couples barely acknowledged them leaving.

Mike and Holly waited until they exited the dining room before they began to laugh.

"Wow," Mike said. "Could they be any more pompous? The way they shunned us, you'd think we just crawled out of the sewers."

"I think anything living in the sewers would be more pleasant and fun than them," Holly snickered. "Let's go find something sweet."

They strolled the decks until they found exactly what they searched for. A café and bakery fit for Rue de Seine in Paris. While the soft sounds of "La Vie en Rose" piped through speakers, Holly ordered choux à la crème with pistachio filling while Mike ordered the more modest apple tart, warmed. Each of them craved a cup of coffee to complement their treats. They sat beneath the beautiful night sky to sip their lattes, savor their sweets, and succumb to the sound of the ocean waves melding with the music and ambiance of the Parisienne café. If they were cats, you might have heard them purr.

TABLE FOR EIGHT

SHEILA

Sheila donned her new two-piece bathing suit, the one she recently bought on Rodeo Drive for the price of a small used car. The copper strapless suit with dime-sized white dots complemented her tanned Hollywood body. She wrapped a white embroidered lace sarong around her petite waist, left a note for Cate, and quietly left the room.

The seven-o'clock cloudless morning sky beckoned the sun to share its comforting rays with Sheila. She had always been drawn to the sun, so much so that she exhibited symptoms of depression on days the sun played hooky. As a child, expecting her parents to make the rain stop or blow the clouds away for her, she threw a tantrum if she could not lie in the sun. The sun gave her sustenance, endowed her with hope, and lavished her with love.

She chose a chair on the far side of the pool away from the shallow end where children tend to splash. The padded blue cushion of the chair held a fluffy white towel that absorbed the smell of ocean air. She folded the towel and, placing it behind her head, reclined the chair to a perfect forty-degree angle. As if she had willed him to appear, the deck waiter in white shorts and starched white shirt approached. Sheila noted he made a conscious effort not to block her sun, something she appreciated immensely.

"Good morning, Miss. May I bring you something from the café or bar?" He had a pleasant morning voice.

"Yes, please. Could I have a mimosa with a splash of cranberry juice?" Sheila replied in the same serene manner. She opted to change her morning routine slightly, foregoing the daily macchiato her kitchen maid usually handed her as she made her way to her pool. Her mischievous mind role-played a scene with the handsome young waiter replacing her kitchen maid.

"Right away, Miss."

As she watched the waiter make his way to the outdoor bar, bypassing a few thirsty sunbathers along the way, she noticed a man sitting on a stool at the bar, his back to her. He wore a business suit. *How odd,* Sheila thought. *Who would be wearing a business suit at seven o'clock in the morning on a cruise ship? Maybe he's still wearing yesterday's clothes,* she reasoned. *It is possible he never went to bed, or he went to bed in someone else's cabin, a much more plausible explanation.*

Sheila interrupted her own train of thought. *You're doing it again.* It was a thing her mother did. She loved to watch people and try to figure out their stories—strangers in the park or diners in a restaurant. It didn't matter. She inevitably came up with an entire backstory about the person or people and explained what circumstance brought them to that place on that day and at that time. She encouraged the girls to create their own interpretations, and then they compared stories. Cate and Sheila resisted the game in their early years, but as they grew older, they recognized it as a terrific way to study body language and expressions. Cate had written a college paper on the process and received one of the highest grades she ever got, which thrilled her mother.

The waiter placed her mimosa on the small white table next to her lounge chair. Sheila was so involved in her thoughts that she barely acknowledged him. She stared at the well-dressed man, hoping he would turn around so she could get a look at his face. He had excellent posture. Average build with wide shoulders, although she couldn't tell if the suit jacket made his shoulders look bigger. She willed him to turn his body towards her.

A small group of passengers rounded the corner from the port side deck to the open space of the pool area, and just as Sheila had wished, the man at the bar turned sideways and glanced their way. She got a perfect profile of his classically attractive face, a cross between a young Cary Grant and Hugh Jackman, she thought. Her view revealed stubble on his face, unshaven because of circumstance, not by choice she gathered. His gaze followed the small group. He looked tired. She guessed his age at about thirty and saw him just as comfortable in a suit as in well-worn jeans. He turned back to face the bar, her admiring view gone.

I may have to run into him, she allowed herself to think. *But not right now.*

She took a sip of her mimosa, closed her eyes, and lay back on the chair to enjoy the morning sun.

CATE

Cate woke at eight twenty-two, groggy and momentarily unsure of her surroundings. A smile formed on her face when she remembered she lay in a cabin on the *Perth*, at sea. She happily jumped out of bed, something she hated to do at home, took a shower and, after her lengthy decision-making process, put on one of the four bathing suits she had packed.

It took her twenty minutes to choose the one-piece black suit featuring a diagonal white stripe across the front. It presented a flattering fit, and she didn't need too much of a tan to pull it off. Allowing her to show off her legs, which she perceived as her most attractive feature, the white sheer cover-up reached only to her thighs.

She left the cabin and rode seven floors up to Lido Deck, to the pool where Sheila's note said to find her. As she rounded the corner from the starboard side of the ship, at the bar, she noticed the handsome man in a business suit. *How odd,* she thought. *Who would be wearing a business suit at a bar on a cruise at nine o'clock in the morning?* She caught a glimpse of his unshaven face and knew instantly that he had not slept in his own cabin the previous night. But he sat alone now.

She left a stool open between them as she settled in at the bar. The bartender at once approached her. She flaunted an easy smile and ordered a Bloody Mary. Cate glanced to her right, caught the stranger looking her way, and said, "Good morning."

"Good morning," he replied with a tired but stunning smile. Two dimples decorating his strong jawline gave him a youthful edge. Cate sized him up to be in his late twenties or early thirties.

"A little warm for a business suit, isn't it?" Cate asked.

The man chuckled and said, "I had an early business meeting this morning. No rest for the weary."

An obvious lie, Cate thought, *but well thought out if he wanted to play the field.* "Well, I hope you won't be working this whole trip, that would be such a waste of this beautiful weather. My name's Catherine, but everyone calls me Cate." She reached out her hand.

"Hello," he said. "I'm Derek. Nice to meet you, Cate." He took the last sip from his coffee cup and set it on the bar. "I guess I should find something more suitable to wear. It was very nice meeting you," he said as he got up.

"It was nice to meet you, too, Derek." Cate watched as he walked away. Something about him seemed a little off, but she just could not put her finger on it. However, she thought, she looked forward to trying to figure it out.

Cate found Sheila in a sunbathing trance. She procured a nearby chair and pulled it next to Sheila, blocking her sun in the process. Sheila opened her eyes to identify the sun-stealing culprit and saw Cate standing there, beaming.

"It is still morning, isn't it?" Sheila asked. "What's up with the happy face? You don't usually exercise those facial muscles until at least noon."

"I just met the most gorgeous man on this ship. His name is Derek, and he's a cross between Cary Grant and Ryan Reynolds. He wasn't wearing a wedding ring, although I think he slept with someone last night. He also has an air of mystery around him. Just my type."

"You mean the man sitting at the bar over there?" Sheila pointed to his vacant seat.

"I should have known you would see him, even through your closed eyelids."

"He's been sitting there for at least two hours. In a business suit of all things."

"He told me he had an early morning meeting, but I think that was bullshit. I don't believe he slept in his own cabin last night. Maybe he didn't like what he woke up with this morning?" There was a short pause as Cate pictured waking up next to him in bed. "His name is Derek."

"Yes, you said that."

HOLLY AND MIKE

Holly and Mike arrived at the Meet & Mingle breakfast at eight fifteen, the room was nearly full. The extravagant buffet, laid out with exotic fresh flowers and creative ice carvings of cranes, windmills, and such, pleased the eye and teased the palate. Various varieties of fresh fruit, berries, and colorful produce formed the shape of a cruise ship. Roast stations included carved prime rib, baked ham, steamship round, and beef tenderloin. Plentiful egg choices, some of them cooked to order, included scrambled, Benedict, omelets, and quiche. Fresh baked breads, bagels, and muffins occupied an entire table alongside flavored cream cheeses, jams, jellies, and compotes.

The bathing suit Holly wore beneath her shorts and top convinced her not to fill her plate with everything she wanted, so she took only fresh fruit, cottage cheese, and orange juice. Mike, on the other hand, had no worries about how he looked in his bathing suit, so he piled his plate with scrambled eggs, prime rib, roasted red potatoes, and a stack of thick-cut bacon. He thought about a made-to-order omelet but decided he could always go back if he wanted to.

They shared a table with a young honeymoon couple, Tina and Tom, from Tennessee. They exuded such joy, it made Holly smile.

The foursome had finished breakfast and enjoyed their third cup of coffee when the captain made it to their table to say hello. A handsome man in his early sixties, Holly guessed, he had an engaging smile and professional demeanor. He congratulated the young couple, and they made small talk until the captain became aware of the man wearing a business suit, who had come into the breakfast room. He excused himself and walked over to the man.

Holly thought the man looked familiar, like a movie star, or some famous person she should know, but she couldn't place him. He seemed uncomfortable with his slightly scruffy appearance and rubbed his hand across his cheek and chin, but the whiskers did not diminish his good looks. The two men exchanged a few words before they left the banquet room together.

"Well, Holly, it's a little after nine o'clock. We should head to the escape room. We're supposed to be there by 9:15 to check in," Mike said.

"Or we could just go to the pool and forget about the escape room." Holly hoped he would agree.

"A promise is a promise." He reminded her. "C'mon. It's going to be fun."

"Would you two care to join us?" Holly asked the newlyweds. "It promises to be extremely lame and not a bit entertaining." She was feeling comfortable around the young couple now.

"As fun as that sounds," Tina teased, "I think we're going to go to the pool. But thank you for the invitation."

"Well, hopefully we will see you there later," an envious Holly replied.

Mike and Holly found the nearest elevator to take them to Level 10, the Sun Deck that mimicked a Moroccan beach resort. Portable signs pointed them to the Escape Room and a large reception area hosting a breathtaking upper-level, unobstructed view of the vibrant blue ocean surrounding them. As they entered the room, Holly noticed Bradley and his mother with a man she assumed to be his father.

"Oh, Dad, those are the people I met on deck last night. Come on. I'll introduce you." Holly grabbed Mike's arm. She waived at the trio when they saw her coming toward them.

"Hey, Holly, crazy meeting you here. How's your foot?" Bradley asked. "Are you doing the Escape Room?"

"Yes. Looks like it. And my foot is fine, thanks." She turned to Mike. "Dad, this is Bradley and his mother Lynn."

They exchanged hellos, and Lynn pointed to her husband. "This is my husband, Doug."

"Nice to meet you," said Doug. "Are you the photographer Bradley told me about?"

Holly laughed at the thought. "Amateur photographer at best."

"How are your detective skills?" Bradley asked.

"I guess we'll find out. I've never done anything like this before."

"Don't worry. I have," Bradley remarked with confidence. "We'll nail this thing in no time."

The rest of them chuckled at Bradley's assertion.

Two other couples showed up to join their group. They learned they would have one hour to figure out clues that would open a secret door to let them out. The ship's recreation director would time them, and the team solving the puzzles the quickest would receive free tickets to a shore excursion of their choice on the last stop of the cruise. One team of eight had already attempted the challenge that day with two more days of competition and a total of twenty-four teams. The recreation director would post the winners on the fifth morning of the cruise, the day before the *Perth* would reach their last stop, St. Kitts.

"Awesome!" Bradley could barely hold in his excitement. "I have a plan."

CATE AND SHEILA

The morning flew by like a hummingbird to a feeder. When Sheila checked her cell phone, it was almost twelve thirty.

"Are you hungry?" she asked Cate.

"I could eat a little something."

"I could go for a salad and a Margarita."

"Ooh, that sounds perfect, let's go."

Cate remembered seeing something in the daily newsletter about one of the lunch restaurants on board, something about a turtle. It was on the same deck as the pool, but she couldn't remember where exactly. They decided to walk down the starboard side of the ship first. Three quarters of the way towards the stern, they spotted a sign hanging just ahead, The Happy Turtle. Before they reached the restaurant, they came to another hanging sign, M'all Aboard. The glass windows displayed mannequins wearing everything from bathing suits to tuxedos, any clothing you could possibly need on a cruise ship.

"Let's check it out, Cate."

"Okay, but I won't have any room in my luggage to bring home more clothes."

Sheila laughed knowingly. "Well, we can always ship some things home, right?"

As they walked through the open door, Cate spotted the handsome man in the business suit looking at slacks in the far-left corner of the store. She bumped Sheila's arm and pointed to him. Stopping only to act interested in the kimono hanging from a rack, something neither one of them would ever consider wearing, and trying to appear casual, they each shopped their way towards Derek. They watched as he brought an armload of clothes into the dressing room.

"It looks like he's buying a whole new wardrobe," Sheila whispered.

"I don't get it. He had on a custom fit suit. This stuff is okay for an emergency, but I would hardly do my clothes shopping here." She had already pictured him in a custom-tailored tuxedo at the cruise line's formal dinner. She also pictured him in silk pajama bottoms with her wearing the silk top.

"Lost luggage," Sheila exclaimed. "The airline must have lost his luggage."

Cate nodded. "That's got to be it. That makes sense." Cate felt mildly disappointed she would not get to see the silk pajamas.

They left Derek to his shopping and slipped out before he emerged from the dressing room.

The Happy Turtle had placed a few tables out on deck so patrons could enjoy ocean air as they dined. Sheila and Cate chose one so they could watch the clothing store doorway and possibly have a chance run-in with Derek. To their dismay,

Derek left the store two sips into their frozen margarita, glanced their way only for a second as if to get his bearings, and walked in the opposite direction carrying three full bags. He obviously didn't notice them.

The salads came served on cold plates garnished with edible flowers—nasturtiums, the waiter told them. A lively mix of spinach, kale, frisée, arugula, bib lettuce, and radicchio topped with dried cranberries and pumpkin seeds, and served over a bed of endive. Creamy cranberry dressing clung to the greens, enhanced by a delicate touch of orange rind. Neither one of them ate the crusty cream cheese baguettes and fruit compote that accompanied the main dish.

As they waited for their second frozen Margarita to arrive, a group of six passengers stopped momentarily at the nearby railing. Each held a flute of champagne as a grey-haired man with a boisterous demeanor had their full attention.

"I tripled my money in one year. It was the best choice I ever made." The man laughed and clinked glasses with the rest of them.

"Right place, right time," another of the group responded. "I never seem to be around when those opportunities present themselves."

The boisterous man threw his arm around the unlucky man's shoulder as they started to walk again and said, "You never know, it could . . . " The sound of the churning ocean ate up the rest of the conversation.

"What's it like to be rich?" Cate turned to Sheila. "I mean, really rich." Cate wondered if Sheila would tell her what happened to Sheila and David's money, but she did not want to ask.

Sheila paused. A flicker of sadness passed through her—not a lingering feeling, but enough to remind her of her recent predicament. Cate took notice of the look. It made her feel guilty for prying.

"Well, being rich is wonderful in the sense that you don't have to worry about the everyday distractions, which are a lot. But that makes other aspects of your life take center stage, like love, happiness, and self-esteem. Money can't help with any of those."

"Are you going to miss it?" Cate asked carefully, not wanting to poke the wound but curious as to her and David's plans going forward.

"Oh, I'll be fine . . . we both will."

HOLLY

Bradley's escape room plan worked perfectly. He had divided the group into two-person teams so that each of the teams worked on different puzzles simultaneously. Communication was key, he told them. At every step, they would relay information to him so he could put it in sequence, "even if it seems insignificant," he had said. They solved the murder and stormed through the secret door only thirty-six minutes after they entered.

"Is it a record?" Bradley asked the escape room attendant. "It's got to be, right?

"I really can't say," the young woman laughed, "but I can say you did it in very good time."

Disappointed, Bradley rolled his chair towards the exit.

"He's such a perfectionist," Lynn told Holly. "This is going to drive him crazy until he finds out how we did. I'm going to have to keep him busy for the next few days. Maybe we should have done this on the last day. I hadn't realized there was a competition." She sighed.

"Wow, that sounds familiar," Mike chimed in. "Holly is the same way, a complete perfectionist and very impatient. When she graduated from kindergarten, she couldn't wait for the school principal to finish her speech. She walked right up to her as she was speaking and said, "Can I get my prize now?""

"Oh, my God, Dad. You have to stop telling that story! I was six!"

"An oldie but a goodie," Mike laughed. "Hey. Doug and I were thinking about going to hit some golf balls. Anyone else interested?"

"Absolutely not!" Lynn replied. "I'm heading to the pool. Under all this clothing, is a bathing suit just dying to get out."

"Me, too. Somewhere up there, a deck chair has my name on it. Mind if I join you?" Holly asked.

"Sounds great," Lynn said.

"I'm bringing my own chair," Bradley said as he smiled and tapped the arm of his wheelchair, "and a good book. Let's go. We're losing daylight."

"Hey, are you a John Wayne fan?" Holly asked, surprised to hear the old movie phrase come out of his mouth.

"Only the biggest. *The Cowboys* was one of my favorites."

"I'm a *Chisum* girl myself, but I could make a case for *Rooster Cogburn*." They exited the room, leaving all thoughts of breaking escape room records behind them.

On the way to the pool, Lynn, Holly, and Bradley decided to stop at the café for a snack. They reasoned that if they ate something then, at eleven in the morning, they could skip lunch and not ruin their appetite for dinner.

"Ugh, dinner," Holly sighed.

"What's the matter with dinner?" Lynn asked.

"Nothing's wrong with dinner itself. It's the people at our table. They're not very nice. And they are so boring. One of them, Edward, I think he said, has this high-and-mighty attitude and acted like a real jerk to the waiter. Dad and I left before dessert last night. We just couldn't stand it anymore."

"Hey, we've got three empty seats at our table," Bradley said. "You should sit with us?"

"That would be so great," Holly smiled. "I wonder if we can do that?"

"I don't see why not. We can talk to the dining room manager or host, whoever does the seating," Lynn said.

The tiny pit in Holly's stomach disappeared. She hadn't even realized it was there until it was gone. It also made her realize how comfortable she felt. Making friends with these nice people seemed effortless. Holly surprised herself as she enjoyed every minute of it.

Once at the pool, the three found two open chairs side by side, a benefit of showing up at lunchtime. Bradley parked himself between the two women, thereby launching himself into protection mode to ward off unwanted advances to his new friend and his mom. He mentioned how he had read about cruise ships and the number of sexual assaults that occur.

"Bradley, really? Could you be any more morbid right now? Just because you read something doesn't mean you need to spew it," Lynn stated.

Holly discretely gave him a thumbs up and a smile. She thought it sweet that Bradley wanted to protect her.

The afternoon moved swiftly. Holly wasn't sure, but she thought she may have fallen asleep for a while. She looked over and found Bradley ensconced in his book, a title and author she hadn't heard of.

"How's the book?" she asked.

"It's great. It's about a guy who had always wanted to hike the Appalachian Trail but then has an accident and loses the use of one of his arms. I'm just getting to the part where he decides to give it a try anyway. I'm guessing he made it. Otherwise, he wouldn't have written a book about it. Right?"

"Well, I don't know. I read a manuscript like that where the person couldn't accomplish their goal. In the end, it didn't matter. There was a great twist. You may want to read it. The publisher plans to release the book soon.

"How do you know that?"

"Because that's what I do. I'm a reader for a publishing company. I read author's manuscripts and decide if the company should publish them."

"Way cool," an excited Bradley exclaimed. "Who wrote it? When is it coming out? I want to read it!"

Holly laughed at the excitement she created. "Tell you what. You give me your address, and I'll send it to you as soon as it's in print. I always get a free copy of the books I recommend. Maybe I can even get it signed by the author for you."

"So cool. What other manuscripts have you read?"

Holly told Bradley about some of the manuscripts that had passed through her hands. She made a point of mixing in some of the bad ones with the good.

"Someone actually wrote a love story about a zombie and an alien. I laughed through the whole thing. But the author didn't mean it to be funny."

"Maybe someone should write one as a comedy," Bradley thought out loud.

"Do you write, Bradley?"

"Sometimes, but I've never tried to write something like that. That would be fun."

"Who knows? You might be a natural. I've tried, but it's not my thing. I just stick to reading."

Mike and Doug found Holly and Bradley in deep conversation while Lynn remained silent. They couldn't tell if she was sleeping or relaxing.

"So, Doug and I were talking," Mike announced. "It seems our new friends have a few empty seats at their dinner table, so we went and spoke with the maître d' and arranged for us to sit with them for the rest of the trip." Thinking he would surprise Holly with the good news, Mike spoke with an air of satisfaction.

Bradley and Holly laughed.

"What's so funny? What did we miss?" Doug asked.

Lynn opened her eyes. "We came to that conclusion, too, a few hours ago."

"Okay, then. I guess we did good." Doug and Mike clinked beer bottles together in a mock toast.

They found a shady spot on the deck where they could sit together and talk the rest of the afternoon away. Holly felt at ease with their new friends, and she enjoyed herself immensely.

Mike noticed the change in Holly. He realized it as a small step, but still a step. He had high hopes for the remainder of the cruise.

CATE AND SHEILA

"I'm not waiting for you any longer. Dinner is scheduled for eight o'clock for the rest of the week. I told you that. Last night was late because of the boarding process. How much longer are you going to be?" Sheila had an obvious edge to her voice.

Cate emerged from the bathroom to confront her sister. "Well, I can't very well walk into the dining room like this, can I?" She sported the black lace undergarments she purchased just for the trip. "I'm just finishing my face. You go ahead. I'll meet you there soon."

Sheila left in a slight huff but managed to gather her composure before reaching the dining room. As she drifted through the doorway in her white chiffon tea dress with charcoal-grey accents, she resembled sun breaking through lifting clouds of a light summer storm. Men in the dining room turned their heads to watch her breeze by.

The dining room had transformed from the previous evening. Where every table had its own character on the first night, the next night, each looked exactly the same. Burgundy tablecloths, white linen napkins, white bone china, empress-patterned flatware, and brilliant white roses embodied the change from individuality to intimacy, from strangers to friends.

As she approached the table, she noticed unfamiliar faces.

"Hi, Sheila. This is Holly and her dad, Mike," Bradley quickly stated. "They got stuck with snobs at dinner last night, so they're gonna eat with us from now on."

Sheila let out a short giggle. "Well, my sister and I may be a lot of things, but snobs are not among them." She held out her hand to both Mike and Holly. "It's very nice to have you with us. My sister will be here shortly, I hope. She's never on time for anything."

Oscar the waiter appeared to take drink orders. "Well, good evening everyone." He noted Mike and Holly in their new seats. "I'm so glad you found a more suitable table," he said as he gave Holly a wink and a smile.

Holly couldn't help but laugh. "Thank you, Oscar. This is *much* better."

Each of them ordered a beverage, and Sheila ordered a glass of white wine for Cate.

"Here she comes," said Bradley. "She looks hot."

Cate sauntered into the room wearing a bright red, low cut A-line dress, at her neck a long strand of pearls given to her by her parents on her twenty-first birthday. A simple and understated dress on most people, it outlined Cate's body in an elegant fashion. Heads turned.

Holly saw the resemblance to Sheila right away. They shared the same high cheek bones, cute turned-up nose, and emerald-green eyes. She walked with poise and conviction. Holly envied it.

"Oh, hey, Cate. These are our new tablemates," Sheila stated. "Let me see if I get the names right. Mike and Holly?"

"That's exactly right, Sheila." Mike extended his hand to greet Cate.

"It's very nice to meet you, Cate," Holly almost whispered.

"Wow, Cate. Hubba, hubba. You look awesome!" Bradley shared the thoughts of most men in the dining room.

Cate giggled and replied, "I wore this just for you, Bradley. I was hoping you would take me to the movie later."

Bradley shot a quick pleading look at his mother, as if to say, *See, I told you I need to stay up for the movie.*

"All right, Bradley. You don't have to use your laser eyes on me. You can go to the movie tonight," Lynn acquiesced.

Bradley pumped his fist. "Yes!" he said under his breath. "It's a date, Cate."

"You know you have to take me, too, Bradley," Sheila smiled.

"She's always horning in on my dates," Cate laughed.

As they bantered, none of them noticed the maître d' walking toward them, a man following. Once they reached the table, the maître d' stepped aside and said, "Excuse me. We have a latecomer for dinner, and I would like to seat him with you if there are no objections."

He wore dark blue dress slacks and an Oxford style light blue shirt unbuttoned at the top and no tie. *He still looks like a movie star,* Holly thought.

"Derek," Cate almost sang his name. "So nice to see you again."

"Hello, Catherine. I'm sorry—Cate," Derek replied.

"Of course, you can sit with us. No one minds. Right?"

They welcomed the newcomer and introduced themselves around the table.

"Did you get stuck with snobby people for dinner last night? Like Holly and Mike?" Bradley asked Derek. "They got moved here tonight, too."

"Ah . . . no," Derek replied. "I had a dinner meeting last night."

"What line of work are you in?" Doug asked.

"Insurance," Derek replied. "I usually don't explain any further than that, because people think I'm going to try to sell them something."

"I'll bet," said Doug.

"I'm here on a business trip. Seminars, team building, that sort of thing," he explained.

Cate took the opportunity to extract some information. Thinking it the perfect opening, she began, "I had to do one of those team-building events once. We flew to Arizona to some resort, but the airline lost my luggage. A short, little trip from

California, and the airline lost two of my suitcases. I had to buy all new clothes at the resort."

Cate had intentionally provided the perfect segue for Derek to talk about his lost luggage, but all he said was, "I hope the airline reimbursed you."

Cate and Sheila exchanged a knowing glance. *There's more to Derek than he would let on,* they both thought.

Oscar returned to take their dinner order. The conversation flowed freely and comfortably. They ordered a second round of drinks, and Derek ordered a diet coke.

Holly remembered seeing Derek at breakfast earlier that day when she saw him in his nice suit but appearing a bit disheveled. The Oxford shirt he wore to dinner was straight out of the package. She could see the folds in the fabric. *Maybe he got a stain on his business shirt,* she thought.

They enjoyed dinner, the menu as varied as its customers. Bradley followed Derek's lead and ordered osso bucco, veal shanks braised with vegetables, wine, and a tomato-chicken stock. His choice surprised everyone at the table, especially his parents. Both Doug and Mike ordered rib-eye steak with roast shallots and balsamic glaze. Sea bass attracted Lynn and Cate, while Sheila went for the chicken saltimbocca. Holly felt a bit adventurous that evening and decided to try something totally out of character for her. She ordered peppered lamb chops with wild mushroom risotto and grilled balsamic asparagus. She had never before had any of those things. After she placed her order, Mike gave her a big smile of approval.

Conversation continued throughout dinner and never fell into uncomfortable silence. The three young woman paid attention to Derek, who seemed to pay attention to a group of diners a few tables over. When Holly found the opportunity, she turned in the direction of Derek's gaze and saw her former dinner companions only three tables away. If she really concentrated, she could pick out the voice of the boisterous guy, Edward, talking about his investments again or still. *Maybe Derek needs investment advice*, Holly thought.

As dinner wound down, talk turned to outdoor movie plans. "Well, Bradley, Cate and I are going. Who else wants to come?" Sheila looked directly at Derek.

"Not me," Derek said. "I've got some work to do. Early morning meeting, too."

"It's not really my kind of movie," Doug said. "How about you, Mike?"

"I'm with you, Doug. Not my thing. What do you say we hit the casino, see what they've got?"

Doug nodded.

"I'd love to go to the movie," Lynn said. "*Avatar* is a great film. How about you, Holly?"

"Yes, I love that movie, and it's a beautiful night."

"Okay, Bradley. Looks like you have four dates for tonight," said Cate.

Bradley grinned at his dad.

Derek excused himself first, then Doug and Mike. As soon as they cleared earshot, Cate turned to Sheila and said, "Isn't that weird?"

"It is," Sheila replied, "but there's got to be another explanation."

"What are you guys talking about?" Bradley asked.

The sisters exchanged a quick look, then Cate began. "Well, it's probably nothing, but Sheila and I saw Derek at the pool this morning . . . wearing a business suit."

"So?" Bradley questioned. "What's wrong with that?"

"Well, nothing," Cate went on, "but I'm pretty sure he wasn't being totally honest when he said he had been at a business meeting. And . . . we saw him buying new clothes at one of the stores. Three bags full."

"Maybe the airline lost his luggage," Lynn piped in.

"That's what we figured, but when Cate mentioned how the airline had lost her luggage—great idea by the way, Cate— he didn't say a word." Cate exhibited a satisfied smile. "I would think if that did actually happen, he would want to gripe about it, at least."

Bradley jumped in. "Maybe he just needed new clothes."

Holly sat quietly, taking in the conversation and remembering his demeanor at breakfast. Before giving it too much thought she said, "He doesn't buy his clothes off the rack. He was wearing an expensive suit and shoes."

The sisters looked surprised.

"I saw him at breakfast this morning. He wasn't eating though. He came into the room to talk to the captain. They seemed to be in a serious conversation and then left the room together."

The table got quiet as each of them processed the bits of information.

"But he seems so nice," Lynn said. "I'm sure there's a logical explanation."

Nobody had an answer. Holly thought about it and decided to tell them what she noticed during dinner.

"Did anyone else notice that he seemed to be paying a lot of attention to that table over there?" She held her finger close to her body, trying not to make a show of pointing to her former dining companions. "Those are the boorish people my dad and I sat with last night."

Bradley's face lit up. "You don't suppose he's a thief, do you? Like a cat burglar or something?"

"Bradley, really," Lynn admonished, "You watch entirely too much television."

"I doubt he would take the chance of talking to the captain if he planned to steal things," Holly reasoned. "But it is kind of weird."

"So, what's so special about those people over there, other than being snobs?" Bradley asked Holly.

"I don't know. They said they're all successful, probably well-off people. That one guy, Edward, kept talking about his investment properties and how much money he makes." Holly paused, trying to remember what he had said. "He told us he tripled his money in one year. I remember that because my dad and I didn't believe him. We laughed about it later."

Sheila gasped. "Cate, that's the guy we saw at lunch. He said the exact same thing to one of the guys he was walking with. I don't recognize any of the other people, though."

Cate nodded.

"Maybe it's some sort of corporate espionage," Bradley suggested.

"Bradley," Lynn exclaimed. "Your imagination astounds me."

"Well, he may not be too far off. It sounds like this guy could be running a Ponzi scheme," Holly said. "That would make sense. You know, like he's trying to get people to invest in something. But what would Derek have to do with it, if anything?"

"I have an idea." Bradley began to get excited. "At dinner tomorrow night, I'll ask you about those people you sat with. If he's one of them, he will probably ignore the conversation, right? But if he starts asking questions or seems interested, then he's not part of it."

"But we're not going to be here for dinner tomorrow night. We're going to have dinner in St. Thomas," Holly remembered.

"Oh, yeah," Bradley scowled. "Us, too. It will have to wait until the next night."

"That's a good idea, but it still doesn't explain his choice of wardrobe," Sheila countered.

Another pause fell over the table.

"I got nothing," Bradley stated.

CATE AND SHEILA

It was close to one in the morning when the movie concluded. The clear starry night proved a spectacular host for the special-effects-filled film. The outdoor theater provided all typical accoutrements for theatergoers with the added benefit of a nearby bar, an attraction Cate and Sheila enjoyed.

They had said their goodnights to Bradley, Lynn, and Holly as the three decided to call it a night.

"Okay, Cate, let's find a place we can dance."

"I checked out all the clubs on the ship while I was on the airplane. Sylvester's is open until four o'clock, and it's supposed to have the best view of all the clubs on the ship. Deck PA, the Panorama Deck."

"Let's go."

As they approached the door, Cate began to think she had it wrong. She heard no muffled music ahead, and the glass windows appeared blackened.

Sheila reached for the door and swung it open. The soft melody of the ship breaking through the ocean became engulfed by the bass, treble, and vocals of a Springsteen classic. Floor-to-ceiling windows encased the room on three sides showcasing where the ship had already traveled. Purple, yellow, and white lasers danced in unison with the gyrating inhabitants as the musicians morphed seamlessly into Bob Seger and the Silver Bullet Band.

They headed toward the bar, but a waiter stopped them midway. "Would you like me to find you a table?" he asked.

"Yes, that would be much appreciated." Sheila released her best flirting smile.

He was almost six feet tall and impeccably built. The dark curls on his head and one o'clock stubble on his face accentuated his Brazilian blue eyes and tanned complexion. The brilliant white uniform only enhanced his features. He showed them to a recently vacated table next to the darkened windows. Sheila let slip an audible gasp, loud enough to be heard over the musings of Bob Seger as the waiter walked away to retrieve the drinks they had ordered.

"I know, right?" Cate almost groaned.

While they waited for the waiter to bring the drinks, they scanned to room to get a feel for the crowd. It much resembled the atmosphere and clientele found in an upscale California club, except that customers' ages varied more. When Cate mentioned that to Sheila, her sister disagreed.

"I've got to get you into some of the Hollywood clubs. It's not unusual to see a sixty-year-old hacking it up with a twenty-one-year-old. And that's only because the twenty-one-year-old would have fake identification."

"Well, back home in Sacramento the clubs are still overflowing with twenty-somethings, the occasional thirty-something, but never a forty-something. At least not the clubs where I've been," Cate confessed. "I like the variety of people."

When the waiter arrived both Cate and Sheila struck their best casual-yet-stunning pose.

"Merci," Sheila said as she slowly and deliberately lowered her long, mascara-thickened eyelashes and reopened them to draw attention to her luminous green eyes.

Not to be outdone, Cate reached for his attention by placing her hand gently on his arm. "Thank you so much," she cooed. "This table is perfect."

"You are most welcome," he replied, making a conscious effort to give them equal eye contact. "My name is Mateo. If I can be of service, please don't hesitate to ask."

Careful not to assume who would sign for the drinks, he held out the small black tray with the drink receipt and pen. Both reached for the tray at the same time, but Cate captured it first. She signed her name and wrote their cabin number on the receipt.

"I got this, Sis," Cate said.

"Okay, but I get the next one. You paid for lunch today, too."

Cate knew she couldn't afford to pay for every drink and lunch tab, but she felt guilty. It had never occurred to her that Sheila could have problems of her own. She decided right then that when they got home, she would make a better effort to stay in touch.

"Dance with me." Sheila stood and grabbed Cate's hand, breaking her out of her thoughts.

It took all of four minutes for two of the more confident men in the room to approach the swaying sisters and ask them for a dance. They didn't sit down for the rest of the evening.

HOLLY

Holly and Mike began the day with coffee and muffins at Aweigh from the Grind Café. They exchanged stories about their night, although Holly left out the part about the Ponzi scheme theory. The more she thought about it, the more ridiculous it sounded. And then, just as if she conjured him up herself, Edward the loudmouth burst through the door from the inner hallway and sat at a table on the outskirts of the café. She watched him check his watch and scan the deck. When their eyes met, he didn't show even a glimmer of recognition.

"Hey, that's the guy from dinner the other night, right?" Mike asked.

Holly nodded, "Yup. Mr. Wall Street."

Two men joined him. They looked younger and well put together, probably wearing clothes their wives laid out for them. Edward stood, shook their hands, and waited until they got their coffee before he launched into the familiar spiel.

"Good morning."

Holly and Mike turned in unison to see Derek standing behind them.

"Good morning," they replied, synchronized as if in one voice.

"Join us for breakfast?" Mike asked.

"Thank you, yes. I'd like that," Derek replied.

He pulled a chair from the next table and turned it slightly in Edward's direction. He wore a pair of white shorts with a small cruise-line logo on the right leg hem with a royal blue polo shirt sporting the same logo, only larger, on the left chest. The flawlessly bright white sneakers and equally bright white socks also displayed the cruise line logo. *He's a walking billboard*, Holly thought, *and a highly effective one at that.* She noticed her heartbeat quicken.

"Coffee sir?" The waiter hadn't made a sound as he approached.

"Yes, please. Black. How about a muffin, too? I don't care what kind. You choose," Derek said with a grin, showing his freshly shaved dimples. "Another beautiful day, isn't it?"

"As promised," Mike replied. "Are you going into St. Thomas when we dock later today?"

Derek turned his hands palm up in the universal language of expressing, *I don't know*, as he said, "It's going to depend on work. My schedule is kind of up in the air."

Holly became more curious about Derek. Her shy self would normally sit quietly and listen to the men talk, but her curious nature prompted her to ask, "I thought you had a meeting this morning."

"What? Oh." He looked down at his outfit. "I did. It was a casual breakfast meeting."

The waiter set his coffee on the table and said, "The muffin is an island favorite, pineapple-macadamia."

"Thank you. I'm sure it's great."

Holly lifted an eyebrow as she gazed from the muffin to Derek's guilty expression.

"Ah." Slight pause. "I was speaking at the meeting, so I didn't have the opportunity to eat."

He is good on his feet, Holly thought. *Very convincing.*

But she instantly recognized his lie.

SHEILA

Cate slept soundly as Sheila made up her bunk and prepared for her daily sunbathing routine. Even in Hollywood Hills, Sheila got up before the gardeners and servants except for Ava, her kitchen maid. Ava insisted on being up bright and early to have Sheila's macchiato ready for her as she made her way to the swimming pool. Sheila felt guilty about it and told Ava many times that she need not bother, but Ava persisted.

At the thought, Sheila felt the tiniest tinge of homesickness.

She filled a glass with water for Cate and placed it with a bottle of ibuprofen next to the alarm clock. She supposed Cate would need it, as her sister had finished the evening with a few straight bourbons after drinking wine most of the night. Sheila had limited herself to a couple glasses of wine and therefore woke up unaffected by the previous night's libations. Score one for her good decision.

She arrived first at the pool area except for deckhands, bartender, and a waiter. She chose a chair facing east, one that would give her optimum sun and minimum passenger interaction.

CATE

The bunk-side clock read 10:59 when Cate could finally open her eyes. She saw a glass of water and a bottle of ibuprofen sitting next to it. She poured four of the pills into her palm and downed them with a glass of water as she sat motionless on the edge of her bunk. While sitting, she replayed the previous night's events in her head. She smiled as she recalled Mateo, who also appeared in her early morning dream.

Cate saw smoothed bedcovers on Sheila's bunk neatly tucked at the corners and the bathroom door ajar.

"Sheila?" she called.

No answer. She tried to think. *What time was it when they got in?* Then she remembered. Sheila did not come back to the room with her. She wanted to stay and dance. Cate had tried to get her sister to leave the club around two thirty, but Sheila wouldn't budge.

Cate checked her phone for messages: nothing but the usual junk. She dialed Sheila's number, but it went straight to voicemail. She began to panic. *Did Sheila even come back to the room last night?*

Cate quickly brushed her teeth, ran a comb through her hair, and put on a pair of jeans and t-shirt. She checked the breakfast buffet before realizing they had cleared that up an hour before. She looked into every café and lounge on the way to the pool.

Cate's panic increased with each empty outcome. She winced when she emerged onto the deck as the sun forced the previous night's alcohol through her pores and lent energy to the hammer in her head.

Once her eyes adjusted to the bright light, Cate scanned the deck. It didn't take long to find Sheila lying on a deck chair in her unmistakable blue-and-white striped, wide-brimmed hat and a matching blue bikini. Three considerably attractive young men surrounded her and seemed mesmerized by her banter. Of course, Cate decided, Sheila had them laid out in a way that would not block her sun. She sipped on a Bloody Mary. Thinking she recognized the nuances of Sheila's body language, facial expressions, and laughter, Cate watched her closely. It seemed that Sheila was on the prowl.

Cate's panic quickly turned to exasperation. She wanted to confront Sheila and ask her what the hell she was doing but the thought of any of them seeing her so disheveled prevented her from doing so. She felt dizzy. The hot sun, usually welcome, felt like a million tiny razor blades scraping across her face. She took a seat in the shade near the bar, her view obstructed from Sheila. A waiter quickly appeared, so Cate ordered a Bloody Mary to take the sting out of her hangover. *How could Sheila do this to David? Especially now when he will need her the most.*

The Bloody Mary went down tangy and refreshing, just what she needed. She took it with her to their cabin so she could make herself presentable before laying into Sheila.

SHEILA

The sun fed Sheila's lifeblood. She needed the sun's rays just as she needed air to breathe. Without the sun, she became a different person, a person she did not enjoy and one her family and friends would not recognize. She first noticed the phenomenon in her teen years when she likened herself to a sunflower eagerly awaiting sunrise, then tracking and absorbing the celestial energy while it faded beneath the horizon until the next day only to reset toward the east to wait once more.

Feeling morning sun on her skin somehow gave Sheila confidence to glide through the day as she absorbed the energy of the orb to kindle the happiness she craved. A day consisting of clouds or rain kept her motionless, sad, and unsure of herself. She made her worst decisions on sunless days.

Not a morning person, David never got out of bed before ten, and everyone considered that an early rise for him. He fed off the nightlife.

Sheila enjoyed both and could hold up her end either way. She didn't need sleep to re-energize. Only sun. She also did some of her clearest thinking while sunbathing, although the household staff always assumed she slept the entire time . . . she heard the whispered conversations.

Sheila thought about David as she rejuvenated in the sun. *Just what is it about him that makes me want to leave him?* She couldn't answer the question without thinking herself petty and shallow, which made her feel like a horrible person. *Although he's kind, sweet, and attentive when we're together,* she thought, *we just aren't together very often. Oh, we attend parties, events, and premieres almost every evening, but other people continually surround us, none of whom I'd call a friend. But we are hardly ever alone together.*

Outwardly, lying in her deck chair, Sheila looked serene and content. Most passersby would probably think her asleep. However, inwardly she experienced turmoil as boisterous as a Hollywood party at midnight.

You are lonely. Leave the party. The idea unexpectedly invaded her thoughts, a clarity that could only have come from her energy source rising in the eastern sky. *It's up to me, not David. He has no idea how I feel. He always asks me if I want to go to this party or that, but I give him the answer I think he wants, not what I want. I'm still trying to be the person I think other people want me to be. I don't want to be that person anymore. Maybe David doesn't want me to be that person either, otherwise why would he keep asking the question?*

An imperceptible smile swept Sheila's face. The deck began to fill with passengers, but she paid no attention. Like a schoolgirl acknowledging her first crush, she suddenly felt both anxious and excited. Nervousness enveloped her self-assured exterior. She checked the time. It was too early, but she nevertheless reached for her cell phone.

She sunbathed the morning away. Her three dance partners from the club spotted her on deck and stopped to say hello. They invited her to join them for lunch, but she declined. She wanted to be alone with her revelation. And then she would have to get ready for entering the port of St. Thomas to celebrate her birthday.

She reached for her phone again, this time to dial Cate's number, expecting to leave a message about where to find her.

Cate answered.

HOLLY

Holly decided to spend the rest of the morning strolling the ship's decks with her high-tech digital camera. She had an eye for candids, catching people in interesting and sometimes vulnerable moments that made her photographs memorable. Her boss wanted her to produce a coffee table book to showcase her art, but Holly resisted. She lacked the confidence to put herself out there. She assumed publishers would throw her work into the discard pile, as she herself had done with so many manuscripts. No one knew better than she the difficulty of getting a publisher's backing.

She sauntered down the port side of the Sports Deck that housed a center gym encircled by a jogging/walking track. Instinctively framing her subject in the best possible light, she occasionally raised the camera to her eye.

When she reached the stern, she viewed a cargo ship in the distance. The multicolored intermodal containers reminded her of her favorite childhood toy, Legos. Set against the dark blue ocean and vivid blue sky, the stacked containers presented a unique picture.

As she brought the camera to her eye and focused on the ship, she noticed that her frame took in two men and a woman in heated conversation on *Perth's* deck below. She was about to move the camera away to see if she could avoid including them in the picture but lingered long enough to recognize one of the men and the woman as the lawyers from the first night's dining room fiasco. She watched until she began to feel like a peeping Tom and moved the camera away.

After a few attempts, she realized it was impossible to get the picture she wanted without including them. Reasoning she would crop them out later, she tapped the button. Following her custom for each photograph she took, she created a caption. Before editing, she called her photo *Anger in the Sea of Tranquility.*

Almost as soon as she thought it up, she discarded it as lame.

Keeping her eye out for subject matter, Holly followed the track to starboard. She found Derek jogging down the track. He hung on to a camera. He must have been deep in thought, Holly surmised, as he did not notice her until he was almost beside her.

"Oh, hey, Holly." He stopped when he reached her.

"Hi, Derek. You seem like a man on a mission."

"Ah, no. Nothing really. I just, ah . . . " He looked towards the stern and said a little more confidently, "I just wanted to get a picture of that cargo ship back there." Then he pointed to the Lego ship.

Once again Holly felt sure that Derek was lying. But why would he lie?

"That's funny," she told him. "That's what I just did. I'll let you get to it while the light is still good. See you later." She started to walk away and then casually glanced over her shoulder. Derek wasted no time getting to the railing, but he didn't lift his camera. He just stood there.

It's one thing to assume someone is lying to you. It's another to know it. Holly felt positive Derek had not been honest with her. Just two weeks before, she finished a manuscript written by a former FBI instructor detailing how to read body language to determine, among other interesting law enforcement tactics, if someone is lying. Some simple and obvious signs include pausing while answering a question or saying ah, um, or similar.

Derek had done some of that, but he also used hand gestures, quite common while talking but unusual when finished talking. The FBI instructor stated that, when someone lies, the mind is too busy creating or perpetuating the lie and so may not allow gesturing until after completing the lie. The author also wrote that a liar would most likely use the nondominant hand to gesture. If Holly had noticed only those two clues, she would not feel convinced that Derek lied. However, Derek also broke eye contact, changed his tone slightly, and tilted his head just enough to be noticeable.

But his lips provided the real indicator. Just before he spoke an untruth, he pursed his lips, an involuntary action when one does not wish to discuss something or lies, the author wrote.

Holly had approved the manuscript for publication.

She began to think she, her dad, and their friends should keep their distance from Derek. But how would she explain that to her father? *Maybe I won't have to,* she thought. *Maybe Derek's business on the ship will keep him preoccupied and I won't have to explain anything.*

Holly made her way back to their stateroom to get ready for St. Thomas. Still early yet, she thought she might relax on the balcony for a while before they docked. They would be in port overnight, not sailing again until the next evening at six o'clock.

CATE AND SHEILA

"What!" Cate hollered into the phone.

"Well, good afternoon to you, too." Sheila chuckled. "I guess someone's got a bit of a hangover."

"What are you doing, Sheila? Did you even come back to the cabin last night? What the fuck?"

Suddenly all the positive energy Sheila had built up zapped out of her as if Cate took a hose and siphoned it from her body.

"What are you talking about, Cate? Of course, I went back to the cabin last night. Didn't you see the water and ibuprofen I left for you?"

"Oh." Cate silently chastised herself for missing the obvious clue, which just made her more upset.

"Well, thank you, but that's not the point. What the hell are you doing throwing yourself at those guys? You're a married woman, Sheila!"

"What are you talking about, Cate? What guys am I throwing myself at?" It was Sheila's turn to get angry.

Surrounding sunbathers took notice of the heated conversation.

"I was just at the pool, Sheila. I saw you with those guys. You were ready to pounce. I've seen it a hundred times."

Sheila was not only livid. She was deeply hurt. *How dare Cate treat me this way. She has no cause.*

"Where are you?" Sheila barked.

"In the cabin."

"I'll be right there. Don't move!"

With every step, Sheila's anger grew. However great her anger, it didn't match how much Cate had wounded her. She may as well have stuck a pitchfork through her. But she was also very confused. So, what if she had been flirting, not that she was. Cate knew Sheila planned to leave David. She had said she understood.

She arrived at the cabin door radiating that infuriation and burst into the room.

"Where the hell do you get off talking to me like that? What is your problem?"

"My problem? No, Sheila, what the hell is your problem? How can you treat David like this?"

"Like what, Cate?" She threw her arms up in the air. "What are you talking about?"

"I saw you with those guys at the pool, Sheila. You were wrapping them around your little finger, like you always do when you're on the prowl. You were beaming."

"Cate, you are delusional. First of all, what business is it of yours if I am flirting? And second, I wasn't flirting. I was declining a lunch invitation. Why the hell do I have to explain myself to you?"

Wondering if she had misread the situation, Cate paused. Her head began to pound again.

"But you had that look, Sheila, that *new love* look. I've seen it on you many times before and your body language corro... corrob... corrob... "

"Corroborated, Cate? Is that what you're trying to spit out? What the hell are you talking about? I was happy, I was just..." Sheila went silent. *I was happy.* An involuntary smile donned her face.

"What the fuck are you smiling about?"

"Not that it's any of your business, but I was happy because I decided I was not going to leave David."

"Leave David! Are you out of your mind? How unbelievably shallow are you that you would even consider doing that under these circumstances."

"Now wait just one goddamned minute, Cate! I've had it with your insults. First, you're pissed off because you think I'm cheating on David, and now you're pissed off because I tell you I'm not leaving David? Get off the merry-go-round, Cate."

"How low is it to even consider leaving David just because he's broke now. You should be standing by his side, helping him cope. Not throwing him out."

"What are you talking about, broke? Who's broke?"

Cate looked confused.

"You and David!"

"Where the hell did you hear that?" Now Sheila looked confused.

"You told me."

"I absolutely did not! Why would I say that?"

Silence.

In her head, Cate replayed the conversation they'd had at the bar. Sheila was right, she never actually said that they were broke. *But what did she say?*

Cate broke the silence. She spoke softly and deliberately, recounting the scene as much for herself as for her sister.

"At the bar the day we boarded, you got all upset when I said we could have stayed at your house with all the servants instead of taking this cruise. And then at the muster you told me you had to tell me something. It all added up to David losing his money, no more servants, no more house."

"Cate, I was upset because you made me sound like a spoiled brat. And I was worried about telling you I had decided to leave David. I knew that wasn't going to sit well with you."

"You're not broke?"

"No."

"You're not leaving David?"

"No."

"You weren't flirting?"

"No."

"You're not going to kill me?"

"Maybe."

After a long pause, Cate cried, "Oh, Sheila, can you ever forgive me? I'm such a horrible person." Tears streamed down her face, with a few splashing on her bare feet.

"You're not a horrible person, Cate. Just a horrible sleuth."

They reached out their arms at the same moment in a genuine sister hug.

"Happy Birthday!" Cate said.

They laughed so hard their stomachs hurt, and when they finished laughing, they sat on their bunks. Leaving one small detail out of her story, Sheila told Cate about her morning.

ST. THOMAS

HOLLY

The ship docked at the St. Thomas port. Holly and Mike planned to poke around town that evening, wander through the shops, and then find a place to have dinner. Then Holly received a text.

Please come help me celebrate my birthday at the Yacht Club tonight at eight o'clock. I hope you can both make it. Sheila.

After a brief discussion, Holly and Mike decided they would join the celebration after they did a little shopping in town. They really wanted to go to the outdoor market, but it had already closed by the time they disembarked. Instead, they decided to go to the shops near the marina and yacht club. The beautifully landscaped development resembled a small-town main street. Benches lined the way with an occasional water fountain to create serene space, one suited to loosening the wallets of travelers who ventured to the area. They noticed several older gentlemen sitting alone on outside benches, presumably waiting for their wives to finish shopping in a nearby store. They came upon a cute little clothing shop named *Isle Take It*.

"This looks like a nice place to pick up a birthday gift for Sheila," Holly said.

"What are you thinking? A hat or something?"

"Oh, God, no. Have you not seen the way Sheila and Cate dress? If they wear a hat, you can be sure they have an entire outfit to go with it, shoes included," Holly explained.

"I was thinking of a scarf," she continued. Scarves are very versatile. She could wear it around her neck, in her hair or dress up a hat or a skirt with it. And if we get a multicolored one, she can wear it with more than one outfit." Holly hit the last word with a head bob, accentuating its importance.

"Okay, then. A scarf it is. Did I just get a fashion lesson?"

Holly laughed as she turned to enter the store.

"It's not complete yet. Follow me."

Feeling as comfortable as a trucker at a tea party, Mike dutifully accompanied his daughter into the boutique. He watched as she stopped occasionally to admire a garment during her perusal of each clothing rack. He had never seen her so relaxed, given she would soon attend a near stranger's birthday party at a ritzy yacht club. At home, he knew, she would have spent her time trying to rig an excuse to put the brakes on the party. But here they were, in tandem, picking out a gift for that stranger. Mike felt tremendous happiness, and his face reflected it.

"What are you smiling about?" Holly interrupted his thoughts.

"Oh, nothing in particular, I'm just enjoying myself."

"But you hate shopping."

"I know. But I'm not shopping. You are."

"Sometimes I wonder if you understand the concept of shopping, Dad." Holly picked a scarf from a rack. "What do you think of this?"

"I think it's white and yellow and red and orange."

"Uh huh. Glad I asked," she chuckled. "I like the way it looks like colors have been brushed on the fabric, like a painter wiping excess paint from a brush."

"Uh huh."

"And these colors will complement her beautiful eyes."

"Uh huh."

"Okay, okay. You sold me," Holly quipped.

Mike loved seeing that side of Holly.

A witty, light-hearted, wonderful person, she spent most of her time with her nose in a book. He had hoped that would change on this trip. And so far, things looked good. Of course, she did all of it with him, her father.

Baby steps.

Holly asked the shopkeeper to put the scarf in a decorative bag with a tag so they could write a short birthday greeting. As they left, they spotted Bradley, Lynn, and Doug just outside the shop. Happy to run into each other, they exchanged pleasantries.

"Are you going to Sheila's birthday party?" Bradley asked.

"Yes, we are. We just picked her up a little gift," Holly replied.

"We got her something, too. A scarf?" Bradley looked at his mom to make sure he got that right.

"That's right, Bradley. It's a scarf," Lynn smiled.

As Mike and Holly laughed, Lynn wondered about her choice.

"That's what we got her," Holly said through her laughter. "That is so funny."

Lynn began to laugh. "It is the *only* gift for this situation."

The three males looked puzzled as if Holly and Lynn had just reasonably concluded that one plus one equals three.

"I wanted to get her a dress, but mom said that wasn't appropriate. I don't get it. She likes dresses." Bradley sulked.

The two women shared a knowing glance.

"I can explain. You said you love to read, right?" asked Holly.

"Yeah," Bradley replied.

"Let's say it was your birthday today and I decided to buy you a book. But I don't know you very well, so I buy you a book I really like, hoping you will like it, too. Something like a romance novel."

"Ewww. Why would you do that?"

"That's my point exactly. A woman's clothing choices are a lot like book preferences. So, what kind of books do you like, Bradley?"

"Anything but romance novels."

They shared another laugh as they all walked together toward the yacht club.

CATE

Overlooking the marina, the yacht club restaurant perched on stilts. Vessels of all shapes and sizes moored at the docks. A few people wandering the decks appeared to be curious travelers presumably dreaming of life among the yacht set.

Model ships and wooden steering wheels throughout, the teak-filled dining room strutted the expected nautical theme. Chandeliers fashioned like antique gas lamps illuminated the room with an amber glow, brilliantly animating scattered tropical plants. The teak wood floor exhibited an old-world quality, well worn but well kept, and the ceiling boasted a mix of teak and corrugated tin with vintage flags draped from above. Surrounded on three sides by walls of windows, the view at any time of day reigned spectacular. The old and worn illusion gave way to a new, clean, and impressive reality.

Sheila stopped at the reception desk to speak with the hostess and sent Cate to the bar to order cocktails. The bar, also created from teak, ran the length of the room, and hosted black leather, well-padded stools with high backs and rotating seats. Cate chose two available stools closest to the entrance so they could watch for the others. If she had her way, they would sit at the bar all night as they watched the sunset and sipped on tropical concoctions.

Cate and Sheila spent most of the day repairing their relationship. Cate felt awful about the way she jumped to conclusions and vowed never to assume anything about Sheila again. But she found it difficult to keep her promise. She couldn't help but feel that Sheila had kept something from her. She had no idea what it might be, but she felt Sheila hadn't told her everything.

During their long talk, Sheila had revealed that she took the cruise to tell Cate she planned to leave David for good. She explained she felt David had no direction, that the two of them just coexisted without living a meaningful life. She also clarified that, when Cate spotted her on the deck as she declined a lunch invitation from the young men, she had just had a revelation—a thought that had surprisingly never occurred to her, the thought that she was master of her own fate—that she didn't need to wait for David to make things right, that she could manifest her own happiness and maybe even David's. She also told Cate she had decided to take responsibility for the failure of her first two marriages, a painful admission.

Sheila had a busy and productive morning, Cate mused as she sipped her Island Breeze and waited for her sister to join her.

SHEILA AND DAVID

"Look who I found at the door!" Sheila strolled to the bar with Mike on her arm as the rest of the group followed.

"Our table is ready," Sheila announced. "This handsome man is waiting to take us to our seats." She pointed to the waiter holding a large stack of thick leather-clad menus.

Sharply dressed in black slacks, white shirt, and a short white sport coat with tails, the waiter steered them to a table for eight next to south-facing windows. Painting the sky in hues of blue, purple, and orange, the sun had begun its descent into the ocean.

They insisted that the birthday girl, Sheila, sit at the head of the table. Bradley wheeled himself to the empty spot provided by the waiter to Sheila's left. Everyone else took a seat.

"Who is sitting there?" Bradley pointed to the empty chair at the other end of the table. "Did you invite Derek?"

"Yes, I did, but he said he couldn't make it. Something about work. But I did invite someone else," Sheila divulged, directing her remark toward Cate.

As if on cue, a tall, blonde, and well-tanned man in khaki slacks and coral dress shirt approached the table.

"David!" Cate screamed, jumped up from her chair, nearly knocking it over as she gave him a hug and a kiss. "What . . . how . . . when?"

David interrupted Cate's stuttering. "Sheila called me this morning and asked me to come down and spend her birthday with her. So, I chartered a plane, and here I am."

Sheila beamed. She and David embraced and shared a silent moment.

"Thank you for coming," Sheila shyly whispered.

"Always," David whispered back.

Sheila felt like a sixteen-year-old girl at a school dance. Her heart beat quickly, and her face flushed. Something in that moment told her that her life would never be the same, and she couldn't wait to get started.

She circled the table with David on her arm, introducing her new friends, finishing with Bradley.

"Hello, Bradley." David shook his hand. "I understand you took my wife out on a date." David tried to feign displeasure.

"That's right, I did. You snooze, you lose." The wisecrack spewed easily from Bradley's lips.

The table burst into laughter with merriment that set the tone for the evening.

Cate moved from her chair to the open seat at the end of the table, thus allowing David to sit next to his wife.

David ordered two bottles of champagne for the table and a bottle of sparkling cider for Bradley. They toasted Sheila's birthday seven times as each took a turn to wish her well.

As the sun showed its last bit of life for the day, their meals arrived with great fanfare. Four waiters, each carrying two platters, made the customary presentation parade as they circled the dining room to show off the extravagantly garnished dinners.

After the meal, the waiter appeared from the kitchen with a flaming baked Alaska and set it down in front of Sheila. David had called the restaurant earlier in the day to arrange for the elaborate dessert. Had anyone looked closely, they would have noticed happy tears forming in Sheila's eyes.

Sheila genuinely appreciated each of the scarves, and after admonishing each of them for buying her a present, she donned both and promised to cherish them forever.

The birthday celebration ended.

"You're on your own tonight, Sis. David has a condo in town. I'll give you a call tomorrow?" Sheila raised the pitch of her voice at the end, as if asking an actual question.

Cate gave Sheila and David a hug and wished them a great evening. They left arm in arm like newlyweds on a honeymoon.

A fresh start, Sheila sensed.

HOLLY

After Sheila and David departed, the discussion moved to plans for the rest of the evening.

"I'm all wound up," Cate stated. "I need to dance. What do you say, people?"

"Well," Lynn replied, "unfortunately it is getting late, and we'll need to be getting to bed soon."

"You mean, *I'll* have to get to bed soon. Right?" Bradley paused before speaking again.

"Why don't we go back to the ship. I'll go to the cabin and go to bed at a reasonable hour, and the rest of you can go dancing. When is the last time you danced, Mom?"

"Ages ago," she looked at Doug hopefully. "At someone's wedding, I think."

Doug nodded approvingly. "Okay."

"Mike, Holly? What do you say?" Cate asked with an encouraging tone.

"Okay," Mike said. "I'll go, but I can't promise that I'll dance."

"Same here," Holly laughed.

"Okay!" Bradley laughed, too.

Since David had taken care of the dinner bill, they needed only to gather their belongings and head back to the ship.

They chose a different nightclub from the one Sheila and Cate had patronized the night before. With music Holly happened to love, sounds of the 1960s and 1970s, the band catered to a more mature audience. They found an open table on the far side of the room away from the band so they could carry on a conversation without having to scream over the music.

Holly excused herself to go to the restroom while Mike and Cate waited for Doug and Lynn to arrive after helping Bradley get settled in their cabin. Mike and Cate sat alone at the table.

"Well, what do you say Mike? Ready to hit the dance floor?" Cate held out her hands.

"This kind of music I can dance to." He stood, bowed at the waist, took her hand, and in the most gentlemanly manner asked, "Excuse me, Miss. May I have the pleasure of this dance?"

"Why, Sir, I thought you'd never ask." Exaggerating batting her eyelashes, Cate replied in her best Scarlett O'Hara impression.

With perfect rhythm and impeccable charm Mike quickly had Cate swirling around the dance floor.

"You're a wonderful dancer." Cate couldn't hold back her surprise. "I could do this all night."

The compliment caused a twinge of pain to run through Mike. Cate noticed immediately.

"I'm sorry," she said, "I didn't mean to . . ."

Mike quickly regained his composure, twirled her again, and said with a smile, "Don't be. My wife said the exact same thing the first night we danced together. I had forgotten about it. Thank you for reminding me."

"What was she like? If you don't mind my asking."

"Not at all. She was a wonderful dancer, almost as good as you," he chuckled. "She made me feel like I was, too."

"Well, she was right. And I was serious. I could do this all night."

"Only if they play waltzes all night," Mike laughed.

As Holly left the ladies room, she noticed a young woman ahead trailing a tail of toilet paper from the spike of her heel. Holly hastened her pace to try to step on the paper to release it from the woman's shoe before anyone saw it. She lunged toward the slithering paper with her right foot, trapped it, and succeeded in removing it from the unsuspecting spike. As she did so, however, her right foot skidded on the slick floor, and she fell flat on her rear end in the process, one leg stretched in front, one folded beneath her. Pure instinct swiveled her head to see if anyone noticed.

She caught the eye of the most handsome man in the room heading straight toward her.

"Are you okay? Here, let me help you up." He held out his hand.

"Um, thank you." Mortified, she couldn't look at his perfectly proportioned, tanned, and dimple-marked face, although she obviously noticed it.

"That was an amazing thing you did," he said.

"Oh, I don't know. I think it's the least amazing thing someone can do, falling on their ass in the middle of a crowd of strangers." She wasn't trying to be funny, but he laughed.

"I'm Jack." he held out his hand to shake hers.

"Hi. I'm Holly." she shook his hand and felt a few callouses against her palm.

"Now we're not strangers. And I wasn't talking about the falling part. I was talking about what you did for that woman. What's more embarrassing, falling on your butt while doing a nice thing for someone or trailing toilet paper around the dance floor?"

"Well," Holly said, "having done both, I would say they are pretty close."

Jack laughed once again, then asked, "Can I buy you a drink? Just to take the sting out of your backside, of course."

She finally turned to take in the full force of his face. He had an irresistible smile with golden eyes accentuating his chestnut brown hair and suntan. She guessed him to be somewhere in the twenty-eight-year-old range.

"Um, I'm here with some other people. I should get back," she said nervously.

"Well, Holly, I would love to meet them unless you are with someone in particular."

"Ah, no. Okay. I guess that would be all right." She began to hyperventilate as her stomach started to do a waltz of its own.

"We're over there." She pointed to the table where Doug and Lynn settled in.

The song came to an end, and Mike and Cate reached the table at the same time as Holly and Jack.

"Hey, everyone. This is Jack," Holly managed to say without fumbling.

Mike's eyes opened wide as he watched Holly's hand move to her stomach. He grabbed Jack's hand and shook enthusiastically.

"Hey, Jack. I'm Mike. Meet Cate, Lynn, and Doug. Have a seat."

Mike pointed to the seat between himself and Holly.

"We were just about to order some drinks," Mike said.

"Well, for medicinal purposes, the first round is on me." Jack looked at Holly, smiled, and faintly bowed his head.

Holly's hand slipped away from her stomach.

The waiter took their orders and quickly moved on to the next table.

"So, Jack," Cate asked, "what brings you on this cruise?"

"It's my parents' thirtieth anniversary, and they insisted this is how they wanted to spend it. My whole family is here."

"Oh?" Lynn piped in. "How many siblings do you have?"

"There are three of us. I have a brother and a sister, both younger than me. And my aunt and uncle came, too. A real family affair." Jack grinned, showing his captivating smile.

"How nice," Lynn said. "We should think about that for our twentieth anniversary, Doug."

The distribution of conversation took the pressure off Holly. She began to relax. Mike noticed the difference in her demeanor.

"So, Jack, where are you from?" Mike asked.

"Daytona. I have an auto repair shop there."

"If you're going to have an automobile shop, that would be the place to have one." Doug said. "Are you involved in the racing racket?"

"Yes. I have some interest in that," he said. The men understood Jack's understatement.

The band began another waltz.

"Okay, Doug. it's your turn. Let's dance." Cate jumped up and Doug had no choice but to comply.

"Mike, you were dancing so beautifully with Cate. How about we give it a try?" Lynn asked.

"It would be my honor, Lynn." *This will be a good test for Holly,* Mike thought.

Leaving Holly and Jack alone at the table, the others headed to the dance floor.

Holly's stomach began to rumble.

CATE AND DEREK

Although she didn't love the music, Cate did love the dancing. She had ballroom danced before, so she knew the waltz and foxtrot. She had even danced swing before. Out of the three, she preferred the livelier swing dances. However, she began to realize, it had most likely been her previous dance partners who made the waltz and foxtrot seem uninteresting.

Expertly snaking between other dancers, directing her movements with the slightest touch of a hand on her back, Doug and Mike each had her whirling the breadth of the dance floor. She had never experienced such a sensation, and she didn't want it to end.

A lost art, she found herself thinking. At least with her generation. And she thought that sad.

The song finished. Cate and Lynn switched places. Cate traversed the floor once again with Mike.

"What are you doing hanging out with us old fogies? I find it hard to believe this is your kind of place," Mike observed.

"Old fogies, my ass," she laughed. "You and Doug dance the pants off any of the guys I've ever danced with. It may not be my kind of music, but the dancing is mesmerizing."

"Well, I'll bet those other guys are much better at today's way of dancing than Doug or me. I think I'd throw my hip out doing that stuff," Mike laughed.

"Come on. You're still a young guy. It's a shame you let all that talent go to waste. Wouldn't it be nice to share it with someone?"

"Maybe someday," Mike replied. For the first time since he lost Abby, he considered the possibility of dancing with a woman he loved.

"Look who just came in." Mike pointed to the doorway.

Derek stood in the doorway scanning the room as if casing a bank he might intend to rob. It was his habit. He spotted Mike and Cate, gave a quick hello wave, and headed over to the bar where he took a seat.

"I wouldn't have pegged him as a club kind of guy," Cate noted.

"As clubs go, I'm guessing this one has music about as mellow as you will find on this ship," Mike laughed.

Cate giggled innocently. The song came to an end.

"I'm sorry, Cate, but I must excuse myself and find the men's room. Thank you for the dance."

Cate headed back to the table until she saw Holly and her new friend Jack in what appeared to be deep conversation. She decided to go to the bar instead.

"Hi, Derek, she said. "Is this seat taken?" She pointed to the stool to his right.

"Hello, Cate. No. Please. Have a seat. You are a terrific dancer."

"No, not really. Mike did all the work. I just followed."

"Can I get you a drink?" Derek offered.

"Yes, thank you. A merlot please," she told the attending bartender. "So, what brings you here? You don't strike me as a ballroom dancer type."

"Funny, I was just thinking the same about you," Derek replied.

"Yes, but I'm here with a group of people who are that type. You're here alone." *Touché, she got him.*

He chuckled. "It's the closest bar from my cabin," he remarked. "I am notoriously lazy."

"I find that hard to believe . . . the lazy part, I mean," she said good naturedly.

Cate spun her chair to turn her back to the bar so she could watch the dancing. She noticed a familiar face sitting with a large group of people not far from the bar. Edward, the suspected Ponzi scheme guy, sat twenty feet away. *This can't be a coincidence,* she thought.

Cate's muscles stiffened uncomfortably. *Who is Derek and what is he up to?* She determined to find out.

"What's the matter?" Derek asked.

"What? Nothing, why?"

"You just got all tense and pale."

"Did I?"

"Yes. Are you sure you're okay?"

Cate took a moment to gather her thoughts. She would have to approach the situation carefully.

"I'm perfectly fine, Derek. I'm just hot from dancing, and I got a muscle cramp."

Derek accepted the explanation even though it wasn't very convincing.

"So, you're in the insurance business, huh? What kind of insurance?" Cate asked.

"Ah, property insurance."

"What does that mean? I mean, what kind of property?"

Derek directed an inquisitive stare her way.

"Come on. You're not really interested in hearing about the insurance industry, are you?"

"Absolutely. I've always wondered how it works, how you decide costs and what gets covered as opposed to what doesn't. I think it's fascinating."

She had trouble convincing even herself.

"Well, we cover commodities like artwork collections, rare artifacts, and jewelry."

"Fascinating," she said. "What's the strangest commodity you've ever dealt with?"

She made it sound like an inquisition. She was done with his ruse.

"Oh, uh, nothing out of the ordinary," Derek answered.

"Just out of curiosity, Derek, what is the minimum per-object value requirement to determine if an item must be appraised?"

"Excuse me?" Derek asked.

"Also, does the insurance company need to verify the provenance of the insurable item before appraisal?"

"Cate, are you playing with me now?"

"No more than you are playing with me."

Derek contemplated Cate's response.

"I'm not sure I know what you're getting at."

"Look, Derek. We both know you're not in the insurance business."

"Why would you think that?"

"Because my father made his living as an insurance broker. I asked you two basic questions, and you had no idea what I was talking about."

"Maybe I just don't feel like talking about work when I'm sitting next to a beautiful woman."

Derek concentrated his captivating smile on Cate, but she would not yield.

"That's a great line. Does it work on most women?"

Derek replaced his smile with sternness and turned Cate's chair to face him.

"What is it you want from me, Cate?"

Cate crossed her arms and glared defiantly.

"The truth, Derek."

HOLLY

"They're all very nice," Jack said. "Are they your family?"

"No. I mean yes. Well—one is." Her nerves were getting the best of her, and her stomach rumbled at a faster pace. *It won't be long now*, she thought.

She began to panic. She had just come from the ladies' room, so she couldn't run back in there without him wondering why.

Did she want him thinking she had diarrhea? No!

The more she thought about the gas buildup, the quicker it traveled. The quicker it traveled, the more she thought about it.

Oh no, oh no, oh no . . .

Holly dragged her chair back three feet, scraping the wooden legs across the floor with a horrible grating sound, jumped out of her seat, quickly moved to the opposite side of the table, and, with animated movements and volume befitting the voice of a hard rock star, began: "Sitting here is Lynn who is married to Doug who is sitting here, and we met on the main deck at sunset when I was taking pictures before dinner, and they have a son Bradley who is in a wheelchair and is really smart and he likes to read."

She took a deep breath after her verbal torrent meant to conceal her physical challenge.

Did he hear it? He's looking at me like I'm crazy.

"Are you okay, Holly? You seem nervous," Jack said.

"I am nervous," she replied. "I get that way when I make a fool of myself in front of people."

"You didn't make a fool of yourself. You did a kind thing, and I thought it was great."

He's still talking about the toilet paper thing. He didn't hear it! Relief overtook her. She slowed her breathing and continued.

"Well, thank you. So, sitting here is Cate. And Mike: he's my father. He and I are on our first vacation outside of New England. This is all very new to me." She sat back in her chair and took a sip of her drink.

"Sorry, I got a little carried away," she said.

"No need to be sorry. I'm usually not too good with people myself, especially women. But something about picking a girl off the floor makes it much easier."

They shared a laugh.

Holly explained about the dinner table debacle, how they moved from their original seating arrangement, and how they all ended up together. She declined to mention Derek, though, and she wasn't quite sure why.

"Would you like to dance, Holly?" Jack asked timidly.

Holly took stock of her stomach. No rumbling.

"Yes, I think I would," she smiled.

He took her hand and led her to the dance floor. She didn't know how the dance would proceed. Most men her age didn't know how to waltz or foxtrot. They just swayed their partner back and forth, moving in a circle. But not Jack. It delighted Holly as he put one hand on her waist and, holding her hand with the other, raised her hand in the air.

Mike taught Holly how to waltz, since she never finished ballroom dancing lessons after the Tommy DePoula incident.

She and her dad danced around the kitchen and living room. It hadn't occurred to her that Mike had more than dance lessons in mind. Her father wanted her someday to experience the joy she felt at that moment as she moved across the dance floor with a special partner.

Holly beamed as she glided across the parquet on the arms of a handsome not-so-much stranger, but her smile did not begin to equal her father's when he saw her.

THE TRUTH

CATE AND DEREK

Cate found a table in the far corner of the café and waited, possibly the first time she arrived early for anything, especially at that hour of the morning.

She hadn't slept well. Without Sheila in the room, she had no one to tell her news, and it drove her crazy. Not that she had anything concrete to tell. She still didn't know what Derek was up to. As they sat at the bar the previous night, she and Derek made plans to meet at the café at seven o'clock the next morning. Her phone read 6:45 a.m. She sipped her latté as her head spun with wild thoughts.

He was an art thief on his way to sell a priceless painting. Or some sort of corporate espionage—after all, he was wearing a suit when we first met. Ooh, maybe a spy selling secrets to some foreign country.

But none of them felt right. *He seems like a decent guy, even though he lied to all of us.*

Derek walked into the café and went to the counter to order coffee. He spotted Cate in the corner and acknowledged her with a slight wave of the hand. *He looks tired*, Cate thought.

"Good morning, Cate," he said as he took a seat across from her.

"Good morning, Derek. You look terrible."

"Well, thank you for that. You look fantastic."

Cate blushed involuntarily. She felt a stirring inside.

"I just meant you look tired."

"Well, I didn't sleep too well last night, as you might imagine."

"Well, it just so happens I didn't sleep too well myself."

"I'm sorry. I didn't mean to ruin your trip. I was trying to be low key. Apparently, I wasn't successful."

"Not very, but I am a perceptive person," she proudly stated.

"Hmmmm. Or I'm a rotten liar."

"So—I'm waiting." Cate managed to sound slightly stern, even though she felt a little sympathy for Derek, putting him on the spot like that.

"Okay. I'm not in the insurance business. I just said that because I thought people would leave me alone."

Derek leaned in and spoke barely above a whisper.

"My name is Derek Richards, and I work for the department of justice. You tell people you work for the federal government, and you get endless questions. It's exhausting."

"Well, what are you doing here? What do you do for them?"

Derek glanced at Cate as if to say, *See? I told you so.*

"What did I tell you about the questions? This is why I wasn't truthful from the beginning. I'm working, Cate. That's all."

"Now wait. Just wait a minute." Cate's head filled with images of Derek since their first meeting. She saw him at the bar. Tired and unshaven the first morning at sea, he wore a rumpled high-end business suit. Then buying clothes at the ship's store. And then at dinner when the maître d' brought him to the table as a newcomer.

"No, no, no. You're going to have to tell me a lot more than that," Cate insisted. "What's with the shopping spree? Where are your own clothes?"

He sighed with resignation. "Okay. Originally, my office assigned two others to be here, but they had a bad car accident on the way to the port. I flew in from the Northeast to take their place, but the ship had already sailed by the time I reached the dock. A small barge brought me out to the ship during the middle of the night. I boarded without luggage or even a toothbrush. When I saw you at the bar that morning, I hadn't slept all night. I was waiting for the ship's cabin steward to get me into the room that had been booked for the other guys."

Cate sat silent for almost a minute. Derek appeared drawn and defeated.

"Are they all right?" Cate asked.

"What? Who?"

"The guys in the accident. Are they all right?"

Derek smiled admiringly into Cate's empathetic green eyes and reached for her hands across the table.

"I don't know. I haven't heard any news since I boarded the ship. You are an amazing woman, Cate. I just finished telling you a somewhat unbelievable story, and your first instinct is to ask about those men."

Cate extended her hands. They sat quietly and looked into each other's eyes. Each felt a connection bordering on longing.

"Cate, please don't tell anyone about this. It's important to me that this stay between us. I must rely on your confidence in this matter. Please promise me you won't tell anyone.

Cate had to ask. She was dying to know.

"Is it that guy, Edward, the Ponzi scheme guy? It's okay. You can tell me. We're pretty sure we've already figured it out anyway."

"We? Who's we, Cate?" Derek let go of her hands and sat back in his chair. He looked worried.

Cate suddenly felt uneasy.

"Just me and Sheila." She paused. "And Holly." Another pause. "And Lynn . . . and Bradley." She winced. She felt like a schoolgirl ratting on her friends.

"Shit." Derek slumped his shoulders. "What exactly is it that you think you know?"

It was Cate's turn to tell a story, exhibiting pained expressions throughout her tale. Derek listened.

She explained how they had each seen Edward in different and what they considered suspicious, conversations on the ship and how they noticed Derek paid a lot of attention to the people at the dinner table assigned to Holly and Mike on their first night when Edward bragged about money he made in some investment and how Derek seemed to follow Edward everywhere, even the night before at the club.

"It is too much for it to be coincidence. Holly suggested the idea of the Ponzi scheme. I wouldn't have thought of that."

"So, you all think I am the kind of guy who would trick people into giving me their money so I can get rich?"

"Ah. Um. Well, it was just a theory." She raised her shoulders and tucked her head like a turtle trying to hide.

"Wow. I gotta to tell you. That stings a little."

"What the hell do we know? We only know that you are consistently lying to us. We were just trying to figure out why," Cate explained. "And the clothes thing really threw me off."

"Okay, Cate. I get it. But now you need to listen to me very carefully. I don't know this Edward guy or anything about a Ponzi scheme. I'm not following him, and I'm not in business with him. That's the truth. Please, Cate, I can't tell you any more, I've already said too much. You have to promise me, Cate."

He wasn't lying. Cate could tell. He was alarmed and worried. Cate became worried too.

"Okay, I promise. Derek, are you in danger?"

He smiled, lightened his mood, and reached for Cate's hands again. Then he pursed his lips and said, "No. Not at all. We just need to keep all of this to ourselves and everything will be fine."

HOLLY AND MIKE

Holly felt unusually blissful as she sat on their balcony with a fresh cup of coffee and Jack dancing in her head. Morning sun had never felt so energizing, and the soft island breeze carried a tropical floral scent.

She willed herself to imprint the moment to memory so she could return to it any time she wished.

Mike had just gotten out of the shower when someone knocked at the door. With a towel around his waist, he opened the door slightly.

"Your tickets for the ferry," the cabin attendant said and handed him an envelope.

"Thank you." Mike closed the door and returned to the bathroom to dress for the day.

They had booked an excursion via the ferry from Charlotte Amalie to Cruz Bay on St. John. They had endless options for how to spend the day: sunbathe on one of the most beautiful beaches on the planet, snorkel in crystal blue water with tropical fish at their fingertips, explore the island with a tour guide in a jeep, or enjoy an afternoon at an outdoor deluxe seafood buffet while listening to the island music of a steel band. Or, if planned well, the brochure stated, do all the above.

Holly and Mike intended to sunbathe, swim, and eat. But first, they would take the forty-five-minute ferry ride departing at ten o'clock to the island.

At quarter of nine, Mike sat beside Holly on the balcony, a lukewarm cup of coffee in his hand.

"So. Did you enjoy yourself last night?" Mike asked.

"Oh, my God. That restaurant was amazing. My Jamaican shrimp salad was to die for, and the baked Alaska—well, what can I say?" Holly said, knowing full well that her dad was fishing.

"All right, Miss Wise Ass. I won't push."

Holly giggled. An actual giggle, much to her surprise.

"I had a wonderful time. I know this is going to sound stupid, but the only word I can think of to describe it is *magical*."

"That doesn't sound stupid at all. I remember that feeling very well. In fact, I was reminded of it last night."

Holly gave him a sideways look as if to say, "Explain."

"I forgot how nice it was to dance with a woman, someone who isn't my daughter," Mike laughed. "Not that I don't enjoy dancing with my daughter. But I remember your mother and me dancing the waltz on the night we met. I fell in love during that dance."

"You never told me that," Holly exclaimed. "You just said you met her at a party, and you spent the whole night talking."

"Well, you can talk while you're dancing," he smiled. "It was an anniversary party. I don't even remember whose— some distant family member. I remember not wanting to go, but I ended up glad I did."

"Did you feel like you were floating?" Holly asked as she looked out towards the open water.

"I felt like we were the only two people in the world," he replied.

CATE

Cate got a call from Sheila at ten thirty in the morning. She told Cate that she and David had a wonderful night. They talked about a lot of things, and Sheila felt much better about their future.

"What are your plans for today, Cate?" Sheila asked.

"I don't have any."

"Do you want to join David and me? We just left the pool and thought we would find a nice place for lunch, then do some sightseeing."

"No, Sheila. You and David should spend more time alone. I'll be all right. But will I see you on board for dinner tonight?"

"Absolutely. I can't wait to hear what everyone's been up to. Thank you, Cate. You are the best sister anyone could ever have. I feel terrible abandoning you like this."

"I am in a tropical paradise with a beach in every direction. What more could I ask for? Give David a hug for me. I really enjoyed seeing him last night."

"I will. Love you. See you tonight—Late Cate."

"I love you guys, too, TP!"

Cate felt a moment of guilt. *How can I keep Derek's secret from Sheila?* It's all she could think about since their conversation in the cafe. But she had promised him.

And what do I know, anyway? Nothing, except that he's not a bad person. He's sweet, adorable, and a hand holder. And those eyes look right into my soul.

Cate found herself drifting off the point as she digressed into her feelings for Derek. She knew so little about him, but her instincts told her she could trust him. She would just have to find a way to keep his secret and maybe do some research on her own.

She decided to do a little sightseeing, so she dressed in her teal one-piece bathing suit topped with white shorts and white cover-up. She packed a day bag with sunscreen, a beach towel, and other necessities, donned her teal wide-brimmed hat decorated with a white scarf, and off she went.

She didn't have a plan, just a direction—toward the water. Before debarking, she stopped to pick up some pamphlets at the main desk. Most people had already left the ship for the day.

Once ashore, Cate decided to take in the outdoor market before heading to the beach. She hadn't eaten anything. Her coffee shop conversation with Derek abandoned any thought of food, so the market provided a perfect place for her to get some grab-and-go lunch.

Clear skies, hot sun, and a cool breeze made for a glorious day for visitors.

The market teemed with shoppers and entrepreneurs, commercial activity resembling a ballet. A promenade of patrons circled each other as if in choreographed pirouettes, an adagio grace and fluid in movement and purpose. Mesmerized by the scene before her, Cate sat on a bench under a palm tree and ate her Jamaican jerk skewered chicken.

Jolted suddenly from her trance by the sight of the apparently omnipresent Edward, the loudmouth, Cate watched as he led a group of four men into a building just outside the boundaries of the marketplace. Curious, she strolled toward the building to read the sign hanging above the door, THIRD STREET BANK.

DEREK

Things are becoming complicated, Derek thought. He would have to distance himself from Cate and the rest of his dinner companions to ensure they didn't get mixed up in his business. Involved in the case from the start, he knew its danger. He hoped to get help when the ship docked in a few days in St. Kitts. That's where he would need it most. He already had to use one of *Perth's* security officers to watch the lawyer couple's room that morning, to make sure they didn't leave the ship while he spoke with Cate. Luckily, they hadn't risen early.

He followed the two at a comfortable distance through the marketplace toward the marina. The man carried a large satchel, switching it from hand to hand as if it were a burden to carry. Derek watched as they boarded a small yacht called *Close Enough.* He snapped pictures of the captain and two-person crew before they pulled away from the dock. He could see no one else on board, but someone may have been below deck. Either that, or the couple expected to meet a contact somewhere else.

Derek quickly made his way to the harbor master's quarters.

"What can I do for ya?" asked an old gentleman with a Maine accent. He wore a captain's cap.

Derek showed the man his FBI badge and Boston credentials. As he did, he felt a twinge of regret that he hadn't broken protocol and told Cate the entire truth.

"Is there someone here who can take me out on a boat right now?"

"Just me here," the man replied. "It important?"

"It is. But we'll have to be discreet."

"My middle name."

The captain locked up his office and led Derek to a fishing vessel moored close by.

"Hop on. Name's Jed."

"Derek."

"Where to?"

"Follow that boat." Derek pointed. By then the yacht had a good lead on them, but that was all right. He did not want to be spotted.

"I don't know where they are headed, and we'll have to keep our distance, but the more information I can get about their activity, the better." Derek watched Jed as he bobbed his head in understanding.

"Looks like they're headed to the West End," said Jed.

"Is there anything significant about the West End?"

"No tourists."

"Hmm. Good place for a private meeting?"

"Yep. Good place to fish, too." Jed nodded toward the fishing poles in the rack at the back of the boat.

"Well, then," Derek smiled. "Let's go fishing."

Derek lifted his camera and zoomed the lens to its maximum.

"Got binoculars under that seat there," Jed offered.

The binoculars confirmed no other presence on the boat, unless they stayed below deck, surely not very likely. Making sure to include the landscape for location purposes, Derek snapped pictures for the next thirty minutes.

Jed took notice of the yacht changing its course and slowed his engine almost to a stop.

"Looks like they're pulling up to a private dock." Jed pointed.

Derek focused on a large waterfront estate lined with glass windows. He took photos of everything and everyone who came into view.

Jed stopped the boat and put out four fishing rods, but only one had bait on the hook.

"Might as well make use of my time," Jed exclaimed.

Derek positioned himself between two of the useless fishing rods and watched. Bag in hand, the man left the yacht with the woman to climb a steep stairway to the deck of the estate. Derek watched a large figure emerge from inside the house. He held a pair of binoculars and wore a business suit so shiny the sun reflected from it.

As the big man raised the field glasses to his eyes, Derek stashed Jed's binoculars behind his back and picked up a fishing rod. Knowing full well that without any weight at the end of the filament it would not fly, he went through the motions of casting the line. He smiled and gestured as he launched into his best imitation of a vacationing businessman on a fishing excursion in the Virgin Islands, although what he fished for could not be caught on the end of the pole.

The man in the shiny suit noticed a man on a fishing boat lower his binoculars. He leaned inside the doorway to quietly report to his boss.

Once confident that the man no longer inspected them nor the two other fishing vessels in the vicinity, Derek looked through his zoomed camera lens and saw an older man of small stature come through the estate door. He wore a gaudy flowered shirt and white shorts.

Derek rapidly triggered the camera shutter.

Always staying within camera range of the buildings in Derek's sights, Jed moved the boat from time to time, Derek couldn't help but think Jed had some experience in surveillance.

"So, Jed. Tell me about yourself. Looks like we've got some time to kill."

"Not much to tell. Retired navy man who owns a fishing boat and works as a harbor master."

"You in the war?"

"Yep."

"Ever have to sneak up on someone before?" Derek supposed he already knew the answer to the question.

"Captained a PBR in the Mekong River."

Having read a lot about the Vietnam War and seen any number of documentaries, Derek understood the weight of Jed's statement. The river patrol boat, nicknamed PBR, played a vital role in the US war effort to disrupt enemy weapons shipments. PBR crews often found themselves in firefights with the enemy either from shore or boat to boat. The PBRs also inserted and extracted US Navy Seals from areas along the Mekong which required absolute vigilance.

Derek felt great admiration for Jed and his abilities.

"Well, this time you'll be well compensated for your efforts." Derek smiled.

"Yep."

Though thorough, Derek's surveillance failed to take account of another pair of binoculars focused on Jed's fishing boat.

HOLLY AND MIKE

Mike and Holly boarded the ferry and looked for seats on the open-air upper deck, all disappointingly full. They descended into the hull of the boat, into a dark, welcoming coolness. Benches lined the hull on either side with an aisle in between. The benches, too, quickly filled. Everyone faced front toward a view of two closed doors. One had a sign reading PRIVATE. The other said RESTROOM—not the view one desired on a journey to one of the world's most beautiful beaches.

Shortly after boarding, the ferry left the dock. It would take approximately forty-five minutes to reach the island of St. John and then another half hour by jeep to get to the beach and buffet. Not surprisingly, they recognized most of the other people as passengers from their cruise ship. They made small talk with a few of them but mostly each kept to their own companions.

About twenty minutes into the trip, a woman seated a few benches away got up and approached the door marked RESTROOM. She opened it and instantly turned her head away as if she had been slapped in the face. Holly saw her reach to the inside wall, searching for a light switch she never found. Soon, Holly and most of the other passengers in the hull noticed a stench from the tiny, closet-sized room. Holly squinted her eyes to get a look into the darkened space as the woman stood in the doorway trying to decide whether to enter. She decided against it, closed the door, and retreated to her bench.

A few moments later, a man wearing a straw fedora descended the stairs from above and opened the same door, had a similar reaction, drew a similar conclusion, and returned to the upper deck. Passengers in the hull whispered about the foul odor. A few had drawn tissues from their bags and placed them over their noses.

Able to get a partial look inside the so-called restroom, Holly saw only well-used mops, buckets, and a few brooms with cloth rags hanging from the handles. She said a silent prayer that her bladder would hold out until they reached the island.

Two more passengers from above approached the restroom door, but no takers. Then the man in the fedora couldn't take it any longer. A pained expression on his face, he rushed down the stairs and to the door.

"The hell with it," he hissed as he slammed the door behind him.

A minute later, he reappeared looking simultaneously disgusted and relieved as he ascended the stairs into daylight.

With the trip almost over, a young woman from the upper deck made her way down the stairs and to the restroom. She opened the door, shook her head in disgust and slammed it shut. She hesitated and then moved to the door with the sign that said PRIVATE. She opened it and reached her hand in to turn on the light that illuminated a sparkling white porcelain toilet and sink with hanging towel and soap dispenser.

She entered.

The hull of the boat erupted with laughter at once tear-producing, stomach-hurting, out-of-breath, and raucous laughter that only toilet humor evokes.

The uproar had just begun to settle down when the unsuspecting woman timidly emerged from the clean bathroom. Without pausing to catch their breath, the hull contingent erupted again. The woman scampered up the stairs to join the oblivious open-air travelers.

It wasn't until the final passenger disembarked from the ferry that the tittering subsided.

CATE AND DEREK AND SHEILA

Even though she had set her phone alarm, Cate got back to the ship late. She wasn't the only one. Beating the last-minute deadline to catch the ship before it sailed, several groups and individuals hurried to board before the deck hands removed the gangway, one of them Derek.

She first decided to duck out of sight, but she thought that would be childish, so she caught his attention with a wave of her hand as he reached the deck.

He smiled and waved.

"You got some sun," Cate observed.

"Yes, I did. I went fishing," Derek responded, placing his hand on the small of her back as they walked the deck.

"I'm sure you did." She raised an eyebrow. "But for what?"

Derek scanned the deck.

"Please, Cate."

"Innocent question, Derek. I've got to go. My sister should be back by now."

As they parted ways, neither of them noticed the man about to board. He surveyed their brief encounter.

As Cate entered the room, Sheila jumped off the bunk and wrapped her arms around her sister.

"Oh, Cate, I had the most wonderful time," she exclaimed. "David and I talked and talked. It was like meeting each other for the first time but without all the apprehension. We both agreed that we need to pay more attention to our relationship. I think we're going to make it."

She looked as happy as Cate had ever seen her.

"I am so happy for you, Sheila. I love you both so much."

"So, what have you been up to, Cate? What did you do last night after we left?"

Cate decided to stick to the truth but omit some of the details.

"We all went dancing. It was amazing. Mike and Doug are incredible dancers. And Holly met a gorgeous guy. He seems really great."

"Holly? Shy Holly?"

"I know. Right? She went to the restroom and came back with a guy. Who knew?"

"What about Derek? Did you guys end up hooking up with him?"

"Ah, no."

"Too bad. You know, I've been thinking about that conversation we had after dinner the other night. I just can't imagine Derek being a jerk. He seems too clean-cut. What do you think?" Sheila asked.

"Oh, I don't know anything about him," Cate replied.

"But you think he's handsome, right? I mean, how could you not?"

"Sure. I guess."

Cate is hiding something. Sheila thought. *But what. And why?* She felt confused. She knew Cate wanted to get to know Derek better. It had been obvious. *Something happened.*

"What did you do today?" Sheila decided to dig a little.

"I went to the outdoor marketplace and then to the beach."

"By yourself?"

"Yes, Sheila. I'm a big girl. I can do things by myself."

Cate thought about telling Sheila she had seen Edward and the other men going into the bank, but she decided against it. It might just lead to questions about Derek, and she didn't think she could deflect them well, especially after she had spent a good part of the day researching who Derek Richards really is.

"You seem a little tense, Cate. Are you all right?"

"Of course I am. I guess I'm just hungry. I haven't eaten anything since this morning. Let's get ready for dinner."

"Okay. As long as nothing's wrong."

"Absolutely nothing." Cate managed a smile. The promise she made to Derek already proved problematic. She didn't know if she could keep it.

DINNER—NO DEREK

Cate and Sheila thought they would be last to arrive for dinner, but Derek still wasn't there. They decided to wait just a little while longer before ordering, but Derek didn't show, so they ordered without him.

If Cate hadn't seen Derek boarding the ship earlier, she would have been worried.

"That was a great party last night, Sheila. I had a blast." Bradley opened the conversation. "I think baked Alaska is my new favorite dessert!"

"It really was very nice," Lynn said. "Your husband is so sweet. He didn't need to pay for everything, though."

"He wanted to. He was just so happy to meet all of you. He told me he felt much better after he met you, knowing I was in good hands." Sheila laughed. "He actually said that—good hands."

"He's handsome and sweet," Holly stated. "What are the odds?" She laughed.

"Well, I heard you may have found a keeper, Holly," Sheila replied. "Tell me about him."

Holly became embarrassed. Though excited to talk about Jack, she felt uncomfortable with herself in the spotlight.

"He's really nice." She felt the need to understate her assessment. "He picked me off the floor!"

"What?" they all said in unison, including Mike.

Holly went on to explain how they met. Usually she kept her mishaps to herself, but she decided to share her embarrassing moment with her friends. Her shy nature seemed to slip away.

"Well, if you end up getting married, you will have a hell of a story to tell," Doug laughed.

"I wish I could have been there. It sounds like you all had a good time," Bradley commented.

"And where were you during all this, Bradley?" Sheila asked.

"In the cabin, reading." Then realizing what he said and sneaking a look at his mom, he added, "But I went to sleep at a reasonable hour." Everyone laughed.

"I wonder what happened to Derek tonight. I hope he didn't miss the boat," Mike joked.

Before she even realized it, Cate responded.

"Oh, no. I saw him boarding the ship late."

Sheila glanced Cate's way. Cate's body language silently screamed she knew more than she let on. Sheila became positive Cate hid something.

They all talked about what they had done on St. Thomas. Holly and Mike relayed their ferry experience while Bradley, Lynn, and Doug talked about their adventure on the skyride and the beautiful view from Paradise Point. Bradley pronounced he looked forward to the St. Kitt adventure. The family planned to book an excursion to swim with dolphins, and Bradley couldn't wait.

"You guys should come with us!" Bradley extended the invitation to everyone at the table.

"It does sound like fun." Sheila looked at Cate, who nodded in agreement.

"What do you think, Holly?" Mike asked. They had talked about other options for their day on St. Kitt, but they hadn't settled on anything yet.

"Sounds great," she said.

DEREK CHECKS IN

Derek ate dinner in his cabin. He needed to contact the office with an update on the developments of the day. He set up his laptop on the coffee table and connected to the conference call at eight o'clock, Eastern Standard Time.

"They made contact," he reported. "But there's someone else on the ship. I haven't been able to get a picture of him yet, but he's in his late forties, maybe early fifties, greying hair, about five feet seven and wears glasses."

"Great, Derek. You just described ninety percent of the men on board that ship. Get the photo. We got your pictures of the estate. That's Benny White, just like we figured. Good job. These are the first new pictures we've gotten of him in ten years. Tell us what happened."

"Their surveillance is good," Derek replied. "It's going to be hard to make a surprise appearance anywhere near the estate. Unless you go in with an army, you may want to plan to take him outside the compound. The suspects brought a heavy bag with them, stayed for about ninety minutes, and left with what looked like full shopping bags from the local market. Do we know how they got the product down here?"

"Working on it. We think it was a tanker, then a courier. Find out more about the third guy on the ship. He could be the key. Anything else?"

"Yes. We have a minor situation with one of the passengers on board."

"What kind of situation?"

"Totally under control. It's just that I had to reveal a little about myself to one of the passengers. She saw through the insurance scam but has promised to keep it to herself."

"*Her*self? What the hell happened, Derek?" His boss was not happy.

"Apparently she is an unusually perceptive person. I just told her I work for the DOJ. I didn't say in what capacity." Derek neglected to mention the others' suspicions about his initial lie. *They didn't really know anything anyway*, he reasoned.

"Be careful, Derek. I do not need to remind you how many hours we have on this thing already. We can't afford any screwups."

"Yes, boss. How are Ron and Kyle?"

"Ron is in intensive care, but they think he is going to pull through. He bashed his head pretty hard against the car window. Kyle comes home from the hospital today. They'll both be out for a while. I'm working on personnel for St. Kitts. I should know by tomorrow. Keep your head in the game."

"I will. Thank you."

Derek breathed a little easier. He had not looked forward to telling his boss about Cate, but he had to. He also had to find a way to get a picture of the third subject, the one the lawyer couple met with. That's when he remembered Holly. She had been snapping pictures off the stern when he almost ran into her. He wondered if by miracle she had gotten the picture he missed.

Again, he would have to be careful how he went about finding out.

He decided to join his dinner companions after all. Maybe he could connect with them before dessert.

DESSERT

Derek surprised Cate when he appeared just before dessert. She had surmised he would keep his distance from the group to minimize any further complications.

"I had a dinner business meeting," he said to explain his tardiness, "but I didn't stay for dessert." Derek showed his contagious smile and winked at Bradley as he poured himself a cup of coffee.

"Well, you missed the best dessert last night at Sheila's party. We had baked Alaska, and it was awesome!" Bradley said enthusiastically.

"I'm sorry I missed it—the dessert and the party. Happy belated birthday, Sheila." Derek raised his coffee cup as if to toast.

"Thank you, Derek. We missed you, too." Sheila felt genuinely happy to see him. She noticed, however, that Cate barely glanced at him.

Cate may not have looked at Derek, but she did scan the nearby table where Edward and his wife sat. For the first time, she concentrated on the other two couples at the table and took in their mannerisms. She knew instinctively who Derek had an interest in. Just as she had the insight, she caught Derek glancing at her.

"So, what's everyone doing after this?" Bradley asked.

Derek took advantage of the segue.

"Well, I'm going to take some pictures of the moon. It's a nice clear night for a camera buff like me." He felt he may have laid it on a little thick, and he knew Cate would not buy it, but it worked just as he intended.

"Do you mind if I join you? I'm not meeting Jack until ten thirty. He has a family obligation." Holly seemed delighted.

"Great. I would love the company. Anyone else?" Derek had to ask to make it believable, but he had already hooked his fish.

Sheila waited for a response from Cate, but her sister remained quiet.

"Well," Sheila said, "I heard that Mike and Doug dance wonderfully. I would like to find out for myself if you guys are up to it."

"Well, Mike, our reputation precedes us. To think my dancing has been a secret for so long, but now the cat's out of the bag," Doug said chuckling. "What do you say, Lynn. Can you stand another night of me?"

"I thought you'd never ask. Will you be bored if you come with us, Bradley?"

"No way. I've got to see this!"

Derek and Holly made plans to meet on deck after retrieving their cameras while the others went to find a club, one family friendly enough for Bradley. They found a suitable music fest in the same open-aired area as had movie night. With music varied in style, they could not have picked a more perfect atmosphere.

DEREK AND HOLLY

Although Derek had no idea when he made the statement, it really was a picture-perfect night. Engaging in small talk, he and Holly snapped away. Derek professed himself a novice photographer. Holly talked of her love of the camera.

"It's amazing to me that you can capture such emotion through a lens," she stated. "People become vulnerable when they don't know someone's watching them. It sometimes feels like borderline voyeurism, but the results expose authenticity, and authenticity develops into art."

"Do you mind if I see some of your pictures? I don't want to pry, but I'd love to see them," Derek fished again.

"Of course." Holly felt pleased with Derek's interest in her work. And she thought it a terrific opportunity to get a completely objective opinion.

She handed Derek her digital camera, and he slowly scrolled through the images.

"These are beautiful." He spoke sincerely. She had a gift.

Then he came across the photo he hoped to find, the cargo ship in the distance and on the deck below Holly's viewpoint, there he stood. She had captured a full frontal, clear picture of John Doe.

"This. This is the picture I was trying to get." He tried not to sound too excited. "I love the way the light reflects off the boxes."

"I know. It's as if it's alive," Holly agreed.

"Can you send me that picture? And . . . " He thought it better to add some others, " . . . this one and this one. I promise I won't steal them—I mean use them to make money or anything. Do people do that?" he laughed.

"No, most people don't want to open themselves up to a lawsuit. Not that I would sue you," she laughed. Holly felt honored though a little surprised he skipped over some of her favorites. *To each his own*, she thought.

"Sure, give me your contact info."

She sent the pictures to his phone, and just as quickly, he forwarded the picture to his office in Boston.

"Thank you, Holly. I really appreciate it. So, who's this Jack fella?"

Derek flashed his smile.

SHEILA AND CATE AND BRADLEY

Exhausted from continuous dancing, Sheila slumped in her chair.

"I told you so," Cate laughed. "These guys blow away any of the guys our age. And they're still out there! Who's the woman dancing with Mike?"

"I don't know. She just cut in. She's pretty, though."

Cate, Sheila, and Bradley watched as Mike and his mystery woman moved around the floor. Doug and Lynn hadn't sat for more than a minute since they arrived.

"Okay. Break's over. What do you say, Bradley? Shall we cut a rug?" Sheila asked.

"Cut a what?" Bradley asked.

"A rug. It means dance. Shall we dance?" Sheila laughed.

"Ah, well, I've never . . ."

"Well, then, It's about time." Sheila stood. "Let's go."

Only slightly apprehensive, Bradley followed Sheila to the dance floor. She held one of Bradley's hands so he could work the wheelchair with the other. It didn't take long before he got into a rhythm with his chair. Occasionally Sheila got behind him and spun him in circles only to join him again holding his hand. Bradley had never had such an experience.

Cate became emotional as she watched the scene play out. She couldn't sit any longer.

She leapt out of her chair and onto the dance floor. "May I join you?" She asked Sheila and Bradley.

"Heck, yeah!" Bradley beamed.

On the opposite side of the dance floor, Lynn watched and wept.

DEREK

Derek and Holly parted ways, Holly for her date with Jack and Derek to his cabin.

He logged onto his laptop to initiate a face-to-face conference call with the office at a rather late hour. He didn't expect his boss to be there. When the call connected, his boss's face filled his screen.

"We got the picture, and we're running it through facial recognition as we speak. Any idea yet who he is?"

"No. He's been keeping a low profile. I haven't seen him in the open except for that instance. He had a heated discussion with the lawyer couple the day before the contact with Benny White took place."

"Why are we just getting the picture now?" His boss did not sound happy.

"The pictures I took with my phone weren't clear. I had to extract these from someone else's camera."

His boss paused before speaking again.

"No problems?"

"No, no problems," Derek said, not really knowing if he told the truth.

"We'll let you know when we get a hit on the photo."

"Okay, thank you."

Derek logged out. He hoped he'd been subtle enough in obtaining the photo. He had learned that he should not underestimate his dinner companions, whom he began to think of as friends. Either proposition could develop into a dangerous prospect.

When working in the field, he knew the importance of staying focused, not making unnecessary contacts, and most of all, not getting involved emotionally with contacts made.

Derek had always excelled at those mandates, no matter what his assignment. In fact, he adhered to the rules in his personal life in order to keep his work life as uncomplicated as possible.

But meeting a group of genuinely nice people, strangers when they boarded, he felt a bond in spite of himself. *It's not often something like that happens in this complicated world,* he thought. He wished he could fully participate.

He paused to wonder what prompted his feelings. He had met nice people before, and yes, maybe sometimes he had been a little sad about the direction he had chosen for his life but never before so quickly and penetratingly.

You idiot, you know why—Cate. He wasn't sure whether he said it out loud. Unfettered for the moment of obligation to his work, he allowed himself to think about her. He could allow no more. Saddened, he did his best to bury the images in his head. He made the decision not to see her again.

But the decision came too late.

FORMAL NIGHT

HOLLY AND MIKE

Exhausted from the week's events, Holly and Mike both decided to spend the morning sipping coffee on their cabin balcony. A flawless blue sky once again provided invigorating energy.

"How was your date with Jack?"

Holly snickered.

"I wondered how long it would take you to ask. You held out longer than I thought you would."

Mike smiled.

"Well?"

"It was beautiful. We sat under the stars at the outdoor café at the back of the ship. The piped-in music wasn't loud, so we could carry on a conversation. We just talked all night and laughed. He's very witty, and he thinks I am, too. The best part is I never once felt uncomfortable. No stomach rumbling, not even at the beginning."

"I am so happy for you, Holly. And proud. And Jack is an exceptionally good judge of character. You are witty, smart, and courageous and . . ."

Holly held up her hand to make him stop his praise.

"I got it, Dad. You're not going to start tearing up on me, are you?"

"Maybe just a little." He smiled and winked.

"Jack asked if I had any plans for St. Kitts. I told him I'd have to check."

"Well, we sort of committed to swimming with the dolphins with the rest of the gang, but we don't know what time or where. Other than that, we just planned to go sightseeing. But if you want to meet up with Jack, that's all right with me."

Mike felt ecstatic about Holly and Jack. It was her first meaningful experience with a man, and he didn't want to stand in her way, especially with the hardest part over, the initial getting-to-know-you part.

"I think I'll ask him to join us for the dolphins. If he can't, maybe I can meet him for a drink or even dinner later that night."

"I think it's a nice idea. But if you go out later, I will want to know where you're going, because I am your Dad."

"Okay. I'll let you know once we've made a decision. Why don't you make some plans of your own for dinner with her tomorrow night?"

Holly held up her cell phone to display a picture of Mike dancing with a pretty brunette.

"How did you get that?"

"Sheila texted it to me. She wanted me to know you weren't sitting at the table alone while I was out with Jack."

Holly modeled an ear-to-ear grin. "So, who is she? What's she like?"

"She's nice. Her name is Jenny, and she has her own business, a music store. She sells all kinds of instruments, sheet music, and even some old vinyl albums, too."

"How cool."

"She teaches, too, occasionally. She used to play clarinet for the New York Philharmonic."

"Wow, impressive. Why did she leave the philharmonic?"

"She got married, had kids. She decided she didn't want to commit to the travel required. She wanted to be with her family. Her husband passed away three years ago."

"That's so sad. Is she on the cruise by herself?"

"No. She came with her sister-in-law. She's nice, too. A retired teacher."

"Have you made any plans to see Jenny again?"

"No. We just had a few dances together. I think Sheila got the wrong idea."

"Or maybe she has a good eye and could see you were enjoying yourself."

Mike quietly pondered the thought. He decided not to ask any more questions about Jack because he might then have to reciprocate with answers about Jenny—answers he didn't have.

SHEILA

Sheila spent her morning the usual way, by the pool gathering energy for the day. *I'll have a lazy day at sea,* she decided. She left Cate a note informing her of her whereabouts, even though she knew Cate would know where to look.

She pondered the possibility of something going on between Cate and Derek. She had noticed the way Cate looked at him when he showed up for dinner the second night and the way she watched him shopping. But something must have happened after her birthday celebration. Cate barely looked at him during dinner the following night. And any time Sheila mentioned his name, Cate evaded the topic.

Cate joined Sheila at the pool midmorning.

"This is the life," Cate remarked.

"The sunbathing or the dancing?" Sheila asked.

"Both. And the food and weather."

"What about the guys, Cate? Some very gorgeous and single guys?"

Cate smirked.

"Them, too. There does seem to be a disproportionate number of nice-looking men on this boat. Why is that?"

"That's because you don't live in Hollywood, Cate. You should come live near me. You could have such a view every day of the week."

"And go broke in the meantime," Cate stated.

"So, what's happening with Derek? Things seemed a little weird with you two when he showed up last night."

"What? No, nothing weird. I haven't even seen him much. I guess he's been working a lot."

"With his insurance pals?" It was Sheila's turn to push.

"I guess."

"Come on, Cate. You don't believe that for a minute. What's going on?"

"I guess he's just not interested, Sheila." Cate had a hard time lying to her sister, but she couldn't risk putting her in danger—nor Derek.

Sheila didn't know what to make of the conversation. Even though it didn't feel finished, she decided to drop it.

DEREK AND THE PISCELLI FAMILY

Derek received a text message shortly after waking. *Conference call . . . 9 am.*

He had called room service for a pot of coffee and a pineapple-macadamia nut muffin. He found himself thinking he would miss the muffins once back in Boston.

He logged into his laptop and joined the conference call at exactly nine o'clock.

"Here's what we got," his boss said without preamble. "We confirmed the drugs were delivered to St. Thomas via a tanker under a foreign flag. We can assume the drugs made it to Benny White's where the lawyer couple . . . ." He turned to look at someone behind him. "What's their name?"

"The Websters, Patrick and Sharon," came the answer from someone not in camera range.

"Right," the boss went on. "Where the Websters picked up the drugs. We have that on camera."

"Well, we have them picking up something," Derek interrupted. "I didn't see drugs. Only bags."

"Right!" Derek's boss seemed annoyed at the distinction.

"To go on . . . ," the boss said, "the information we received corroborated the drug exchange for the jewels will take place on St. Kitts, but we don't know where, when, or how. And the big question is *Who?* Who is fencing the goods? Have we got any further on that?"

Of the four other participants on the conference call, no one spoke up.

"Right. Let's skip that for the time being. The next move will happen on St. Kitts. The Websters will bring the drugs to someone, somewhere, at some time in exchange for the jewels. They will then bring the jewels back to the states, get them through customs somehow, and then to the buyer."

Derek began to worry that too many unknowns would prevent a successful FBI operation.

"Some good news," the boss continued. "We got a hit on the facial recognition of the suspect agent Richards was able to obtain a photo of. His name is Duke Montalvo. He is a known associate of the Piscelli family. I don't think I have to tell any of you about the history of the Piscellis. They have their hand in everything on the East Coast. But the key here is that old man Frankie Piscelli has a taste for gems, the unobtainable kind, like the Grand Duchess Sapphire necklace stolen from the Birmingham Museum in England three years ago. We believe the Grand Duchess Sapphire is one of the pieces, the main attraction, if you will, of the product the Websters want to buy."

The boss took a deep breath and continued.

"We must allow the transaction to occur. I repeat. The transaction must occur to get the jewels onto US soil. We cannot do anything without local authorities involved, and we don't want local authorities involved just yet."

"What kind of help am I going to get on St. Kitts?" Derek asked.

"Two agents will arrive today in St. Kitts. Ross and Jenkins. I'll send you their contact info and you can coordinate with them. We need names, pictures, locations, the works."

"What's the plan when we get back to Florida?" Derek asked.

"We'll worry about that after St. Kitts. Okay. We've got two major crime families involved in this case so far plus an unknown third party obviously comfortable working both sides. No mistakes, and everyone comes home in one piece."

"Yes, boss."

"Got it."

"Yes, boss."

"Yes, boss." Derek followed suit.

"Derek, stay on the call. The rest of you, get back to work."

The computer pinged three times as the other callers logged out of the conference call.

His boss waited until they were alone.

"Has Montalvo made you?"

"I don't think so. I haven't seen much of him. Only the Websters."

"Stay as far away from him as you can. He's Frankie Piscelli's personal handyman, if you know what I mean."

"I'll stay clear."

"We just sent you Ross and Jenkins's info. You know them?"

"I've worked with Jenkins a few times. Ross I don't know."

"Surveille only. Pictures, addresses, cars, and his barber, for chrissake. I want to know it all before you leave that island."

"You got it, boss."

Derek logged off. He had expected some heavy hitters in the game, but he didn't know it would get so big. He wondered about the third party, someone able to bridge the gap between two large crime families.

He logged into the FBI National Crime Information Center database and searched for known affiliates of both families that might cross over. Nothing. None still alive, anyway.

He spent the rest of the morning searching NCIC for other useful information. He also searched a map of St. Kitts for possible areas of concern and potential meeting places.

When he felt he had gotten all he could from the database, he logged off and contacted Fred Jenkins. They made plans to talk again before the ship docked.

HOLLY

Holly and Mike made their way up to the pool late in the morning. They had no plans for the day except to relax, work on a tan, and maybe take a nap. Bradley spotted them as they looked for a couple of open deck chairs, hard to find that time of day.

Holly and Mike waved to Doug and Lynn as Bradley wheeled himself over.

"Guess what? You'll never guess. Guess what?" He was as excited as Holly had seen him.

"What?" she laughed, "What?"

"We won! We won the escape room challenge. We beat the next best team by a whole nine minutes. I went first thing this morning to check the standings, and there we were, right on top of the board."

"Well, that was all your doing, Bradley. You are a natural born leader. Congratulations," Mike said.

"That's so awesome," Holly grinned. "Are we going to get the swim-with-the-dolphin tickets for free?"

"Of course. What else would we do? The woman said I could pick them up for all of us later, if you want me to."

"That would be great," Holly said. "I would probably forget."

"How could you forget free dolphin tickets? Hey, I think I saw a couple of open chairs over there." He pointed to the back corner of the pool area.

"Thanks, Bradley. Are you hanging out here for a while? Maybe we could have lunch together?"

"I can't. I have a date."

"A date? With who? Where are you going?" Holly sounded as excited about Bradley's date as Bradley was about winning the escape room challenge.

"Her name is Kylie. We met on St. Thomas, and I ran into her in the activities room earlier. I asked her if she wanted to get some ice cream later, and she said yes."

"Well, maybe we will get to meet her later?"

"Maybe. We'll see. I wonder how she feels about dolphins," Bradley said as he wheeled back to his parents.

Mike had meanwhile commandeered the two empty deck chairs Bradley had pointed to. When Holly told Mike about Bradley's date, he sprouted the smile of a proud uncle.

Holly checked her phone and saw a text from Jack. She spent the next hour texting back and forth, unable to stop smiling and sometimes laughing out loud.

Too content to move from their spot, Mike and Holly skipped lunch. Around midafternoon, Holly opened her eyes when she no longer felt the sun shining on her face. Between her and her tan stood a beautiful woman with long, thick brown hair and stunning figure.

"Hello, Mike," Jenny said, as she stirred him from semi-consciousness.

"Oh, hello, Jenny." He blinked his eyes in the bright sun, her body slim enough to block out only the portion of sunlight that would have reached Holly's face."

"I was hoping to find an open chair, but they all seem to be taken. That's what I get for not getting here earlier, I guess."

"I think we got the last two," Holly spoke up.

"Jenny, this is my daughter, Holly. Holly, this is Jenny."

"So nice to meet you, Holly."

"Nice to meet you, Jenny. Here, you can take my chair. Dad, I just got a text from Jack. He's got a little time between family things, so we thought we'd get a snack or something."

"Oh, please, I hope I'm not running you off." Jenny felt a bit uneasy.

"No, really, Jenny. It was perfect timing," Holly said to ease her mind. "It was very nice to meet you." She hurried off.

"I don't mean to intrude. I'm sure I can find another spot if you'd like."

"Not at all, I would love the company," Mike smiled as he fixed his chair to a more upright position.

DEREK

By noon Derek found himself famished. He decided to take a break from work and get lunch. He had stayed in his cabin all morning and collected all the available information about his case he thought relevant. He needed some fresh air.

He decided to try The Happy Turtle for lunch. He had noticed the restaurant the day he went shopping for clothes.

Suddenly, he stopped dead in his tracks as something in the back of his mind pulled at him. Hitting the rewind button in his brain, he thought back to that day. And then in his mind's eye he saw it: the sign hanging from the side of the ship. He shifted to slow motion and watched the mind movie again as he saw two beautiful women sitting at a table, on the deck, under the sign eating lunch: Cate and Sheila.

How could I have missed that? He berated himself. *And if I missed that, what else have I have missed?*

Derek began to suspect that Cate had thrown him off his game right from the start, more than he wanted to admit. From the moment she sat next to him at the bar that first morning, she had occupied his thoughts. Her gorgeous green eyes penetrated his armor like a couched lance through chainmail. Unlikely, but possible. Even more reason to stay clear of Cate—and the rest of them. He could not risk their lives because he might have feelings for her. And even if he did, *What could ever come of it anyway?* he thought forlornly as he walked down the passageway.

For the first time in his life, Derek began to think about what it would be like to have more in his life, more than work, more than the adrenaline rush of closing a case, more than the occasional casual relationship he held himself to. He wondered what it would be like to have a family, to go home to someone every night and have dinner together, talk about his day and hers, maybe even take a cruise. His daydreaming took him all the way to The Happy Turtle, where he abruptly dismissed his thinking as crazy. *I love my work*, he thought to himself, as he entered the restaurant alone.

While he inspected the menu, he found it difficult to concentrate as a boisterous conversation took place two tables away. He glanced over to see an older man speaking loudly to a group of three men who listened intently. He recognized the loud-voiced man as a dinner companion of the lawyer couple. *That must be Edward*, he realized.

Edward talked as if reading a bullet-point list. He tapped the first two digits of his left hand on the tabletop with each point he made. Derek heard him state, "I tripled my money in one year."

As he ate his lunch, Derek listened.

CATE, SHEILA, AND HOLLY

Cate, Sheila, and Holly arrived midafternoon at their salon appointments. The schedule had that night's dinner as formal dress code, and Cate and Sheila intended to make a splash. They had looked forward to this day of indulgence since they arrived.

At her own expense, Sheila invited Holly to join them to experience her first spa treatment. Holly felt nervous but excited. She hadn't told her father about the expected makeover. Instead, she made up a little white lie about meeting Jack to go for a walk. She texted her dad later in the day to say she would spend the rest of the day with Cate and Sheila and meet him for dinner in the dining room.

Holly never felt comfortable in circumstances focused on her femininity. She imagined that formal night on a cruise ship meant showcasing oneself, something she had always tried to avoid, mostly because she had never been taught how. Cate and Sheila recognized the fish out of water and determined to help educate her in feminine ways of baiting the hook.

Pampering began with a steam bath. Holly felt moist heat purify her skin and clear her pores, producing a soft, healthy glow. She had never felt anything like it. Steam removed the stress of inadequacies she felt about the upcoming formal dinner.

They moved on to a brief cooldown, passing time with a glass of champagne and talk of nail polish colors to complement their evening dress. Sheila spoke with the spa attendant about the herbal baths in preparation for each of them. When Holly slipped into hers, she detected a distinct lavender scent. Cate sank into a tea tree bath, while Sheila chose rosemary and rose essence. Sheila carefully chose scents to balance the full ensemble of the evening, each aroma distinctly different from the other but not overpowering or clashing.

The next two procedures demanded that Holly release her inhibitions about being naked. She wore only a robe until time for her full body scrub and massage. The massage therapist showed her into her room and directed her to lie on her stomach and cover herself with the sheet provided. The therapist would knock on the door in a few minutes so as not to enter before Holly had readied herself.

Holly had a beautiful body, slender but not so much that her bone structure dominated. Her subtle, smooth curves flowed from one extremity to the next.

She hung her robe and climbed up on the table, then covered herself up to her neck and, at a gentle knock, admitted the massage therapist.

A young Asian woman with incredibly soft hands, small build, and immense strength provided the massage. With the unintrusive body scrub, Holly almost fell asleep and didn't think once about a stranger touching her naked body. The young woman rinsed her with a warm water solution carrying a slight fragrance of lavender mixed with an herb that Holly could discern but not identify.

It was heavenly.

If the body scrub and rinse put Holly to sleep, the massage woke her up. The tiny woman seemed to dig deep into her frame with each press of thumb or finger. Holly had heard about deep tissue massages but never before understood their intensity. Involuntary squeals escaped her lips as the therapist came upon tight knots Holly's body had held for years. She worked them until they unraveled, leaving Holly exhausted, aching, and exhilarated.

Massages complete, the three young women relaxed on comfortable padded lounge chairs, each with a small pillow for their heads. A server brought them another glass of champagne and a plate of finger sandwiches: cucumber, pâté, and avocado-crab.

"Oh my God, is it always so intense?" Holly asked about the massage.

"Not if you get them regularly," Sheila answered.

"I could get used to this," Holly murmured, her eyes closed as she took a tiny bite of the avocado-crabmeat triangle.

"That's the problem," Cate said. "It's easy to love, hard to afford. I try to treat myself at least once a year, usually around my birthday."

"I like the way you think, Cate. This may become my new birthday routine. It's much better than lying in my hammock with a book and a bottle of wine."

"Well, I think we should plan a reunion, once a year, to meet at a spa resort. Or, better yet, come to Hollywood and stay with me, and I'll book my people to come to the house. We can make a whole weekend of it."

Sheila's excitement rose as she spoke. "When is your birthday, Holly?"

"The beginning of July, the seventh."

"That's so perfect! Cate's is the end of June. We could do a whole birthday weekend—or week! I love this idea."

As much as they could during their facials, the three women continued to discuss the idea. Then the topic turned to men.

Cate described her last few dates and how difficult the dating scene really is, especially when working as a restaurant manager. Because she worked weekends, she missed out on meeting executive types. Most of the guys she met worked in the hospitality industry or tradesmen, which she preferred anyway. She had a penchant for electricians, she said. She wasn't sure why, but she was drawn to them, like a moth to a porch light, although she hadn't given up just yet on meeting a wealthy young executive.

Sheila talked about her plans with David, what they had discussed on her birthday, how they were going to bring excitement and purpose back into their marriage.

When it was Holly's turn, she didn't have much to say.

"I haven't dated much—well, not really at all. I mean, I have some guy friends but it's nothing romantic or sexual. It's hard for me to meet new people. Sometimes I get physically ill when I'm put in that position. This week has been exceptional for me. Unusual. Even with you two. It's been so easy getting to know you. I don't know why I can't do this at home."

The three of them went silent for a moment.

"It must have been difficult growing up without a mother," Cate finally said. "I can't imagine."

"Yes, but I really have nothing to compare it to. My dad and I have a great relationship. I guess I wouldn't have it any other way."

"So, what makes this week different than any week at home?" Sheila asked.

"I don't know. It's weird, right? But I did come on this cruise with the idea of changing my personality. I just didn't think it would work," Holly laughed.

"Maybe, here, the pressure is off," said Sheila.

"What do you mean?"

"Well, at home you always have the chance that meeting someone special will change your life—and the life you have with Mike. But this ship is like living in a fantasy world—no pressure."

"Huh. Interesting," Holly replied.

"Maybe your issue isn't about you. Maybe it's your way of worrying about your Dad."

Holly thought about that for a moment. She supposed that Sheila might be partially right, but would that account for her biggest and most embarrassing symptom? She wasn't about to bring that up for discussion.

The final stage of pampering took place in the salon, a hive of activity, with hair, nails, and makeup. Chairs—all of them occupied—lined either side of the large room. Down the middle of the room between hair stylists' chairs, manicurists sat busy at work repairing cuticles, filing, and painting nails. You could opt for acrylic if that were your preference, Holly noticed, with a wide range of choices.

Holly decided to give her hair stylist full rein to pick a style that suited her best. She instructed her only not to cut too much off. She had always worn her medium-thick and shoulder-length hair straight, often tucking it behind her ears to keep it out of her face. On *Perth*, though, she felt adventurous and open to possibilities, another first for her.

Cate opted for a trim and highlights that lightened up her hair substantially. Sheila got a trim and style.

As suggested by the salon, they had brought their attire with them. It was time for the finishing touches.

DEREK

He paced. To the door. Back to the bed. All of four steps. Again. And again.

The images in his head would not stop. Cate in a black strapless gown. Cate in a flowing red, thin-strapped A-line, although his imagination could not put a name to the design. Cate wearing a blue tea-length cocktail dress.

Cate, Cate, Cate.

Derek didn't know what to do. He found himself almost desperate to see her.

Was it too dangerous? It was only dinner with six other people at the table in a large, crowded room.

After all, he hadn't chosen that table. The maître d', damn him, put him there.

Never in his life had he felt so indecisive. He always knew exactly what to do and when to do it. But now he felt like a schoolboy hiding from the head cheerleader because he feared she would see how he felt about her just by looking in his eyes.

They would dock in St. Kitts by morning.

Anything could happen.

He checked his closet for the second time. His suit hung clean and pressed, covered with a dry-cleaning bag.

ELEGANCE

Rearranged dining room tables made way for a wide red carpet down the center of the room. Each decorated table held beautiful fresh flowers and tea lights. White linen tablecloths appeared exceptionally bright against black linen napkins.

Mike arrived at their table first. Self-conscious as he walked the red carpet, he stepped off halfway to cut between the tables and take his seat. Handsome in a traditional black tuxedo with a wing-tip collar and French cuff white shirt with black pearl-like buttons, he had perfectly perched his black bowtie just below his Adam's apple.

Bradley rolled through the door. Not a hair out of place and wearing a dark navy-blue suit and tie, white dress shirt, and polished black shoes, the boy appeared to Mike more eighteen than twelve. Doug turned out also incredibly put together in a tuxedo with a spread-collar shirt and white pearl-like buttons.

But it was Lynn who particularly caught Mike's attention. He had thought her a pretty woman, but he hadn't realized how striking her features. A petite woman, she certainly stood out in a crowd, especially that night. Her dirty-blonde hair piled high on her head called attention to her slim shoulders, narrow neck, and ample breasts. She wore a black off-the-shoulder, floor-length evening gown accentuated by a diamond- and-ruby-studded necklace with matching earrings. He thought her exquisite. Doug and Lynn followed Bradley the entire length of the red carpet before turning to the right to head to the table.

"Lynn, you look exquisite," Mike expressed his thoughts out loud as he leaned over to give her a kiss on the cheek. "And you two aren't so bad yourselves."

"Oh, my goodness, Mike," Lynn blushed. "Thank you. You look very handsome yourself."

"Well, I don't get to wear this very much. I was happy to remember how to tie my tie."

"Where's Holly?" they all asked in unison.

"She's with Sheila and Cate. She texted that she would meet me here."

"Look," Bradley pointed. "Derek is here."

Derek walked through the door and opted not to walk the red carpet. He scooted around the tables and made his way to them. He wore his clean, pressed business suit.

"Good evening, everyone. You all look amazing," Derek proclaimed as he approached.

"Hi, Derek. You look great, too," Bradley said.

"Lynn . . . wow!" Derek gushed and then felt silly after he said it. But Lynn blushed, and Doug beamed.

"Thank you, Derek."

They sat around the table making small talk as the room filled with resplendently attired diners. It didn't surprise any of them that the sisters hadn't arrived yet. The group had grown used to Cate's tardiness. But Lynn had a notion that the two, wanting to make an entrance, might show later than usual. *And why not*, she thought. *Wouldn't Lynn herself want to if she were in Cate and Sheila's shoes? Holly, on the other hand, might not be as comfortable.*

The dining room had filled to near capacity when Cate, Sheila, and Holly stepped in. In single file, shoulders back and heads high, they strode the red carpet. They walked confidently. At least Cate and Sheila did. Holly, last in line, began to shake in her high-heeled shoes.

Cate wore a seagrass-toned crepe with a plunging V-neck, high waist, and side slit to her thigh. Splashed with tiny white seashells and dark green blades of grass, the color accentuated her green eyes against radiant tanned skin. She wore a necklace of colored glass beads and more seashells, understated yet effective. Her lightened hair enhanced the beachy ensemble.

Derek could not take his eyes off her. She rolled over the red carpet like the foam on a wave then landed at Derek's feet.

Seeming to hover over the floor, Sheila portrayed elegance in her charcoal grey strapless gown that featured sequined, embroidered paisley. The large emerald completing her diamond necklace rested comfortably in her copious cleavage. Her glistening blonde hair, intricately braided and resting between her shoulder blades, had a decorative emerald-colored, intertwined ribbon throughout. Six-inch heels added to her natural height and an illusion of floating rather than walking along the crimson runway.

But all eyes turned on Holly, and she could feel every one of them like darts on a board. Her legs trembled, and she found it difficult to move. As Cate reached the dinner table and Sheila advanced through her last leg of the walkway, Holly, a runway vision, froze.

Her lavender gown was stitched with dark purple and white pansies. Its off-the-shoulder sweetheart collar framed her heart-shaped face as did her new layered hairstyle that curled under her chin.

The A-line gown with a high-low design fell to her knees in the front and the floor in the back. She wore a string of pearls around her neck, the only item she had from her mother. She had never before worn them.

Holly's four-inch white pumps stuck to the carpet. She began to panic and scanned the room.

Mike began to rise from his chair when he felt Lynn's hand on his arm. Her eyes motioned for him to look across the room.

Jack had seen it all. Just in time, he took hold of Holly's arm and escorted her along the carpet. With each step, Holly regained confidence.

They gazed at each other, laughed, and smiled.

"You are dazzling," Jack said as he delivered her to the table.

"Thank you." Holly teared up. "And thank you for picking me up off the floor again."

"Anytime. Every time."

Jack kissed Holly on the cheek, pulled out her chair for her to sit with the others, and then returned to his table.

Holly looked over at Mike. He had tears in his eyes. He wanted to hide it, but he couldn't. He needed a minute to speak without choking up.

"You look beautiful. Amazing," Mike told her.

She noticed him eyeing the pearl necklace. She drew her fingers up to it as she caressed it.

"She would be, and I'm sure is, so proud of you," Mike whispered.

They had a superb dinner followed by an evening of dancing under the stars. Jack joined them as did Jenny and her sister-in-law. They would always remember the night. Cate told Derek he needed dancing lessons from Doug and Mike, Bradley managed to find Kylie in the crowd and showed her his dance moves, and Holly and Jack did not notice anyone else in the room.

The women's shoes came off by ten thirty.

ST. KITTS

MARKETPLACE

Derek made contact with Ross and Jenkins at seven o'clock the next morning. The plan called for them to have two vehicles. Fred Jenkins would park at the pier to wait for Derek while George Ross would be within sight in case the couple split up or if Duke Montalvo showed his face. They planned to follow the couple, watch the expected exchange, and get photographs and information regarding third-party contact. Then, when all went according to plan, Derek would reboard the ship and Jenkins and Ross would report their findings.

Simple, Derek thought. Except he knew that nothing was ever simple with the involvement of large crime families.

The ship had docked overnight in St. Kitts. Passengers could disembark at eight in the morning. Derek had made sure he could get off early to have time to fit himself with an earpiece for communication, prepare a service weapon, and watch as passengers walked off into the port.

He had everything in place when the first passengers appeared. It started with a light trickle of people leaving the ship, but by eight thirty, he saw a steady line.

Derek watched as Cate, Sheila, Holly, Jack, Mike, Bradley, Lynn, and Doug promenaded down the gangway at eight thirty-five. He knew they planned to spend the morning at the outdoor market and then swim with dolphins somewhere in the afternoon. They had asked him to join them, but of course, he had to decline.

Cate had looked concerned when he said he had to work.

He watched as his new acquaintances boarded a shuttle bound for the market and surrounding areas.

And then he spotted Duke Montalvo moving quickly and cutting people off as if he were late for something, and he headed for the shuttle.

Derek could see the shuttle driver counting people as they got onboard and hoped that the driver would cut the line off before Montalvo made it to the front, but much to the vocal dissatisfaction of the people behind, Duke stepped to the head of the line and boarded the shuttle.

This can't be good, Derek thought. *Why would Duke risk drawing attention to himseelf? Why does he feel the need to be on this shuttle? Had Duke seen Derek with one or all of them, and did he intend to use one of them to get to Derek?* The possibility alarmed him.

"Change of plans, Fred," said Derek. "I need the car. I have to follow that shuttle. You and George take the Websters. Stay in touch via the radio. Give me the keys."

Fred wanted to question Derek but saw the look of fear in his eyes. He handed him the keys. Derek followed the shuttle. It stopped first at an old church where a half dozen people got off. At the next stop, the outdoor marketplace, he knew Cate and the gang would exit.

He watched as most people stepped out, including his friends and Duke Montalvo. He saw that it took several minutes for the driver to work the chair lift to allow Bradley and his wheelchair off the bus. That gave Derek enough time to park his vehicle, illegally, in a spot close by. As he turned the engine off, Derek contemplated his predicament. Duke Montalvo presented a dilemma concerning his assigned surveillance duty. If Duke compromised Derek's anonymity or his friends' safety, Derek would have to take action and remove Duke from the equation. Preferably quietly. Otherwise, Derek could risk exposing his FBI affiliation to Cate and the others—and possibly to his surveillance subjects. He decided that, if necessary, he would eliminate any threat Duke Montalvo imposed.

His friends stuck to their group and didn't wander far from each other as they entered the market area. The plethora of shoppers gave Derek confidence that he could blend in with the crowd.

He watched Cate. She wore a white tank top with blue-jean shorts, sandals, and sunglasses. He allowed himself to think of her in that low-cut gown from the night before, but he thought she looked just as amazing in the tank and shorts.

He compelled himself to focus attention on Duke Montalvo, who moved slowly, as if following someone—much like Derek himself. Derek hoped he had misread the situation, but when Cate stopped at a booth to look at a hat, Duke stopped dead in his tracks, watched, and waited.

Shit!

While Cate bought a white floppy hat, Sheila, Holly, Jack, and Mike listened to a steel band. Derek allowed himself a quick scan of the crowd. He could not see Bradley, Lynn, or Doug.

When Derek turned his attention back to Cate, she had vanished, and so had Montalvo. He anxiously scanned the crowd where he had last seen Cate and spied the white hat bobbing up ahead, away from the crowded market and toward the green-painted cinderblock hospitality building displaying a sign that read *public restrooms*.

Montalvo followed about twenty paces behind.

Derek tried to get to her, but he couldn't get by all the people. He called her name, but she couldn't hear him over the music.

His heart raced. Almost out of his sight, she moved toward the opposite side of the building. If Montalvo made it around the corner, the brute could grab her—or worse.

Derek called to her again.

She disappeared behind the building, and so did Montalvo.

Desperate to get to Cate, Derek pushed people out of his way.

With each shove, he imagined the worst. *Would he be too late? Would he find Cate in a lifeless heap?* The terror he felt in his chest spread to his throat. He struggled to breathe.

I will kill the bastard.

With that thought, Derek's fear turned to anger, for him a more manageable emotion and one he had trained for. He reached the hospitality building, stopped, and took deep, methodical breaths. The structure stood in a tree-speckled clearing twenty yards from the offended, pushed-aside shoppers. He had seen no one as he approached the left side of the building.

Derek placed his hand on his Glock and slowly rounded the front corner. But instead of drawing his weapon, he froze. There on the ground lay Montalvo holding his knee, writhing in pain.

His hand still on his weapon, Derek ducked back around the corner. He quietly positioned himself so he could lean his head to watch what transpired in front of the restroom doors.

"You fucking moron! What the hell are you doing running into people with that fucking thing? I ought to kill you," Montalvo screamed at the boy in the wheelchair.

Bradley looked up, saw Derek emerge from around the corner and held up his hand in the universal language of stop, but he didn't look at Derek.

"Gee, mister, I'm real sorry. I didn't see ya. Ya want me to get somebody to help ya?" Bradley said, exaggerating youthful innocence.

Then he started to yell, loudly.

"Hey, can someone help this guy? He needs some help. Help! Someone help! He needs some help!"

Bradley caught the attention of everyone within earshot. As good Samaritans began to approach, Duke Montalvo got up and limped away as fast as he could.

Derek started to move, but just then Cate rushed out from the building. He inched back around the corner, out of sight. Cate, who had been waiting in the restroom, recognized Bradley's call for help and panicked.

"It was nothing," Bradley told Cate. "A guy fell, but he's okay. I called out to get him some help. Nothing to worry about."

"You're sure, Bradley?"

"Yes. Yes. I'm fine."

"You're really sure???"

"Yes. Honest."

She returned into the restroom.

The small crowd had dispersed by then. Bradley rolled his chair over to Derek.

"Are you okay?" Derek asked.

"Yeah, but he's getting away. Go get him."

"Are you sure you're okay?"

"Yes, go!"

"All right. But you're going to have to explain this to me later."

"I will. Go!" Bradley insisted. He waited for Cate.

Derek turned and ran in the direction Duke had hobbled. He had just disappeared from sight when Cate emerged from the restroom with questions for Bradley.

"What the heck happened?"

"I don't know. Some guy tripped or something. I didn't see him, but I heard him fall. He went down hard. I thought I heard something snap."

"Where is he?"

"I tried to get him help, but he didn't want any. He got up and limped away."

"Well, you got my attention. You scared me to death. I recognized your voice and thought someone was attacking you."

"I'm sorry, Cate. I didn't mean to scare you."

"No, Bradley. You did the right thing. I'm proud of you."

"Thanks, Cate."

Bradley felt bad about lying to Cate, but he didn't want to scare her again. *Besides,* he thought, *I stayed close to the truth.*

He would not leave Cate's side for the rest of the day.

Derek lost Montalvo in a sea of shoppers. He doubled back and saw Cate and Bradley reunited with the rest of the group. Cate looked relaxed and happy. It seemed to Derek that Bradley had not told her the truth about what happened.

He made a mental note never to underestimate a twelve-year-old.

As he watched his friends stroll through the marketplace, he radioed Fred.

"We have a problem," Derek announced.

BRADLEY

Bradley had learned long before that adults often don't pay attention to kids, especially a kid in a wheelchair.

Bradley had kept an eye on Derek. He and his female dinner companions had already figured out Derek lied about the insurance company gig. Easy enough to detect. But who was Derek, and what was he up to?

Once Derek got to know him, Bradley could no longer secretly follow him around like the day after they met, but he could pay attention to his words, actions, and inactions. For instance, Derek had identified himself as a camera buff, but Bradley never saw him with a camera, even that day by the pool when he just sat pretending to read the newspaper in the shade.

That was Sheila's birthday. Bradley had shadowed Derek most of the day until he had to get ready for Sheila's party. It became apparent to Bradley—or at least likely—that Derek was watching someone. *Probably that guy Edward,* he had originally thought. *But sometimes during that day, the blowhard was nowhere in the vicinity of Derek.*

Then there was St. Thomas. He couldn't be sure, but he could have sworn he saw Derek at the marina boarding a fishing boat. Considering Derek said that he had to work, Bradley thought that strange, why lie about going fishing?

Many minor things didn't add up to satisfy Bradley's suspicions and curiosity. When he saw Derek at the marketplace even though he had told them he couldn't join them there, Bradley made it his business to watch him.

As the shuttle driver helped Bradley out of the bus, he saw Derek park the black Dodge Charger in a no parking zone. Then Bradley watched Derek move slowly following someone through the crowd.

Bradley began to pay attention to the short old guy he figured Derek was tailing, and it seemed to him that the old guy was pursuing Cate. He wondered if Cate were in danger.

He had heard Cate tell Sheila that she had to go to the restroom, so he parked his chair behind a tree by the hospitality building and waited while Cate bought a hat. Then he watched the short old guy follow Cate to the restroom.

Bradley instinctively knew the man meant danger. When he realized the man meant to enter the women's bathroom, Bradley acted.

The guy never saw him coming as Bradley rolled right up on the back of his legs and spun his chair at impact, so that his footrest swiped the guy's legs out from under him.

Bradley thought he heard something snap.

He didn't know why the guy pursued Cate but concluded that Derek had attempted to protect her. For the first time, Bradley felt he could trust Derek.

Over the next few hours, the gang enjoyed a day of shopping and lunch at a crowded outdoor restaurant. Bradley stayed close to Cate and surveilled their surroundings discreetly—like a true professional.

DEREK

"What's the problem?" Fred asked Derek.

"First, tell me what's happening with the Websters."

"Nothing. They haven't left the ship yet."

"Good. That gives me some time. You two stay on them and let me know when they're on the move."

"What's going on, Richards?" Fred demanded.

"Montalvo went after the girl, the one who has a pretty good idea who I am. He didn't get her, but he may try again. I've got to stay on Cate, the girl."

"Why don't you just take her off the street? Hide her away somewhere safe." Fred asked.

"Too many other people would be involved. It's too risky to bring her in, and it's risky to leave her out. You guys handle the Websters. I'll take care of Montalvo."

Derek hung in the background for the rest of the morning as he monitored the situation with Cate and the others. He watched as Bradley stayed by Cate's side and noticed how the boy constantly scanned their surroundings.

This kid's a natural.

Derek felt better having another set of eyes out there, but potential danger concerned him. He did not want Bradley confronting Montalvo again. He consoled himself with the fact that they would soon leave for the dolphin park.

While the group ate lunch, Derek used his phone to search the internet for *swimming with dolphins on St. Kitts.* The *Discovering Dolphins* facility was approximately three miles away from the marketplace. The shuttle bus would most likely take Bay Road unless it had out-of-the-way scheduled stops. He could not risk losing the shuttle, so he would have to follow close behind. He decided he didn't care if Montalvo spotted him: better him than Cate.

Using website photos and a crude tourist map of the water arena, he checked out the layout of the dolphin attraction. He saw a picnic area to the west of the main attraction with a building set off to the side. To enter or leave the park, you had to go through a gift shop. He looked for alternate entries and exits but could not discern any from the online photos.

His phone buzzed.

"Yeah, Fred!"

"They're on the move. They left the ship carrying packages, about eight of them wrapped like gifts, different sizes and shapes. Like gifts for a kid."

"Oh, Christ!" Derek lamented. "They're going somewhere with kids."

"They have their own vehicle, a black SUV someone must have left for them. Looks like a CRV or RAV 4—can't tell from here. They're packing up the car now."

"All right. I'm keeping this line open. Talk me through it as you go."

The Websters prepared to leave.

Cate, Sheila, Holly, Jack, Mike, Lynn, Doug, and Bradley were on the move, too. Derek knew they would make their way over to the shuttle stop, so he jumped out ahead of them and headed to the car, the one with the parking ticket on the windshield. *Thank God they didn't tow it*, he thought. And then, as if he had jinxed himself, a tow truck pulled up.

Derek waved to the tow truck driver and drove off. He didn't have time to explain extenuating circumstances to the guy—not that he would listen. Derek's credentials didn't matter to him.

A series of one-way streets brought him back to where he started.

The shuttle had just arrived, but the tow truck had left. Derek idled in the illegal parking spot. As he got loaded onto the bus, Bradley discreetly gave Derek a thumbs up. Derek returned the gesture.

"Subjects took a right out of the port and now heading east on Bay Road. Black CRV, plate number Q 814. Just the two of them." Derek heard Fred's voice through his earpiece.

"Got it! I may be headed in that direction soon! Keep it coming."

Derek tried to picture the map of the island.

What is east of the cruise ship port that could attract children? They could be going to a private residence, too. Or maybe I'm wrong and the wrapping paper is a ruse. But if it were me, I'd want it to be a public place. Somewhere with a lot of distractions—or at least a place where you could manufacture a distraction.

Derek felt a pit in his stomach. *Oh shit, no!*

"Fred, I want to know exactly how far you are from the Discovering Dolphins attraction."

"Ah, let me check. About a mile and a half."

"I think that's where they might be going. I don't remember seeing anything else on that side of the island that would be kid friendly. Pull it up on your phone and view the layout. Let me know as soon as possible whether you think that is the intended location."

"Roger that."

The shuttle was on the move.

Derek pulled into the roadway directly behind the bus. He could see Bradley in the back by the window. Bradley pointed at him. Derek pointed at himself with a questioning look. Bradley shook his head side-to-side and pointed his finger again with a double-tap.

Derek looked in his rear-view mirror. Two cars back he saw Montalvo driving a dark sedan. Derek gave Bradley the thumbs up.

"The Websters are pulling in to Discovering Dolphins now," Fred said through the car speaker. "I'll get a better look at the layout in a few minutes."

"I've got Montalvo on my back. I'm going to confront him before we get into the parking area. I don't want him anywhere near those kids."

"You want backup?"

"I don't know yet. Stay on the line, just in case. The Websters are our priority."

Derek began to form several plans to intercept Duke before he reached the parking lot. He would have to improvise according to the situation ahead of him, of which he had no clue. He felt like a professional golfer attempting a hole-in-one without knowing the location of the flag. Derek knew he would have to take his best shot.

"Okay." Fred's voice came through Derek's phone. "I see two separate entrances, one for passenger cars, one for shuttle buses. Cars to the right, buses to the left. Ross and I are parked about ten rows back on the near end. Subjects have parked four rows back, middle."

Fred paused.

"Derek?"

"Yeah."

"This place is packed with kids."

CATE

"You're awful quiet, Bradley. I thought you would be out-of-your-mind excited about this," Cate commented.

"Oh, I am." Bradley pulled himself away from his thoughts. "I'm just thinking about what I'm going to do first.

And I have a surprise for you and Sheila. We got two extra free tickets to get in. One of the couples that did the escape room with us didn't want them, so they told the lady to give them to us. Cool, huh?"

"How very nice of them," Cate said. "I guess we won't have to stand in that long line over there, then."

They each looked toward the ticket office. The line extended all the way into the parking lot.

As they inspected the waiting line, they heard a loud crash, the unmistakable sound of metal on metal. Everyone turned toward the commotion to see two vehicles crushed together, the front car obviously rear-ended.

"People are always in such a hurry," said someone seated on the bus.

They watched from a distance as the two drivers seemed to scream at each other. Then the encounter became physical. By then, the driver instructed shuttle passengers to dismount the bus where they were corralled into two lines, one line for patrons with tickets, one line without.

Cate noticed that Bradley couldn't take his eyes off the car accident. She tried to distract him, but nothing worked. He stared as he waited for the driver to let him off the bus.

What Bradley saw worried him as he waited. Two men went down in the scuffle, but he did not see anyone get up.

DEREK

Derek kept a close eye on Montalvo. A car remained between his and his quarry as they turned into the Discovering Dolphins driveway. A man in a work uniform drove the vehicle behind Derek, and he could see no other passengers in the vehicle.

As expected, the shuttle took the left lane reserved for buses. Derek worried that Montalvo would ignore the rule and follow the shuttle into the parking lot. He slowed the car down in case he had to make an emergency U-turn to pursue Montalvo, who conveniently drove past the shuttle entrance and remained two cars behind Derek.

Derek chose his best option.

Before reaching the car parking area, he braked completely to prevent anyone from moving forward. He saw confusion on the face of the man in the car behind him. Glancing in his rear-view mirror, Derek whispered a quiet apology. Then without hesitation, Derek shifted his car into reverse and pressed the gas pedal to the floor. The car's wheels screeched as its tires spun furiously, grabbing the pavement and propelling Derek's' vehicle backwards, crushing the front end of the confused, furious driver behind him.

Derek knew exactly what he had to do, and he had to do it quickly. He shifted the car into park, jumped out, walked to the passenger side of the workman's vehicle, and approached the open passenger window.

Derek counted on the uniformed driver to confront him. He did not disappoint.

He shot out of his car, screamed, flailed his arms, and met Derek by the right rear door where the two stood face to face hollering obscenities at each other before Derek wrapped him in a bear hug and rocked him side to side as if trying to tip over a large stone statue.

Anyone observing would think they watched a wrestling match minus the ring and referee.

Derek leaned into the man and yelled as loud as he dared, "Listen to me, now. You are in danger. I'm a police officer and need you to lie down on the ground, now! Don't get up until I tell you. This is no joke. Lie down now!"

"What the fuck . . . ?"

"Now!" Derek yelled, staring directly into his eyes, pushing him away, and pinning his shoulders against the car. The baffled man capitulated. The two went down in a heap.

Derek couldn't afford to waste time. Careful to stay close to the vehicle and out of Duke's line of vision, he crawled like a soldier under barbed wire back to Montalvo's car. Derek pulled the Glock from his holster, leapt to his feet, and concentrated the .45-caliber pistol through the open passenger window on Montalvo's right ear.

"Not a twitch!" Derek commanded.

"Fred," Derek shouted into his phone. "You got me?"

"I'm on him. Coming your way now."

Derek quickly maneuvered into the front seat of Montalvo's car, and holding the Glock with his right hand, reached into Montalvo's waist holster to remove his Heckler & Koch.

The gangster didn't budge.

"Nice piece," Derek grinned. "Now slowly shut the car off, then put your hands back on the wheel. This will all be over soon."

Not wanting to create too much of a scene, Fred directed the backed-up vehicles around the accident before he approached Montalvo's car. He opened the driver's door, leaned in, and grabbed Montalvo's left hand from the steering wheel.

"Now the right, behind your back," Fred told Montalvo.

"You got this?" Derek asked Fred.

"Already got a cleaner on the way. I'll join you once they get here."

"Where's George?"

"He's watching the Websters in the picnic area."

"There's a guy lying on the ground over there. He took one for the team. Do something nice for him, huh?" Derek smiled as he re-holstered his Glock.

Derek held out his hand to stop the next car about to cross over to the parking lot. He glanced at the driver and gave him an appreciative nod. If he had noticed the shiny suit the large man wore, Derek might have recognized him. He may have anyway if he weren't so concerned about Cate.

Derek broke into a jog and headed for the gift shop entrance.

DOLPHINS

Even though they had pre-paid tickets for the park, the shuttle occupants had to stand in line to get in. Discovering Dolphins attracted more visitors than any other tourist options, so everyone expected long waits for each activity offered by the attraction.

When Bradley and friends reached the reception desk three hours before their four o'clock appointment, Doug made arrangements for Bradley and stressed that the eight people in their group wanted to stay together during the dolphin visit.

The receptionist explained that Discovering Dolphins typically served groups of twelve, so four other people might join them. In the meantime, she explained, they could visit the gift shop or food court or movie theatre, play interactive games and take part in other activities, or go to the picnic area. She pointed out the location of the dressing rooms for changing into swimsuits and instructed them to congregate at the end of the dolphin dock at three thirty for their four o'clock scheduled swim.

Without stopping to browse, they entered through the gift shop. As they emerged from the store, the Caribbean ocean lay before them, crystal clear water gently rippling as if unable to sit still from the sun's tickling. Wet wooden platforms jutted from the beach into the water, each walkway attended by multiple uniformed employees tasked with ensuring safety and a pleasant experience for all.

From where they stood, Bradley's group could only get a glimpse of the silver mammals they'd soon visit. A closer look would have to wait until three thirty.

"Where shall we start?" Lynn asked.

"I heard someone suggest the overview movie. They said it runs about thirty minutes," Holly said.

"Sounds like a good place to begin," Doug said. "What do you think, Bradley?

"Huh? What?"

"The movie—do you want to start there?" Doug questioned.

"Oh, yeah, sure."

"Bradley, are you all right?" his father asked, concerned.

"Sure, Dad. Of course."

"You seem upset. What's the matter?"

Bradley scolded himself for being so transparent. He knew better. He worried about Derek, but he would not betray him to the others. He had to think quickly.

"Sorry. I was just thinking. I hope they're not going to make me use that stupid water wheelchair. I don't want to. I want to do it like everyone else."

"I already talked to them about that, Bradley. They said they would assess the situation when we get there at three thirty. No sense in worrying about it now." Doug felt a tug on his heart.

"Okay, Dad. Movie it is."

The movie interested Bradley sufficiently that he temporarily set aside his worries about Derek and learned some interesting facts. He found out, for instance, that dolphins have two stomachs, one stomach for storing the food they eat and the other for digesting it. He was surprised that he didn't already know that. Bradley knew most of the other facts about dolphins, such as they are social, playful, and quite intelligent. Dolphins use echolocation, a kind of built-in sonar to help them maneuver underwater. The bottlenose dolphin, able to produce a thousand high-frequency clicking noises per second, also uses sonar to communicate. That always amazed Bradley. He could not imagine that many clicks in a single second.

The group emerged from the movie theatre back into the sunlight and took a moment to adjust their eyes.

"Hey, I see a picnic table opening up over there. We should grab it while it's available," Cate said.

"Great idea. We'll go with you," Holly confirmed with a look at Jack.

Pleased by their good luck, Cate, Sheila, Holly, Jack, and Mike hustled over to the table. A sizable group of children ran around two nearby tables piled high with wrapped presents for someone's dolphin-themed birthday party.

Lynn, Doug, and Bradley said they wanted to explore a little and would meet the others at the table shortly. They decided to investigate interactive activities located near the outdoor food court. Bradley stopped at a ring-toss game that reminded him of the annual carnival in his hometown. The ring landing area depicted an ocean and featured thirty upright plastic dolphins each waiting to be encircled by a bamboo ring. Each competitor had three chances to ring a dolphin and choose a prize.

Bradley accepted the three bamboo rings as he thanked the attendant. About to toss the first one, he saw a familiar figure out of the corner of his left eye. Derek stood talking on the opposite side of the food court with a man Bradley did not recognize. Relief washed over Bradley. He had not realized the extent of his anxiety since watching Derek wrestle with the man after the accident. He took a deep, calming breath and let the ring fly.

DEREK AND THE THIRD PARTY

"This place is a madhouse," George said. "There are over a hundred kids just in this picnic area alone. And you and I are going to stick out like whores at a cotillion."

Derek chuckled at the reference. He watched from a distance as Cate, Sheila, and a few of the others sat down at a picnic table not far from where the Websters stood. George indicated which packages arrived with the couple. He also pointed out the exceptionally large individual who stood next to the table guarding those packages.

The Websters conversed with a heavy-set woman who wore a colorful wrap over her one-piece, plus-size bathing suit. The bleached blonde hair piled high on her head resembled an industrious beehive. She wore what Derek considered an excessive amount of makeup and gaudy jewelry. He thought it made her look as if she just stepped off the movie set of the *Godfather*, having portrayed an old mob wife. Derek knew he had seen her face before but could not place where.

"I've got an idea . . . ," Derek said. " . . . a risky idea, but I think it's the best shot we have. I don't think the Websters have made me. We've got Montalvo under wraps, so he won't cause a problem. Just stay out of sight and keep snapping pictures of everything and everybody."

Then he explained his plan to George.

Derek approached Bradley, Lynn, and Doug just as the ring-toss attendant handed Bradley his large stuffed dolphin.

"Derek, we didn't expect to see you here." Doug sounded surprised.

Confused but happy to see him, Bradley whirled his head in Derek's direction,

"Hey, Derek, what are you doing here?" Bradley asked.

"Well, my work took me close by, so I thought I'd see what you guys were up to." He didn't lie.

"How wonderful," Lynn said. "The rest of the crew is over there." She pointed to the picnic table.

"Oh, here, Mom. This is for you!" Bradley said as he presented the stuffed dolphin to his mother.

"Thank you, sweetheart." She leaned down to give him a kiss on his cheek. "It will be a great reminder of a wonderful trip. Let's go join the others."

Cate noticed Derek first as he approached with Doug, Lynn, and Bradley. Her surprise exceeded only by her smile, she jumped to her feet and banged her knee on the table.

"Hey, everyone. Thought I might join the party after all," Derek proclaimed.

"Hey!"

"Hi, Derek!"

"Glad you could make it!"

"Yay, you made it."

They greeted him all at once.

A young woman serving drinks from a cart stopped at the table. Derek bought soft drinks for everyone along with a few bags of snacks from the cart.

"Hey, Holly, let's get a group picture. Do you have a timer on that thing?" Derek asked.

"Of course I do. Great idea."

Derek herded everyone into place—two lines, shorter people in front, taller in the back, and the Websters and their unidentified contact behind them. Using the timer on her camera, Holly clicked a few shots once they all got settled and then, to assure the best possible photo, asked a stranger if she would mind taking their picture.

"Okay. Everybody say cheese," the woman directed.

"Cheeeeeeese!"

She snapped a few pictures.

"I hope they look all right," she said.

Holly reached for the camera. Derek stood behind her as she studied the pictures.

"Perfect!" Derek said.

Holly disagreed. She felt they weren't focused properly. Since they would suffice, though, she politely thanked the woman.

"Would you like me to take a picture of you and your Dad? How about you and Jack?" Derek asked.

"That would be great. How about all three of us?"

Derek took a few more pictures before he sat down beside Cate. He had so worried about her that he waited only a minute before he moved his hand to his lap and let it slide down his thigh to touch Cate's. Cate moved her pinky finger to brush his. Derek took her hand and rested it on his leg. Only then did they steal a glance at each other and smile.

They killed time with idle chitchat. Derek managed to get a few more photos using his telephone camera. As part of the cruise ship gathering, he had closer access to the partying suspects than Fred and George. After about an hour, when it looked as if the Websters prepared to leave, Derek excused himself to go to the restroom.

Fred followed him inside.

"Everything work out with Montalvo?" Derek asked.

"Yeah, yeah. Fine. How the hell did you manage that? Who are those people?"

"People from the ship. Friends," Derek allowed himself to reveal. "It looks like the Websters are getting ready to leave. My guess is they will go back to the ship. From what I can see, they picked up only one small package. Whatever it is, it's got to be worth a bundle. I can't imagine they will want to wander around the island with it."

"Okay. So what are you thinking?" Fred asked.

"One of you follows the Websters, one stays here. There's something we need to do."

HOLLY

Holly's excitement about swimming with dolphins grew almost as much as Bradley's. At three twenty-five, the friends, all in their swimsuits, gathered their things and headed for the dock. Holly had taken a lot of pictures, but she really looked forward to getting up close and personal with the mammals. Unfortunately, they would not allow her to take her camera out onto the dock.

Only Derek hadn't paid to swim with the dolphins, so he graciously offered to use Holly's camera to take pictures of everyone from his place on the beach near the dock.

While the rest of them remained on shore awaiting instruction, attendants worked with Bradley, Lynn, and Doug to evaluate whether Bradley needed a special sea wheelchair. They had him wade in water while wearing a life vest and an inflatable donut around his waist. Though no expert, Holly thought he held his own. When she saw the huge smile light up Bradley's face, she knew she had guessed correctly. Holly focused on the boy's joy and snapped a picture. When she viewed it, she thought it one of her best. She set the camera options to generic so Derek could point and click, then handed him the camera.

Bradley, Lynn, and Doug received instruction in the water while the rest of them took their fifteen-minute instruction on land.

Four others joined the group. One of the two couples was the honeymooners from Tennessee that Holly and Mike had met at the Meet & Mingle earlier in the trip, so they introduced Tina and Tom to their friends. The other couple, Helen and Bob from Kansas, had never seen the ocean before traveling to Florida for the cruise.

The Dolphin Discovery crew told Derek he had to stay on shore while taking pictures. Discovering Dolphins had professional photographers on the job during the swim. They'd make their photos available for a fee at the conclusion of the experience.

The first part of the program had them standing still in the water to let the dolphins swim around them so the dolphins could familiarize themselves, Holly supposed. Next, the human participants could touch the animals, snuggle with them, and maybe even kiss them if so inclined. The final part offered the prospect of the most fun when each person could hold a dolphin's dorsal fin and swim alongside, sometimes forward, sometimes backward.

Holly and Jack floated side by side when the first dolphins swam by. She glanced up at Derek and saw him focusing the camera and taking distanced pictures as he moved along the shoreline to get better angles. Once she finally got to touch a dolphin, Holly forgot all about Derek and the camera. She became the vulnerable object at the other end of the lens.

The friends swam, laughed, and urged each other on.

"Go ahead. Kiss him!" Mike hollered to Sheila.

"Only if you do!" Sheila shot back.

They each kissed a dolphin.

One of the dolphins, the largest of the bunch, made fast friends with Bradley. It seemed he didn't want to leave Bradley's side.

"Well," Bradley said to explain the dolphin's evident preference. "They are highly intelligent animals."

His remark drew laughter. Soon their amazing time would come to an end.

Holly thought to look up to shore where she saw Derek looking as if he enjoyed himself with her camera. She also saw a man carrying a load of something, then stumble in the sand and drop his packages. She smiled as Derek put the camera down to help the gentleman. Then her newest friend, a female dolphin named Sophie, nudged her. Sophie had the biggest, kindest eyes Holly had ever seen.

"Grab the dorsal," the attendant said to Holly.

She rode side by side with Jack as each held the dorsal of one of the most beautiful creatures in existence.

DEREK

Derek watched as Doug and an attendant helped Bradley back into his wheelchair. He noticed a momentary wave of sadness move across Bradley's face. When he lifted his head, however, he grinned from ear to ear.

"Oh, man, Derek, I wish you could have been in there. It was awesome! It was the most awesome thing I've ever done in my life!" Bradley beamed.

Derek begged to differ. Bradley may not have realized the importance of his actions back at the marketplace, but Derek knew that saving someone's life qualified as more awesome. But who was he to spoil the moment?

"You guys were amazing. I think I got some great pictures. I just wish I could have gotten closer," Derek said.

"I can't wait to see them," Bradley said.

"Me, too," said Holly. "Where is the camera?"

"Oh, I put it down over there at the end of the dock. I had to help a guy with some packages." And he pointed to the end of dock.

"Where? I don't see it, Derek," Holly said, slightly worried.

Derek spun around and replied, "Right th . . . ." He stopped midsentence.

"It was right there . . . " he pointed to the empty spot, " . . . just a minute ago. What the hell?"

"Oh, no, all my pictures are on there. I haven't downloaded any of them yet. We have to find it!" Holly started to panic.

They looked for the camera to no avail. They hoped someone had picked it up by mistake, but no one had turned it in to lost and found. There was no sign of it. *And*, Holly thought, *with all the people who had been there, anyone could have taken it.*

"Holly, I'm so sorry. I only put it down for a minute to . . ."

"How could you, Derek? You know how much that camera means to me, you know!" Holly began to cry. Mike and Jack proved unsuccessful in trying to soothe her.

Derek looked like someone kicked in the stomach. Cate wanted to help, but she couldn't think of anything to say. Derek watched as Holly's tears fell.

"Shit!" Derek rammed his fist into the dock. He hated to see Holly so upset, and it was his fault. His hand bled.

"Oh, my God, Derek. Your hand!" Cate exclaimed. "It's swelling up fast. Did you break something?"

"I don't care."

"Derek," Lynn went to him. "You need to have someone look at that."

"I don't care if it's broken." He paused and looked at Holly and her father trying to comfort her.

"I'm so sorry, Holly."

Derek walked away.

CONNECTIONS

CATE

Cate worried about Derek. She hadn't seen him since he left Discovering Dolphins, and he didn't show up for dinner on the ship. She supposed he could have stayed on shore that night but dismissed the thought. Light conversation accompanied the evening meal. Bradley's talk of his experience with the dolphins could not lift Holly's spirits. It only reminded her of the memories she caught on camera that she would never see. Cate barely spoke a word. The others kept to topics other than the events of the day. After dinner, Cate decided to find Derek.

"Sheila, I need to talk to Derek. I'm worried about him. I'm going to see if he's in his room."

"Cate, he may not want to see anyone. He seemed pretty upset."

"I have to go."

Sheila watched as Cate hurried out of the dining room. She knew no words would stop her.

Cate stood listening at Derek's cabin door. She thought she heard a soft cough from inside.

She knocked.

Silence.

She knocked again.

"I know you're in there, Derek," she said confidently, even though she didn't know for sure.

"I'm not leaving. Open the door," she commanded.

She heard him rustle around, make his way to the door, and slowly open it.

She gasped.

"Derek, you look awful."

He had an ice-filled towel wrapped around his right hand, and he was sweating.

"Cate, you should go. It's not safe to be around me."

"No, Derek. I'm not going."

Before he could object, Cate picked up the cabin phone and summoned a doctor to Derek's room.

"Did you take anything for the pain?"

"No. I deserve the pain."

"Goddamnit, Derek, don't be so melodramatic. It was a fucking camera."

Derek chuckled as if she had missed the joke.

"What? What is it?" she pleaded.

Derek winced as he tried to move his hand.

"I can't talk about this, Cate. You should go, it's not safe."

"I told you, I'm not going. I don't care if Whitey Bulger crashes through that door. I'm not going anywhere."

Derek grimaced. He felt tired, weary, and not up for games. *Was Cate fishing for information?*

"What? How do you know who Whitey Bulger is?" he asked almost disparagingly.

Realizing what she had said, Cate paused.

"I googled the Boston Federal Bureau of Investigation, and that's what came up."

"Why would you google the Boston FBI?"

Cate gazed deliberately at Derek. With that look, Derek felt the depth of Cate's understanding of his work—and of him. As if shoved off balance, he shifted uneasily from foot to foot.

"What makes you think I'm with the FBI, Cate? And how do you know about Boston? I told you I worked for the DOJ, and I'm pretty sure I never mentioned Boston."

"Even a California girl can identify a Boston accent no matter how hard you try to mask it. But I'm guessing you didn't grow up there."

"Connecticut. I grew up in Connecticut. We pronounce our r's there. What about the FBI part?"

"I had a suspicion, so I googled you. A small newspaper article popped up—well, I had to dig a little. A few years ago, you solved a cybercrime case, and the story associated you with the FBI."

"Huh. I thought we killed that story."

Cate changed the subject. "Derek, let me see your hand. Please."

For the first time since she entered his room, he allowed himself to look into her eyes—*those green, penetrating, remarkable eyes.* He knew he could never say no to her.

He sat on the bed and rested his forearm on his thigh, palm up. Dropping bits of ice onto the floor, Cate unraveled the towel. The color of a bruised plum, the first two fingers on his hand had tripled in size.

At a knock on the door, Cate let the doctor in. A woman in her fifties, give or take, she carried a multicolored medical bag with children's cartoon characters printed on the exterior. The interior provided everything she would need to take care of Derek's broken fingers.

She saw Derek eying the medical bag and asked, "Would you like a lollipop?"

"No, thank you, but if you have a bottle of bourbon in there, I could sure use it."

"Who couldn't?" she joked. "Have you taken any pain medication yet?"

"No," Derek and Cate answered in unison.

The doctor worked on his hand, placed a double-wide metal splint to hold the two fingers in place, and wrapped the hand all the way to the wrist to keep things from moving.

"Here's some Vicodin. If you're going to have bourbon, don't take the Vicodin. I would recommend you forego bourbon. I'm required to ask. Did this injury happen while aboard the ship?"

"No."

"Just out of curiosity, what does the other guy look like?"

"An immoveable object," Derek replied as he swallowed the pill.

HOLLY AND JACK

"I can't believe how selfish I am. I ruined dinner for everyone with my mopey attitude. We only have three nights left together, and I ruined one of them."

Holly leaned on Jack.

"I'm sure you didn't ruin anything. Besides, the night isn't over yet. They're all sitting right over there. If you feel that way, you should say something to them. It might make you feel better."

"Ugh, you're right, of course. Will you come with me?"

"You bet I will. I'll even cover for you if you get nervous and have to fart!" A smile spread across Jack's face.

"What? What did you say?"

"You heard me! And I heard you! That night I picked you off the floor. You managed the single most awesome evasion I have ever seen. Much better than any I could've come up with."

"You heard me? And you didn't say anything?" Holly felt mortified.

"I didn't want you to run away. I had a feeling you might if I acknowledged it, so I didn't."

Holly's face turned angry, then embarrassed, then curious, and finally elated with unparalleled exuberance. The range of emotion she felt in that moment distinguished itself as, well, momentous. They shared a laugh as loud and hard as any Holly had ever mustered. People stared, but she didn't care.

People pointed, but she didn't care. People laughed, but she didn't care.

She could not hold herself back. She jumped into Jack's arms and clung to him like a wet bathing suit. They kissed—a deep, passionate, penetrating kiss that every single woman in the room envied—and some of the not-so-single women as well.

Holly and Jack laughed as they reached the booth where the rest of the gang congregated.

"Hey, everyone. I want to apologize for being such a mope at dinner. I didn't mean to ruin your evening. I made a big deal out of a stupid mishap. I'm really sorry."

"Does that mean we all get a kiss like that?" Doug asked.

More laughter, even from the surrounding tables, and it didn't bother Holly one bit.

She felt liberated.

"Let's go dancing!" Holly shouted.

DEREK AND CATE

The Vicodin kicked in, and Derek began to relax. Cate helped him out of his blood-stained shirt, her eyes loitering to admire his hairless chest and well-toned torso. They sat on the couch that would have acted as the second bed for the agents originally assigned to the room. Derek put his left arm around Cate's shoulders. She snuggled in.

Comfortable in their silence, they sat for some time until Cate spoke.

"What happened, Derek? You don't strike me as the type to lose your cool like that."

"I don't like letting people down."

He looked into Cate's eyes and lingered as he imagined enveloping the rest of her body bit by bit, slowly, as he envisioned her naked and resting in his arms. He pictured himself caressing her radiant skin, gently massaging her breasts, feeling her nipples harden as she leaned into him, his hands stroking the soft skin of her inner thigh, the tip of his tongue tickling her to the edge of decadent satisfaction, teasing her until she could no longer control the outcome, and then finishing her with fullness as he drank her essence.

Just the thought brought him to the threshold. He could not take it any longer. Desiring her as he conjured his thoughts to fulfillment, he leaned into her. His lips touched hers as she became a book whose pages slowly then eagerly filled with his pictures.

Partially dressed, their heartbeats in unison, gasping for air, they lay on the bed, expelling the anticipation, reveling in the consummation. Derek's bruised and beaten hand kept time with his heart.

"I'm . . . I'm sorry," Derek managed. "I shouldn't have. . ."

"Shhhh!" Cate placed her finger on his lips. She slid out of her remaining clothing and removed the pants clinging to Derek's leg. She lay on top of him, kissing and caressing his chest, his abdomen, his pelvis. . .

"I'm not done with you yet," she whispered.

Derek's body arched in response to her tender touch.

A FULL DAY AT SEA

Saturating Derek's face with the morning sun, a bright shard of light pierced the porthole of his cabin. Cate lay wrapped in his arms. He squinted his way into the early morning. His throbbing hand, its blood flow stunted, held the weight of Cate's head.

Reluctantly, hoping not to disturb her, he eased his way free. As he glanced back at Cate, his awakening brain began to race. *She is perfect. How will I ever be able to give her up? How can I say goodbye?* The stark reality tempered the exhilaration he had felt only moments before. *I need to keep my feelings in check. I can't get distracted. That could prove dangerous, especially for Cate.* Derek's self-imposed bachelor status had never come so close to crumbling. He had always carefully honored the disciplined code of his line of work.

He opened his laptop and logged into his secure FBI messaging system where he found three messages.

Message 1: *The dolphin is on the shelf.*

Meaning Montalvo is locked away. Derek found the bureau's paranoia amusing. Even through a secure system, agents felt the need to speak in riddles—or at least nonspecifics. Some got so wrapped up in their riddles that the best code breakers in the bureau couldn't decipher their messages.

Message 2: *Party girl hit.*

They've identified the third-party contact from the photos provided.

Message 3: *Check-in is at eight.*

The boss had scheduled a conference call with Derek in less than two hours. His watch read 6:03.

He closed his laptop, popped a Vicodin, and longingly gazed at Cate. He could not help himself. He set aside his trepidation of entering into a relationship and lay down next to her. She woke.

"Good morning." Derek smiled and leaned in for a kiss.

"Good morning."

"How did you sleep?"

"Completely satisfied." She smiled. "How is your hand?"

"It's fine. I just took a shot of bourbon."

"What time is it?"

"A little after six. Why? You in a hurry to go somewhere?"

Cate curled her body into his and moaned, "Not at all. Although I am supposed to meet everyone for breakfast at seven thirty. Will you come?"

"I can't. I have an eight o'clock conference call. But hopefully I can meet up with you later."

"What are you doing until then?" Cate asked with a mischievous smile.

Derek grinned. "I thought I might practice docking the ship."

Cate winced and laughed.

"Thank God you are so much better in action than words."

"Does that mean you don't want to hear my throttle reference?"

SHEILA

Like a thirsty flower at the watering of the garden, she soaked up the morning sun. As a child, Sheila often heard her mother calling the rising sun Sheila's sun. Her father never understood her dependence on it, and Cate always slept through it. She so believed her mother's assessment that she regimented her life around it.

But today felt different. The sun did not feel as if it belonged solely to her. She had the notion that it concentrated its efforts elsewhere, a strange sensation she could not substantiate. The concept presented quite a conundrum as she contemplated the ramifications.

How did she feel about sharing her morning sun? Or was it even hers to share? Had it ever belonged to her? Had it belonged to someone else who had shared it with her for twenty-five years? Was it ever really Sheila's sun to begin with?

And why had the thought suddenly come to light?

Something had happened to Sheila during the week. A revelation so simple it was complicated. Earlier in the week, she had experienced an epiphany regarding her need to take responsibility for the direction of her marriage. She learned that if she and David were going to be happy, she must take part in creating that reality. She realized she had been a spectator in their union, and in her two previous marriages. She had blamed other people, mostly her husbands, for her unhappiness. It had come as a surprise to acknowledge that she could—and should—play an active role in her own life.

With the help of her new friends, she had learned much more during the week. Sheila had always been taken care of.

When afraid or anxious, Sheila deferred to others to provide a shield. If she had difficulty accomplishing a task, others accomplished it for her. If she lost a love, she filled the void by replacing him with another.

If she felt lonely, she soaked in the sun.

But during the week aboard *Perth*, she had learned about overcoming her fears and anxiety from Holly, a young woman who grew up without a mother, whose father lifted his shield in order for his daughter to grow and become a warrior in her battle for confidence and self-esteem.

Sheila watched as Bradley overcame challenge after challenge with his ever-present smile and apparently effortless resilience, even as she knew in her heart that what seemed effortless took immense determination and strength. His joie de vivre inspired Sheila to emulate him, a twelve-year-old.

She also quickly grew to admire Mike, a man who, after tragically losing the love of his life, took responsibility as a single father for raising a daughter while directing all the love within him to her. Sheila knew instinctively that what she considered sacrifice Mike considered privilege.

Sheila had never felt particularly close with her parents. The more she thought about it, the more she realized she spent her young life trying to impress them with her husbands as she imagined it would make them proud if she landed a wealthy man. She had the notion that, by marrying a successful man, her success would be their success. On *Perth*, however, she came to understand the childishness of her motives.

She envied the relationship Bradley had with Lynn and Doug, how Holly and Mike communicated without words, and even how Jack had willingly spent a week on a cruise ship with his extended family. Obviously close with Cate, she felt potential for much more in their relationship, and she determined to pursue it.

She determined to reunite with her family.

An indiscernible cloud in the sky must have dissipated with Sheila's resolve, because she suddenly felt the full force of the orb soak deep into her soul.

This is happiness, she thought.

BREAKFAST

"Where's Cate?" Bradley asked. "Isn't she coming to breakfast?"

Sheila had just arrived. She wore a cover-up over her bathing suit and carried her large beach bag.

"Well, good morning to you, too, Bradley," she replied.

"I'm sorry, Sheila. I didn't mean. . ."

"I know," Sheila laughed. "I'm just giving you a hard time. I'm sure Cate will be here, but it is a little early for her."

They sat around the breakfast table, minus Cate and Derek. None of them had seen Derek since he walked away from the dolphin park.

"Does anyone know how Derek is doing?" Lynn asked.

"Cate went to look for him last night. I think she may have found him but . . ." Sheila glanced at Bradley and then back at Lynn before continuing, "I haven't talked to her about it yet."

Sheila could tell Lynn understood that she hadn't seen Cate all night—as did the others, including Bradley, but he didn't let on.

"Well, I hope she found him. He seemed quite upset when he left," Lynn said.

"It was my fault," Holly interjected. "I behaved like a child. I shouldn't have made him feel so bad."

"Honey, it wasn't you who made him feel bad. He felt bad because he had responsibility for your camera. You would feel the same if the tables were turned, wouldn't you?" Mike asked.

"Yes, I suppose. But I don't think I would punch a hunk of wood."

"I would hope not," Mike replied.

"Here comes Cate." Doug saw her coming through the door.

"Wow. She looks beautiful," Holly remarked.

"Yes . . . she does," Sheila agreed.

The women at the table shared a knowing smile.

In their best elementary school cadence, her tablemates trilled, "Good morning, Cate."

Cate laughed. "Good morning, goofballs. Sorry I'm late."

"You should just make business cards with that phrase, Cate. You can just hand them to people as you walk into a room. It would save a lot of time," Sheila laughed.

Cate feigned slight amusement.

"How's Derek doing?" Bradley asked.

"Uh, well," she scanned the table, "I saw him last night when he was with the doctor. He broke two fingers. She put some splints on and wrapped him up. He feels terrible about the camera, Holly."

"I know, and I feel terrible about my reaction. I hope I'll get to see him today to apologize."

Cate darted her eyes to Bradley and then Lynn before she spoke again.

"I talked to him earlier, and he said he had to work this morning, but he might be able to join us after breakfast."

"It's okay, Cate. Sheila told us you spent the night with him. You don't have to try to hide it." Bradley confessed his knowledge.

"Bradley!" Lynn exclaimed, shooting him a disapproving look.

"Sheila!" Cate exclaimed, tossing her an embarrassed look.

"I did not say that!" Sheila tried to explain.

Holly giggled at Bradley, Bradley snickered at Lynn, Doug chuckled at Bradley, and Mike, Sheila, and Cate joined in the good humor.

And then they noticed that a break had formed in the buffet line.

DEREK

Once his laptop woke, Derek connected to his call.

"Right to it," his boss started. "Montalvo isn't talking. We don't know what he was doing on the ship. Our guess is Frankie Piscelli sent him to keep the Websters in line. What we don't know is how he tagged you. That's problem number one."

"One?" Derek asked.

"We got a hit on the third party. Her name is Patti Valleri. You familiar with her?"

"Yes," Derek remembered the face. "Vinnie Valleri's wife. Vinnie got caught in the middle of Benny White and Frankie Piscelli in the East Boston war. Got himself blown up. Vinnie worked for Frankie Piscelli, but when Vinnie died, Frankie left Patti high and dry. Bad blood there."

"Right. So why would she help procure the Grand Duchess Sapphire for Piscelli when he broke the code and left her to fend for herself? That's problem number two."

"Two," Derek repeated.

"The pictures we took from the camera at the dolphin park revealed another surprise."

The photo had captured a man in the tree line of the parking lot. Derek zoomed in. Except for the shiny suit, he blended nicely into the background. Derek recognized him immediately.

"That's the guy from Benny White's estate," Derek stated.

"His name is Joey the Suit Carelli. We know he works for White. What we don't know is why he showed up at the dolphin park. Benny's part in the exchange had finished. That's problem number three."

"Three."

"Four. It's possible they slipped someone on board with you. Jenkins staked out the ship until it left port. Not long before it sailed, he got pictures of a vehicle abandoned on the dock. An hour before he spotted the car, the owner of the vehicle reported it stolen.

Derek reached into his suitcase and retrieved the Glock. He fumbled with the magazine as he inserted it into the pistol grip with his left hand, chambered a round, and set it on the table next to him.

"Have I got any help on board?"

"None of our guys. We're checking the manifest for active military and police personnel, but even if we find someone, there's no guarantee you'll have help."

"Any connection between the Valleris and this Carelli guy?" Derek asked.

"Working on it. You still have a weapon?"

"I do."

"Good. Wear it."

"Yes, boss."

They signed off.

Derek sat back in his chair. His right hand throbbed. He found himself wishing he could turn the clock back and discover himself lying next to Cate. He sighed. He picked up the Glock in his left hand and laid his trigger finger carefully alongside the barrel. He had trained shooting a handgun with his less dominant hand. He could not consistently hit a bullseye, but he could hit a pie plate.

He reviewed the information he had just received.

First, Duke Montalvo somehow had identified Derek as a threat. *Had Montalvo told anyone else?* Derek hoped the team could get him to talk.

Second, why would Benny White and Frankie Piscelli deal with Patti Valleri? Derek could almost understand Benny, but Frankie outed her and created the bad blood. That posed no secret. Derek decided that Frankie did not know the identity of the third-party contact. *Therefore*, thought Derek, *it is likely he sent Duke Montalvo along to identify the fence.*

Third, Benny must know about Patti, because his guy, Joey the Suit, showed up at the dolphin park. So, Joey flew to St. Kitts. How did he know where to go? Did he follow Derek or Duke? Or Patti?

Fourth, he needed to keep his head on a swivel. There could be a bogie on board, and he had no backup. *Is Cate in danger again? Are the others in danger?* He had to find them.

Derek stuffed the Glock into his inside-the-waistband holster tucked on his left side and donned his roomiest shirt. He practiced drawing the gun with his left hand and determined himself prepared if the need arose.

He checked the mirror to see if the gun showed. It did not. He didn't have a plan except to do everything possible to keep Cate and the others safe.

CATE

At almost ten thirty, Derek texted Cate. He wanted to know her whereabouts.

She and Sheila sat at the pool with Mike, she told him. Holly and Jack had gone for a walk, and Lynn, Doug, and Bradley enjoyed game day in the activities room.

Derek found them easily as he spotted Cate in her new floppy white hat. For a moment, he stopped to watch her, smiling at his good fortune until he felt a pit in his stomach. Derek sensed a crossroads of some sort. Not quite sure how, he felt his life hung on the verge of change, and that disquieted him. He had always controlled his every thought, emotion, and reaction . . . until he met Cate.

She saw him and waved her arm to make sure he could see her. Her smile melted his heart. With a cloudless sky, light breeze, and many people relaxing by the pool, Derek's presence could endanger all of them.

Resolve replaced the pit in his stomach. Derek determined to protect every one of them. Searching for an individual who looked out of place, he scanned the crowd. No one stood out.

"Hi, Sheila, Mike, Cate." Cate stood to meet him. Her stance invited a kiss, which he happily gave. Sheila smiled.

"How was breakfast?" he asked.

"Too much," Cate replied. "I barely fit into my bathing suit."

"I think it fits you just fine," Derek grinned.

Cate blushed.

Derek turned his attention to Mike.

"Hey, Mike, I am really sorry about upsetting Holly. I feel awful about that. I promise I will make it up to her."

"Holly is fine. It was an accident, Derek. We can't always stop bad things from happening."

"But we can try." It slipped out before he realized it.

Derek hoped that didn't present an omen. *My life is all about stopping terrible things from happening,* he thought.

They spent the next couple of hours enjoying each other's company and getting to know one another better. Cate tried to steer the conversation away from work by asking about hobbies and favorite foods, which Derek appreciated.

"What about golf?" Mike asked Derek. "You play?"

"I try," Derek chuckled, "but I spend most of the round searching for my ball."

"Doug and I are going to hit some balls later. You want to join us?"

"Sounds great, but I don't think I'd be very good at it with one hand." He held up his wrapped right hand.

Mike laughed. "Forgot about that."

Pleased that Derek had joined them, Cate hoped they could spend more time together, since they had so little of it left. She knew that Derek's work came first. But at least for a little while, she didn't have to worry about him.

Derek noticed Holly and Jack walking on the other side of the pool. He excused himself and went to speak with them. Cate watched as Derek said something to Jack. Jack nodded and walked away.

Cate knew Derek agonized over losing Holly's camera. She assumed he apologized to her again, and it looked as if Holly tried to console him.

Derek and Holly hugged. Jack returned with beverages, and the three of them strolled over to where she sat, Holly and Derek arm in arm.

"Well, Holly, if you don't mind sharing, I'll take this one off your hands." Giggling as she did so, Cate reached for Derek's arm.

"Hey, Dad," Holly called. "I hope you didn't make any plans for this afternoon."

"As a matter of fact, I'm hitting some golf balls with Doug at one o'clock."

"Ah, I'm afraid not."

"What do you mean?"

"You have an appointment at one o'clock on the Sports Deck."

"Holly, what did you do?"

"I signed you up for the beer pong tournament."

Sheila and Cate screeched. "Ahhh, that will be so much fun!" Sheila cried.

"We will be your cheerleaders!" Cate nodded.

"Absolutely! Go Mikey, go Mikey!" Sheila cheered.

"It's called payback, Dad." Holly grinned.

"All right. I'll show these kids how it's done. But I better limber up first."

Mike went to the bar and ordered a beer.

BEER PONG

Holly had texted everyone, including Jenny and her sister-in-law, about the beer pong tournament, so Mike had an ample cheering section.

Derek had to excuse himself for another work meeting.

The *Perth's* activities director—her name badge read Kara—announced to the waiting crowd the rules of the tournament.

"We allowed a total of thirty-two competitors for this afternoon's tournament, and I'm happy to say we filled the roster. The rules of the game are simple. We have sixteen ping-pong tables set up. Two competitors at each table will try to advance to the next stage of the competition by sinking their respective ping-pong ball into the opponent's cup before the other can do same. Each twelve-ounce cup is half filled with beer. When an opponent sinks the ball into your cup, you must drink all the beer from the cup and remove the cup from the table. The ping-pong ball must bounce once on the table, and only once, before falling into the cup for it to count. The person first to clear all the opponent's cups off the table wins.

"Are there any questions?"

A male voice shouted from the amped-up crowd, "It works better with whiskey." His surrounding friends cheered. They wore crimson t-shirts emblazoned with the University of Alabama logo. It became obvious that most of them had begun practicing the drinking part of the game much earlier.

"Thank you for the suggestion," Kara laughed, "but I think we'll stick with light beer. I will pick the match-ups at random and we will begin."

Mike beat his first three competitors, two young men from the University of Alabama group and a newly married man who did an admirable job of impressing his bride.

The fourth competitor appeared in the person of an older man of large stature who looked completely uncomfortable wearing cruise-wear shorts, t-shirt, and sneakers. They called him Joe, a last-minute entry. He didn't talk much but gave Mike a run for his money. The game stood tied right up until Mike sunk his ping-pong ball into Joe's remaining cup, thus advancing him to the final match.

"Good game." Mike reached for Joe's hand to shake. Joe had a strong grip, and his massive hand enveloped Mike's.

"Yeah," Joe replied as he stared directly into Mike's eyes. Then he walked away.

"Strange dude," Bradley said.

Mike agreed. Something about the guy didn't sit quite right. Mike's final competitor, a twenty-something blonde woman, wore a Crimson Tide football jersey. She stood all of four feet, six inches. He imagined if a fair wind blew, she would have to hold on to something to avoid wafting away.

Each having consumed a fair amount of beer during the game, they had both made it through four rounds. His cheering section had grown slightly but nothing compared to the young woman's.

Kara introduced them to the crowd.

"Ladies and gentlemen, our final match of the day is between Tawney and Mike. You are encouraged to cheer for your favorite competitor, but let's keep it clean. Tawney won the coin toss, so she will begin."

Mike had mixed feelings about the game. If he won, he would feel terrible for beating Tawney, who seemed so excited to be in the finals. Winning would give her a fun story to tell for the rest of her life. On the other hand, he had his new friends who cheered him on, not to mention his daughter who seemed to enjoy herself. And he had bragged about his beer pong status.

He decided to give it his best shot.

The preliminary games of the final played with six cups, three rows formed in a triangle front to back—one cup, two cups, three cups. For the finals they would use ten cups, so Kara added a fourth row with four cups.

Tawney began. Woosh! Mike drank.

Mike's turn. Woosh! Tawney drank.

For three turns in a row, they each drank.

Fourth shot, Tawney dunked it. Mike drank.

Mike missed.

Tawney sunk the next one. Mike drank.

Mike came back with a hit. Tawney drank.

Tawney missed.

Mike tied it up.

One for one, they took their shots. They each took out four of the other's cups in the next six tries. Two cups remained on the table, one in front of each of them.

It came to Tawney's turn. She took a deep breath, aimed carefully, and skimmed the ball off the rim of the cup.

Mike stood poised to win the game. He aimed, let it go with just the right amount of speed and energy, and watched as it bounced on the table, slightly to the right of Tawney's cup.

Tawney sunk her next shot for the win.

Mike congratulated her and reached in to shake her hand, but she hugged him instead. Her Alabama cheering squad lifted her small frame on their shoulders and paraded around the deck. Mike felt happy for her.

Holly ran over to her Dad and gave him a big hug.

"Wow, that was awesome. You were wonderful," she said.

"But I lost."

"Did you? Really?" She smirked.

"WooHoo! That was incredible," Sheila hollered.

"You are the man!" Cate said.

"Can you teach me how to play that game?" Bradley asked.

"Come see me when you're twenty-one," Mike answered.

"Maybe when you're thirty." Lynn laughed.

"Who wants a drink?" Doug asked.

"Not me," Mike laughed. "I'm ready for a nap."

KARAOKE

DEREK

"Tell me you've got something," Derek spoke into his computer.

"A little. We don't know if it means anything, though."

"I'll take what you've got."

"After some digging, we found that Joey the Suit Carelli grew up in Boston, in the North End, just up the street from Patti Santori, AKA Patti Valleri. Same age, give or take, same neighborhood, same story. From lower- or middle-class families, the neighborhood kids tended to stick together. Most likely they knew each other, but we haven't corroborated that."

"Let's assume they did," Derek said. "North End kids do stick together, always have, always will. Patti marries Valleri, who works for Piscelli, and Joey goes to work for Benny White. So they go to work for different factions of the mob. There's the connection."

"That might explain why Patti would deal with Benny with the help of Joey, but it doesn't explain why Patti and Piscelli are working together," Derek's boss observed.

"Right," Derek admitted. "But what if we're thinking of this all wrong? What if Benny is the fence and Patti works for him? Could be Joey brought Patti into the fold after Piscelli cut her loose? Maybe Patti moves drugs for Benny. He gets a new shipment in and needs to get them to her, so he uses Piscelli's two lawyers to deliver them to her? At the same time, they pick up the jewels."

"Smart, right?" Derek continued. "If the couple gets caught with the drugs, it doesn't touch Benny. They deliver the drugs and pick up the jewels—two birds, one stone. That would explain why they pay with drugs, not money. Benny already has the money."

"Possible. But why would Benny White consider doing direct business with Piscelli's people? That doesn't make sense."

"We're missing something. Is there any indication these two have hooked up, let bygones be bygones in order to get what they each want? Benny gets his money and moves some drugs, and Piscelli gets the museum pieces?"

"None. Every indication is they are bitter rivals, one mishap away from another full-on war."

"Okay, we work with what we've got. Any progress on providing me some backup on this barge?" Derek asked hopefully.

"Not much. No active military or police on board. Got some retired cops and ex-military, but most of them are at least sixty-five years old. Your best bet is a former marine, twenty-year man, in his early forties. His name is Doug Whitman. He's on board with his wife and son."

Derek dropped his head and sighed before saying, "Please don't tell me his wife's name is Lynn and his son's name is Bradley."

"That's the guy. You know him?"

"Yeah."

Derek was not about to bring Doug into it. He couldn't put him in that position. His family needed him too much.

"Can't use him. Too complicated," Derek told his boss.

"Whatever you think, but it's an option if things get out of hand. We've informed the ship's captain up to a point. We told him there may be a stowaway on board. He has instructed his crew to keep an eye out for an unfamiliar face. It's a long shot."

"This whole case is turning into a long shot," Derek replied.

"Check back in before six. We'll keep working the Patti-and-Joey angle."

"I'll do that."

Derek remained in his room for the rest of the afternoon, although he regularly called Cate. He worried about her.

He gathered as much information as he could compile on Joey, Patti, and her husband, Vinnie. Most of it corroborated what he already knew. Patti and Joey grew up in the North End, same age, same background. At the age of eighteen, Patti married Vinnie Valleri, a twenty-year-old grunt in Frankie Piscelli's mob family. A couple months later, Joey began working for Benny White. Twenty-six years later, Frankie told Vinnie to move Frankie's Cadillac around to the back of his warehouse. Vinnie turned the key and boom, bye-bye Vinnie. That escalated the East Boston fiasco to all-out war between the two families, and it took five years to cool down to a simmer. They've been on shaky ground ever since.

HOLLY AND JACK

Mike's thoughts about taking a nap proved serious. He went back to his cabin after the beer pong tournament and slept for a few hours. Holly and Jack sat on the Sports Deck discussing what to do next.

"What's it going to be?" Jack asked.

"I don't care. You pick."

"Are you sure?"

"Um, I think so," Holly smiled. "Whatever you pick, I can get through it if we do it together."

"Okay, then. Follow me." Jack led Holly to an elevator.

There remained only one floor higher than the Sport Deck, the Sky Deck. Mostly used for lounging, the Sky Deck had one major activity, so when Jack pushed the up arrow, Holly knew exactly what she had agreed to do.

The *Perth's* two zip lines—side by side, about ten feet apart—begin at the highest point of the stern and zip you to the bow of the Sport Deck. All week, Holly admired the brave people as she watched them sail overhead. She never imagined she would consent to do it.

The waiting line trailed long, which didn't help Holly's frame of mind. The more she thought about it, the more she thought it a crazy idea. While waiting in line, she talked herself out of doing it four times, right up until a man strapped her into her chair and placed a helmet on her head. Jack strapped himself in ten feet away. He gave her a thumbs up.

Holly would not let go of the handgrips to return the gesture. The countdown began, and Holly whispered *I love you, Dad,* just in case.

Holly felt the release of the mechanism above her and began her forward movement. She looked over at Jack. He displayed a wide grin as he watched her descent begin. Their speed picked up, and she moved out in front of Jack, no longer able to see him. She thought she would scream, but she could muster only laughter. Wind whipped against her face, and she had goosebumps the size of apple seeds. She looked up at the clouds, down at the ocean and at people below as she whizzed overhead. It felt invigorating, and just like that, it ended.

As the deck approached, she could feel the brake system slow her down. She did as instructed and allowed the attendants to get hold of her chair. Eager to see her reaction, Jack pulled up beside her.

"Wooooooooooo!" She jumped out of her chair. "Can we do it again?"

Jack laughed, put his arms around her waist, lifted her off the floor, and twirled.

"We can go as many times as you like."

It wasn't until later that evening, as Holly thought back on the day, that she realized why she had gone through with it. She didn't want to disappoint Jack, of course, but in reality, she didn't want to disappoint herself.

The realization astonished her. Holly had learned a lot about herself, and she loved the person she had become. She wanted to know more about her.

DEREK

"So, what is happening with the Websters?" Derek's boss asked.

"Nothing. As far as I can tell, they haven't left their room. They order their food in and told the steward not to attend to the cabin. They are hunkered down."

"That could work for us. Maybe they don't know that Montalvo is missing."

"Let's hope. We need something to break our way."

"Any luck on the stowaway?"

"Nothing. No one's following me unless he's a ghost."

"I don't like it, Richards. None of it fits. I can't send out two SWAT teams to round up Benny White and Frankie Piscelli with this many unknown factors. There could be a third-party ambush. We need to know where Patti Valleri fits into this. I'll take the risk if you can get me that information. Otherwise, we don't intercept, and we go back to square one."

"Okay."

"Derek, watch your back."

"Will do."

The entire operation hinged on Patti Valleri and her possible connection to Joey the Suit Carelli. They had missed something, he could feel it, and it was up to him to figure it out. He couldn't let his team down—not when they were so close.

The question of why those people would do business together nagged at him. He had to change his approach. He thought, *Who cares why? Forget about why? What about the how?* Derek began to ask himself all the same questions but from a different angle.

He reached for a complimentary pad of paper and pen stamped with the *Perth* logo and wrote down questions as they occurred to him.

How did Piscelli find out about the sapphire?

How did Patti Valleri obtain it?

How did Joey the Suit Carelli know where to find Patti Valleri?

How had Duke Montalvo found out about Derek?

How are they planning on getting the jewels through customs?

He calculated an exceedingly lengthy list of hows and decided to start with them. If he thought about it logically, he might be able to come up with the missing puzzle pieces.

So, he began.

How did Piscelli find out about the sapphire? Derek skipped that question.

How did Patti get the jewels? Benny? Joey? One of her husband's old associates? Possibly.

Joey knew Patti was at the dolphin park. Have Joey and Patti been in contact all along? Are they old friends, good friends, maybe more than good friends?

How did Duke find Derek? Did he see Derek following the Websters?

Derek thought about the information he received about Patti and Joey growing up in the North End. He looked through his notes and searched the secure FBI site to corroborate what he thought he remembered.

Derek produced additional questions and sent them off to his boss with a message that he would check in later that night. He'd hoped he had asked the right questions and hoped the team could come up with some answers.

At seven forty-five, hungry and tired, he finally shut down his laptop. His hand smarted.

Eager to check on Cate, he popped a Vicodin, changed his clothes, and headed to the dining room.

DINNER FOR EIGHT

Lively conversation and stupendous food contributed to the festive atmosphere around the dinner table. Specialty chef's choices included herbed pan-seared salmon with lemon-grass roasted squash and wild rice, beef Wellington with truffle demi-glacé, rosemary roasted potatoes and gourmet baby carrots, cranberry-orange glazed duck breast over shallot polenta with roasted root vegetables and a Chardonnay-sauced chicken and vegetable pasta.

Sheila, Cate, and Lynn opted for the salmon, Holly chose the Chardonnay-sauced chicken, Derek went for the duck, and Mike, Doug, and Bradley each ordered the beef Wellington. The house had provided one bottle of Chardonnay and one of Merlot.

While waiting for the food to arrive, Bradley brought Derek up to speed on Mike's prowess as a beer pong player.

"You should have seen him, Derek. He beat those first three guys without even trying."

"That might be a bit of an exaggeration," Mike laughed.

"The big guy, though, he was pretty good. But he was weird," Bradley said. "He didn't even look like he was having fun."

"He gave me the creeps," Cate agreed. "And he looked silly in those cruise-ship shorts. I don't think his legs had ever seen the sun before. They look much better on you than on him." She directed her last comment to Derek.

"Great. I wear the same clothes as the creepy guy?" Derek joked.

"Yes, but you can pull it off," Cate smiled.

"Anyway, Mike made it all the way to the finals before he blew it," Bradley said.

"Bradley! He did not blow it. He almost won!" His mother corrected him.

Holly glanced over at her dad. He was smiling. She knew he had let Tawney win the match, and she loved him for it.

"It was close," Mike said. "It came down to the last cup, but it was not meant to be. Tawney will be the one bragging about her beer pong victory. She'll probably be telling her kids about it someday." Holly shared a silent laugh with her dad.

"So, what's everyone got planned for tonight?" Mike hoped to change the subject.

"I was thinking about checking out the karaoke lounge. We haven't been in there all week," Sheila commented, as if to suggest it unthinkable that they had gone that long without stopping in.

"Oh, do you sing, Sheila?" Lynn asked.

"God, no! I like to go listen, though. It's fun."

"Trust me, you don't want to be nearby when Sheila starts to sing," Cate interjected, "which is whenever an Alicia Keys song comes on."

"Oh, I love her," Holly exclaimed.

"Do you sing, Holly?" Lynn asked.

"Not even in the shower."

"Do you sing, Lynn?" Derek asked.

Lynn looked at Doug. They smiled at each other.

"We sing a little," she replied.

"They're in the church choir," said Bradley.

"Oh, now we have to go! I would love to hear you guys sing. Would you do it? Would you get up on stage?" Sheila asked.

"What do you say, Doug? Want to give it a go?" Lynn asked.

"Why not? It could be fun."

"You're not going to sing one of those church songs, are you?" Bradley winced.

"Hymns, Bradley. They're called hymns. I guess we'll have to see."

Oscar cleared the dishes and set up a tray beside the table. Then he disappeared into the kitchen. They hadn't noticed at the time, but all the servers in the dining room had done the same. The lights dimmed to mostly darken the large room. An air of anticipation enveloped the diners as the kitchen doors opened and the servers entered the dining room two-by-two, each carrying a flaming dessert. They walked together to the halfway point of the room before peeling off to their respective sides to deliver flaming baked Alaska to each table.

When the lights came back up and Bradley realized what it was, he was thrilled.

"Oh, boy, baked Alaska— my favorite!" he cried as if he had been eating it all his life.

Everyone laughed at his exuberance, a perfect ending to a perfect meal. The first slice of meringue-topped ice cream and cake dome made its way to Bradley.

DEREK GETS SOME ANSWERS

After dinner, Derek excused himself, citing work obligations. He told everyone that he would do his best to meet them in the karaoke lounge as soon as he could but made them promise to record Lynn and Doug if they sang before he got there.

When he entered his cabin, he nearly stepped on a large manila envelope that someone slipped under his door. It had no markings on the outside. By habit, to be sure it didn't contain destructive powder, he felt it with his fingers before opening it. Then he pulled out a facsimile cover sheet and several sheets of paper: printouts sent from his boss.

Derek figured they must be important if his boss broke protocol and sent them through unsecure channels.

The cover sheet included a handwritten note reading, "Check in asap." Derek scanned the pages and felt good about what he saw.

He logged into the secure conference call that awaited him.

"It looks like we got some connections. What are your thoughts?" his boss began.

"Give me a minute to double check something. I just came in."

Derek scanned the paperwork. He had asked them to check on early arrest reports for Joey Carelli, Vinnie Valleri, and Patti Santori. What he looked for were the known acquaintances, KA in agency lingo, of each and for any overlaps. His hunch had worked. The police reports all listed a Rocco Santori as a KA.

Rumor had it that Rocco Santori, cousin to Patti Santori, had become a world-class art thief working in Europe.

Bingo!

Derek had also asked them to check school records and, if possible, talk to any city cops who had worked the North End beat.

Patti, Rocco, and Joey went to St. Mary's School together where they were *thick as thieves*, a quote from the mother superior who still held her post. She elaborated that Joey had what she called "improper thoughts" toward Patti. She could not say if Patti reciprocated.

Derek had said it: North End kids stick together, always have, always will.

There was no information from any Boston police officers available.

"Okay," Derek began, "here's the working theory. Joey, Patti, and Rocco have known each other since the first ruler cracked their knuckles in kindergarten. They grew up together, stole together, and got arrested together, mostly misdemeanors. Vinnie comes along, joins in, and screws things up for Joey, who has a thing for Patti. Patti falls for Vinnie, who takes a job with Piscelli. Rocco, the real talent of the group, goes off on his own, ending up in Europe. Joey needs to make a living, so he takes a job with Benny White, the only place he can go without having to see Vinnie and Patti, who got married two months earlier. Are you with me?"

"Go on."

"Fast forward twenty-six years. Vinnie goes boom, and Patti's left in the cold. Rocco is overseas, maybe sends her some money, but I'll bet my life that Joey stepped up. Right?"

"I'm with you."

"Patti wants revenge. She blames Benny for the bomb and Frankie for leaving her high and dry. She drafts a plan, a plan that involves her closest and oldest friends."

"Joey and Rocco."

"Exactly. Patti convinces Rocco that she can fence his stolen jewels to Piscelli. She knows Piscelli could not pass them up. But she can't go to him directly. Joey puts the word out on the street, knowing it will reach Piscelli.

"What about Benny?"

"This is where the theory gets a little thin. It's possible Joey set up the drug buy to link Piscelli and Benny together. The end game could be to screw them both as each blames the other and throw them into another war. Maybe they take each other out?"

Derek wasn't convinced of his scenario, but he knew in his gut that they had to find a reason to link Piscelli and Benny together. A mantra played over and over in is head . . . *Never screw with a kid from the North End.*

"You've almost got me, but it's not enough. Get me some more. I can't risk it yet."

His boss disconnected the conference call.

Derek spread the faxed pages across the coffee table. He looked at a school photograph from St. Mary's. The three circled students were hard to miss: they pointed their first two right-hand fingers down in front of their chests. The gesture meant to resemble an N, as in North End.

He had updated pictures of Patti and Joey, but nobody could seem to find a picture of Rocco. Rocco was a fugitive from six countries, yet he seemed to move about at will.

Derek struggled with conjuring the endgame. *What is the motivation for Patti and Joey to create such an elaborate scheme?* He needed to clear his mind, get away from it, then come back at it with a new perspective. His thinking bogged down. He wasn't making any progress. He needed a break.

KARAOKE CLUB

Mike had assumed he would never see another disco ball after living through the 1970s. He was wrong. The karaoke club had five of them—one large, silver-mirrored globe over the stage and four smaller orbs hanging over the sides of the dance floor, two on the left side and two on the right.

Multicolored laser lights bounced off tiny reflective fragments creating geometric chaos. Navy blue medium-nap carpeting with red and yellow swirls blanketed the walls. The thick green, glass-like dance floor exposed puck lights in its underbelly, blinking on and off in deliberate cadence to the music. If someone had asked Mike to characterize the disco era, he would have showcased that room.

Every day at three o'clock, the room hosted kids' karaoke. As part of daily activities, the cruise line offered basic singing instruction and encouraged onstage participation to provide a popular attraction for the younger generation. At ten o'clock in the evening, the mirror balls lit up, and the adults got to have some fun of their own.

Mike and Doug pushed two tables together next to the dance floor at the front of the room just twenty feet from the stage with the disc jockey and signup area to the left. A table held four large three-ring binders containing titles of songs available for karaoke.

Doug and Lynn perused one of the books, made their decision, and signed up for their time slot. Their timing was impeccable. Had they not arrived when they did at a little past nine thirty, they would have had to stand in line for the next hour or more and received a much later time slot than eleven twenty.

"What are you going to sing?" Sheila asked.

"We want it to be a surprise," Lynn smiled.

"I know what it's going to be. They've been practicing it at home. Something called 'RV Maria,'" Bradley said.

"RV? Bradley, did you just say RV?" Doug laughed.

"Yeah. The song I don't understand the words to."

"It's ave, a-v-e, 'Ave Maria,' not RV. It is not about a camping trailer, Bradley. It's Latin for hail, as in 'Hail, Mary.'"

"I never knew that," Holly stated.

"Me, neither," said Cate and Sheila together.

Doug looked at Mike.

"Sorry, Doug. Ball four. It's a beautiful song, and I've always understood the sentiment behind it, but I never knew what it meant."

"Exactly," Cate agreed. "I never thought to look it up."

Lynn grinned and reached for Doug's hand.

"It's always been one of Doug's favorites. But that's not what we're singing tonight." She patted Bradley on the arm, glancing at him lovingly while shaking her head at his misconception.

"Well, what then?" he asked.

"You'll have to stay awake for another . . . ," Doug looked down at his watch, " . . . hour and twenty minutes to find out."

The emcee announced the first singer, a woman who appeared to be in her mid-to-late fifties and seemed comfortable on stage. She sang the song, "Natural Woman," originally sung by Aretha Franklin and then later recorded by cowriter Carole King. She did an admirable job and received an enthusiastic response from the crowd.

The next six performances ranged from somewhat talented to painful. A young woman's rendition of "Don't Stop Believin'" had the place singing along, while a young man's version of

Jon Bon Jovi's "Livin' on a Prayer" didn't quite cut it. Some songs were unknown to Lynn, Doug, and Mike, but the young women at the table seemed to know them.

Cate kept glancing at the two entry doors. She hoped Derek would make it in time for Doug and Lynn's song, which was next. As they walked up on stage, their entire table stood up and shouted, clapped, and whistled. Cate started the video recorder on her phone so Derek would be able to watch it later.

The music started, and it sounded familiar to all of them, but it wasn't until Doug started to sing, deeply and slowly, that they recognized the song.

> Now I've had the time of my life.
> No, I never felt like this before.
> Yes, I swear it's the truth.
> And I owe it all to you.

Then Lynn took over, projecting powerful and honest emotion.

> 'Cause I've had the time of my life.
> And I owe it all to you.

The pace of the music picked up as the two began to sing together. Doug's voice, similar but not quite as deep as the great Barry White, complemented Lynn's Adele-like vocals. The comfort and ease of their interaction added an air of intense honesty and genuine excitement.

They were fantastic. The crowd rose to its feet. Some swayed to the music or clapped to the beat, and others sang along. Bradley sat in his chair, chin dropped to his chest and eyes wide open. He had never heard his parents sing like that.

Sheila, Cate, and Holly danced in place while Mike held Cate's phone and recorded his friends taking down the house.

From the back of the room, having ducked inside just in time to watch most of the performance, Derek watched his friends on stage and at the table. He made a decision. He couldn't lie to them anymore. They could be in danger, and he would not allow them to stay ignorant of that possibility.

Tomorrow is the last full day at sea. I'll gather them together in the morning and tell them who I really am.

The music stopped. The room exploded with applause, whistles, and screams.

Doug and Lynn looked surprised at the response. Everyone was on their feet.

Doug and Lynn returned to their table.

"You were amazing!"

"Oh, my God, you guys are unbelievable!"

"That was awesome!"

"Wow!"

They seemed embarrassed by the attention until Bradley looked at them and said, "You guys are really good! Why don't you sing those songs at home?"

And they all laughed.

Derek joined his friends.

"That was one of the most amazing duets I've ever heard!" Derek said.

"Derek, you made it! When did you get here? We recorded it for you." Cate jumped up and threw her arms around him.

"I got here just after they started. I'm so glad I didn't miss that. It was absolutely amazing!"

"Thank you, everyone. The crowd really helped. It was so much fun," Lynn said.

Doug nodded in agreement as a big soft smile flashed across his blushed face. "But I think now we need to get Bradley to bed. Tomorrow will be a big day, last day and all."

"Hey, before you go," Derek said hesitantly, "I was wondering if I could talk to all of you in the morning. Somewhere private."

"What about, Derek? What's up?" Sheila asked.

"I'd rather not get into it tonight, but it is important, and it concerns all of you. Could we meet somewhere at about eight o'clock? Over coffee?"

"Private?" Mike asked.

"Preferably."

"How about our cabin? We've got enough room for everyone, and we can have coffee delivered. Eight o'clock?"

"That would be great, Mike. Is that okay with everyone? I really would appreciate it." Derek was nervous and it showed.

Cate had an idea what was going to happen in the morning.

She asked, "Bradley, too?"

"If Doug and Lynn wouldn't mind," Derek replied.

"Okay, Derek, we'll be there. Is everything all right?" Doug asked.

"Yes, Doug, and thank you."

"We'll be there, right, Sheila?" Cate asked.

"Of course."

Doug, Lynn, and Bradley said their goodnights while a young couple tried their best to imitate Sonny and Cher on stage. Mike and Holly decided to turn in as well.

Sheila and Cate exchanged a few words before Sheila left by herself, but not before giving Derek a warm hug.

CATE AND DEREK

Cate and Derek stopped at a small lounge on the way back to Derek's room and ordered a bottle of 2014 David Ramey Pinot Noir, a Californian Russian River wine, with two glasses.

Once inside, Derek set the bottle and glasses on the coffee table, then excused himself and went into the tiny bathroom. Cate flung off her heels and sat down on the couch with a heavy sigh as if the weight of her shoes had been a burden. She reached for the Pinot Noir the lounge bartender had considerately opened and poured a glass for each of them so they could share a toast when he returned.

Cate leaned back on the couch and noticed a blank white sheet of paper on the floor under the table. She bent to retrieve the paper and place it on Derek's laptop when she realized it was not blank on both sides. She saw two printed photographs. The top showed a group of students in front of a sign reading St. Mary's. Three of the kids in the photo had been circled with a marker, each of the three making a hand gesture of some sort. The bottom photo showed a man from the waist up with a numbered card in front of him.

Oh, a mug shot, Cate thought. Then she looked at the face of the man and recognized him at once. *What the hell is this? Why does Derek have a picture of him?*

Derek emerged from the bathroom and saw Cate looking at the photos. He immediately grabbed for it, but Cate pulled it away.

"Derek, why do you have a picture of this guy?"

"It's just work, Cate. I can't get into it."

"But Derek, why this guy?" She sounded frightened.

"What's the matter, Cate? What do you mean, why this guy?"

"That's the creepy guy in the shorts. The one who played beer pong against Mike today."

Derek froze, looked down at the picture of Joey the Suit Carelli, and asked, "Are you sure? Are you positive this is the same guy, Cate?"

"Positive. I wouldn't forget that face. Who is he, Derek? Why do you have his picture?"

"Cate, I'm sorry. I have to make a call. I'll be right back."

Derek left the room.

Cate glanced at Derek's laptop. It sat on a manila folder, and she could see papers inside. Knowing she shouldn't, Cate opened the folder and ruffled some papers. As her eyes flickered through the documents, she saw the name Joey the Suit Carelli and remembered Joe as the creepy guy's name. She suddenly felt an overwhelming sense of guilt as she realized she was spying—or at least snooping—and that didn't sit well with her. She placed the folder back under the laptop. As Cate waited for Derek, her guilt turned to fear.

Meanwhile, Derek had stepped out onto the open deck, scanned the vicinity, and, seeing no one, dialed his boss's private phone number.

"It's Joey Carelli. That's who's on board. I haven't seen him, but I have confirmation that he's here."

"Confirmation from who?" his boss asked.

"From Cate, the woman I told you about. It's a long story, but it seems he may be keeping an eye on everyone I've been in contact with on this ship. Everyone but me, that is. I haven't seen him. We've got to call this off, boss. I can't put these people in danger."

"Calm down, Derek. He may just be trying to figure out who everyone is, who the players are. They don't pose a threat to him. He's not stupid. Just stay away from them and it shouldn't be a problem."

"I don't know. I think it may be too late for that."

"Can you keep these people under wraps for the rest of the trip?"

"I'm going to try. I'm meeting with them in the morning. I'm going to have to tell them who I am. They're too smart to fall for another story."

Silence. Then, "Do what you have to do. But, Derek, just remember. The less they know, the better off they are."

"Yes, boss."

"I want you to check in with me every two hours, beginning at six o'clock tomorrow morning. Get some sleep."

"All right."

Derek raced back to the room where he found Cate on the couch with a glass of wine. She sat up straight.

"Derek, tell me the truth. Are you in danger?"

"I don't know. I might be. We might be. You might be."

Cate flinched. Derek pushed the coffee table up against the cabin door.

"It's just a precaution, but you're safe with me in here."

Derek removed the Glock from his waistband and set it on the table next to the bed. Cate looked at it as if it were a poisonous snake about to attack.

"Is that loaded?"

"Yes."

"Have you been wearing that this whole trip?"

"No."

"What's going on, Derek?"

"Tomorrow, Cate. I'll tell you all about it in the morning."

He reached for her and wrapped his arms around her.

They are strong, confident arms, Cate thought.

She felt comfortable in his arms. She felt safe in his arms. She felt loved in his arms.

CONFESSIONS

THE LAST DAY AT SEA

Mike had Aweigh from the Grind deliver coffee, juice, and muffins to their cabin at seven forty-five. Holly told him to include the pineapple-macadamia muffins because she knew Derek liked them.

Having foregone her morning sunbathing routine for the first time in many years, Sheila arrived before the others. As much as she loved her morning practice, she felt liberated by breaking the custom and relished a new sense of identity.

She helped herself to a cup of coffee.

Derek and Cate arrived next, followed shortly thereafter by Lynn, Doug, and Bradley. Bradley shot Derek a worried look.

He doesn't want me to tell them what he did, Derek thought.

With coffee, juice, and muffins served, Derek stood.

"Well, there's no easy way to do this, so I'm just going to get to it. I've been lying to you. I'm not in the insurance business, and I'm not on this ship for a team-building experience. My name is Derek Richards, and I work for the Federal Bureau of Investigation."

He paused to let it sink in and because he wasn't quite sure how to proceed.

Sheila shot Cate a wide-eyed, confused look. Cate responded with an affirmative head shake, acknowledging that she knew about Derek. Sheila looked dejected.

Everyone else looked stunned, except for Bradley. He had surmised that Derek was, at a minimum, a police officer, but Derek's admission didn't surprise him. Bradley stayed silent.

"Why did you lie to us, Derek? Why didn't you just tell us who you were in the first place?" Lynn sounded disheartened.

"Because I'm working a case, Lynn. I couldn't take the chance of revealing what I do."

"Why are you telling us now?" Mike asked guardedly.

Derek cleared his throat and suddenly realized how his news would severely affect his friends. He had to just say it, like ripping off a Band-Aid. It was the best way.

"Because you may all be in danger," Derek somberly stated.

Lynn put her arm around Bradley. Extending all his six-foot body, Doug stood and glared directly into Derek's eyes.

"What have you done, Derek?"

Mike stood and put a hand on Doug's shoulder.

"Hold on, Doug. Let's hear what he's got to say before we jump to any conclusions."

Mike urged Doug to sit back down and listen.

Derek cleared his throat again before continuing. He explained his assignment as a surveillance mission, nothing more. Without too many details, he told them that the surveillance included following two of the cruise passengers during the stops on the islands of St. Thomas and St. Kitts. He explained that the case became more complicated than the bureau had anticipated.

"How complicated?" an angry Doug asked.

"There are additional, unanticipated, parties involved." Derek knew what he was about to tell them would enrage Doug and probably do irreparable damage to his relationship with Cate.

"I have been compromised somehow, and I have been seen with all of you. One of the unknown subjects decided to try to get to me by getting to one of you."

Derek looked directly at Cate. She stiffened.

He went on. "At the marketplace on St. Kitts, he went after Cate. If it weren't . . ."

"Derek, wait." Bradley loudly interrupted. "Let me, okay?"

Derek nodded his head, ashamed he hadn't divulged the information sooner.

All eyes fixed on Bradley. Confusion showered the room.

"Bradley?" Doug looked at his son.

"Dad, Mom. This isn't Derek's fault. He didn't know I was going to do any of this, I swear."

Derek could see Doug about to reach his boiling point. He stepped a few feet away.

"I'd been watching Derek since we met him," Bradley continued. "I could tell he lied about the insurance company thing. We all could."

He pointed to Cate, Sheila, and Holly.

"Anyway, that day at the marketplace, I saw Derek as the shuttle driver unloaded me from the bus. I watched him follow an old guy through the crowd. Then I watched the old guy. He was following Cate."

Bradley glanced at Cate. "I overheard Cate tell Sheila she was going to the restroom, so I got ahead of her and waited. He was going to hurt her, Dad. I had to do something."

Lynn gasped. Doug jumped to his feet.

"What are you talking about, Bradley? What did you do?" Doug sounded frightened.

"Before he could grab Cate, I rolled into him with my wheelchair and knocked him down."

"Oh, my God, Bradley. The guy outside the restroom? The one you said fell down?" Cate was horrified. She looked toward Derek. He saw pain in her eyes.

Doug lunged at Derek, grabbed him by the shirt, and pushed him against the closet. Derek didn't fight. Mike ran to Doug, got hold of his shoulders, and tried to keep him from hurting Derek.

"Get away from me, Mike. This doesn't concern you," Doug said.

"This concerns all of us, Doug. I understand you're angry, but we have to let him finish. If we're in danger, we need to know what we are up against."

Doug slowly let up on Derek.

"I'm not done with you!" Doug snarled.

"Dad, it wasn't his fault, I . . . " Bradley pleaded.

"We will talk about you later," Doug warned Bradley.

Sheila wrapped her arms around Cate as Cate shook uncontrollably.

"Go ahead, Derek," Mike demanded. "What else is there?"

"We apprehended the guy who went after Cate at the dolphin park a little while later. He's in custody." Derek hoped that would make Cate and the others feel better, but it didn't seem to have the desired effect.

"The car accident," Bradley revealed.

"Yes," Derek replied.

Bradley could feel the discomfort of everyone's eyes on him as they projected their common sense of betrayal.

"So, that's it, right? We're okay? You got the guy, right?" Lynn asked hopefully.

Derek looked at the floor and cleared his throat again.

"I wish it were, Lynn. But it got even more complicated when Cate identified one of the suspects from St. Thomas from a photo I have in my room."

"The creepy beer pong guy?" Cate asked.

"I knew there was something about that guy," Bradley said.

"Yes. But he hasn't been following me. He's been watching all of you. That's why we are here."

Tension amplified.

"Is that it, Derek?" Doug shouted. "Are you done? Because if you are, I'm gonna beat the living shit out of you!"

Doug had exceeded his boiling point. Mike tried but couldn't calm him down.

He went for Derek, a clenched right fist to his face that drew blood from Derek's nose and dropped him to the floor. Doug knelt next to Derek and drew back to hit him again when Lynn yelled, "Doug, stop!"

His fist raised, he looked back at his wife. Her eyes pleaded him to stop. Reluctantly, he did. He gave Derek one last shove to the floor before getting to his feet.

Cate ran to Derek and knelt beside him.

"Oh, my God, Derek, I think your nose is broken." Blood began to run down the side of his face. "Someone get me a towel and some ice."

Holly ran into the bathroom and returned with a damp hand towel. Cate wiped blood from Derek's face to reveal a deep purple bruise developing under his left eye. Sheila went down the hall to find ice.

Cate helped Derek stand up as he wobbled on his feet. His head and hand throbbed. He wished he had thought to bring the Vicodin.

Out on the balcony, Lynn and Doug held a heated discussion.

Doug stormed back into the room, Lynn right behind him.

"Let's go, Bradley," he growled.

"Wait. I think you should all stay together," Derek urged.

Doug moved toward Derek, stood inches from his face, and screamed, "I don't give a damn what you think! I'll take care of my family." The three of them left the room, passing Sheila without a word in the hallway.

Sheila gave Cate the ice. She wrapped it in the towel and handed it to Derek. He winced as he placed it on his nose.

"Why didn't you tell me, Derek? How could you not tell me?"

Cate began to tear up.

"I was trying to protect you, Cate. Once we got the guy, I didn't think it was a good idea to tell you. I thought the danger had passed."

"You didn't think I should know that someone tried to attack me? And to put Bradley in that position? I thought I knew you, Derek. I thought I knew you."

Distraught, Cate grabbed Sheila's hand, and they walked out of the room.

Derek knew he couldn't stop them. His admissions had done nothing to help protect them. Instead, he had alienated them and made them more vulnerable.

He turned to Mike and Holly who stood silent, watching him.

"I'm sorry," Derek said. "I didn't mean to put anyone in danger."

He turned and walked out the door.

DOUG

"What the hell were you thinking, Bradley? You're twelve years old, for chrissake. How were you planning on getting away from this guy, huh? Fly?"

Furious and frightened, Doug grappled with the thought of what could have happened.

"I wasn't thinking, Dad. I just knew Cate was in trouble and Derek needed time to get to her. I did the only thing I could think of. I couldn't just let him hurt her."

"You could have been killed, Bradley. Don't you get it?"

"I knew Derek wouldn't let anything happen to me."

"How? How did you know that Bradley? How could you know that?"

"I just knew."

Doug took a deep breath. Lynn tried to settle him down. Nothing worked.

"If he's so good, how did the guy get away after you took him down? Tell me that," Doug barked.

"Because he wanted to make sure I was okay. He wouldn't leave me until he was sure I was okay."

"A real hero," Doug sarcastically responded. "I've got to go for a walk. I need some air."

Lynn nodded. She had never seen him that angry. She feared what he might do.

"Just a walk, Doug. Right? Just to calm down."

He nodded and left. He couldn't stop images from forming in his head. An image of Bradley lying on the ground, the wheelchair tipped over, the wheel spinning. Another of Bradley lying in a pool of blood. The more images he imagined, the angrier he got. Before he knew it, he headed down the hallway to Derek's cabin.

He slowly approached the door as he tried to decide exactly what he would do or say. It wasn't until he stood in front of the door that he noticed it slightly ajar.

He heard an unfamiliar voice from inside.

"Drop the magazine onto the floor and clear the chamber," said the voice.

Doug stopped and listened.

"Joey Carelli. I was wondering when you were going to pay me a visit."

Doug heard Derek. His voice sounded different, confident, and stern.

Doug couldn't see inside the cabin, but he determined Joey held Derek at gunpoint. He heard Derek's magazine hit the floor and then the racking of the handgun expelling the bullet from the chamber.

Doug could tell from the sound that Joey stood just inside the doorway. His US Marine instincts kicked in as he put the full weight of his body into the door, which swung open, knocked Joey against the wall and sent his gun to the floor. Derek lunged for the gun while Doug pinned Joey against the wall.

"You like to go after young kids, asshole?" Doug was in Joey's face.

"I ain't goin' after your kid, mister. I ain't goin' after none of ya."

"Damn right you're not," Doug yelled.

Derek held Joey's gun in his left hand. He used his foot to push his own full magazine under the bed.

"Put him on the couch," Derek said to Doug.

Doug glared at Derek.

"Please, Doug. Put him on the couch."

Doug held Joey by the collar of his shiny, rumpled suitcoat. He moved him to the couch and threw him down, then shut the cabin door.

"I ain't here to hurt no one," Joey winced, "I just got a message for ya."

He looked at Derek.

"From who?"

"Patti Valleri."

"Well, go ahead," Derek said, glancing at Doug.

"What about this guy?" Joey said.

"I'm not going anywhere. Say what you have to say," Doug responded.

Derek nodded. He had already assessed Doug's involvement in the case and decided it would not serve anyone's interest to oust him.

"Patti sends her regards."

Derek could tell Patti must have coached Joey on what to say, "She wants to offer you a gift."

"What gift?" Derek asked.

"Frankie Piscelli."

Doug looked at Derek, expecting to see a reaction of some sort, but Derek's expression didn't change.

"Go on," Derek directed.

"Tomorrow morning, the lawyer couple is gonna deliver a package to a cop on the dock, one of Frankie's guys. No customs, see? He just drives out with the goods. Frankie's gonna be waitin' in the parkin' garage. Cop delivers the goods, you pick up Frankie. That simple."

"This cop. Who is he?"

"Dunno. Just some patsy on Piscelli's payroll."

"Am I correct in assuming the package came from Europe?" Derek asked.

Doug shot a look at Derek. *What the hell is going on?*

"Yeah. That's the one," Joey said.

"So why would Patti offer us this gift?"

"Payback for her husband, Vinnie. Piscelli got him blown up. Left her with nuthin'."

"What's to keep us from going after her?"

"You got nuthin' on her. You ain't never seen her with nuthin'. She ain't got no warrants out. What ya gonna get her on?"

"Oh, I'm sure I could think of something," Derek grinned.

Joey laughed. "She said you gonna say that. I ain't done. There's more?"

"Okay, let's hear it."

"Benny White. We givin' him to ya, too."

"We?"

Joey had slipped. He didn't mean to divulge the close connection. It took him a moment to respond.

"Yeah, we," he stated emphatically as he puffed out his chest.

"Tell me about Benny."

"He got a safe in his bedroom closet, in the St. Thomas place behind a fake wall. I got the combination. Benny thinks it's empty, but it ain't. If ya take it tomorrow, he ain't gettin' outta jail in my lifetime."

"What's the catch?"

"You forget about Patti and me. Promise you ain't gonna look for us. You get the combination when we get somewheres safe."

"What if I decline, take Piscelli, and come after you, Patti, and Benny?"

"I warn Piscelli. You ain't gonna do that nohow. We givin' ya two of the biggest mob bosses in the country. No way you pass that up."

"What about Rocco?"

Joey wasn't particularly good at hiding his thoughts. He was shocked that Derek knew about Rocco.

"Don't know no Rocco," he lied.

Derek handed the gun to Doug, surprised that Derek trusted him with it. He inspected the gun's chamber and checked the safety. It was live. He held it on Joey as Derek made a phone call.

As Doug listened to the one-sided conversation, he got the impression that Joey was right, that the black suits were going to take the deal.

Derek hung up the phone, reassembled his own gun, and put it back in his holster before approaching Joey and landing a left hook to his face. "That's for holding a gun on me."

Doug grinned.

"Tell Patti she's got a deal. But I'm not letting you out of my sight until I see you off this ship."

Joey wiped blood from his lip and smiled.

CATE AND SHEILA

Cate had not stopped crying since they left Mike and Holly's room.

"How could he not tell me?" She sobbed.

"Oh, I don't know," Sheila said defiantly, "how could anyone not tell anyone about something so important. How could my sister keep this kind of secret from me? How long have you known, Cate?"

Cate suddenly stopped crying. She hadn't realized how mad Sheila was.

"Um, since the morning after your birthday party. But he swore me to secrecy, Sheila. He said it could be dangerous."

"So, it's okay for you to keep me in the dark about being in danger but it's not okay for him to keep you in the dark? What the fuck, Cate? I would hope you and I are closer than you and Derek!"

Cate sat quietly. Emotions swirled through her brain like a Sahara dust storm, clouding her thinking.

"Cate?" Sheila noted Cate's body language. "Oh, my God, you're in love with him!" Sheila pronounced.

"What am I going to do, Sheila? How can I trust him?"

"Cate, I get it. But he was only trying to protect you, right? It's not like he just didn't care, and he did tell you, just not right away."

"I suppose."

"Is he in love with you?"

"I don't know." Cate thought about it. "I think he might be."

"Well, we'll just have to find out, won't we?"

Cate's phone played her text message tune. Sheila's did the same a few seconds later.

"It's Doug. He wants us to meet back in Mike and Holly's room in thirty minutes."

"Oh, shit. I hope he didn't kill Derek," Sheila said, not entirely sure she could discount the possibility.

"Sheila!"

Thirty-five minutes later, Cate and Sheila arrived at Mike and Holly's door. Everyone was there except for Derek. Sheila wondered if she had been right to worry about Doug.

"Thanks, Mike and Holly, for letting us use your room again," Doug began. "This has been quite a day already, and it isn't even lunchtime. Look, I know we all have different feelings about what Derek told us earlier, but there have been some additional developments."

Doug described what happened in Derek's cabin with Joey.

Not having a clear grasp of the entire case, he told them as much as he understood.

"So," Doug concluded, "it means that the danger he thought we were in today does not exist. He is going to keep Joey in the cabin with him all day just to make sure. There's nothing more to worry about."

"Are you kidding me, Doug? Derek is locked in a room with a mobster and you say there's nothing to worry about?" Cate was frantic. "Why didn't you stay with him?"

"Cate, he wanted me to talk to all of you, to put your mind at ease. Everything is going to be fine."

Doug cleared his throat.

"But there is one thing. He asked that we all stay aboard the ship tomorrow morning until everyone else has disembarked."

"Why?" Mike asked.

"I'm not sure. Maybe the FBI needs to talk to us," Doug said.

"I need to see him," Cate said. "I need to see him now."

Cate began to get up.

"Cate, wait. Let me text him. Maybe I can relieve him for a while so you two can talk?"

"Doug, no," Lynn asserted. I don't want you in there alone with that criminal."

"I can go with you," Mike offered.

"I still don't like it," said Lynn.

"Trust me, Lynn, we'll be protected," Doug promised. Lynn understood but felt no less worried.

Doug called Derek and made plans for Mike and him to relieve Derek for an hour after lunch, at one o'clock. Cate wasn't completely satisfied about having to wait, but she agreed not to go to Derek's cabin without them.

"Wow, and I thought I was going to be bored on this trip," Bradley said.

"I think I could use some boredom right about now," Lynn replied.

"Is anyone else hungry?" Mike asked to alleviate tension.

It was unanimous. They decided to go together for an early lunch.

Sheila suggested The Happy Turtle. Relieved but still anxious, they ate in near silence.

Halfway through their meal, the restaurant began to fill with the normal lunch crowd. A familiar voice bellowed above those of the other arriving diners.

Holly, Bradley, Cate, Sheila, and Lynn looked in his direction. Edward the loudmouth stood waiting for a table with three other men. A chuckle escaped Holly's mouth before she knew it. Bradley followed, and soon the rest of the women at the table found themselves giggling.

"I was afraid of this," Doug said. "They've finally lost their minds."

"It was bound to happen," Mike joked, "with all that's gone down."

The remarks served only to bolster the laughter from the women and Bradley.

Mike and Doug did not know what to make of it.

Once the amusement ceased, the tablemates could hear Edward again, spewing the exact same story they heard every time they saw him. When he got to a familiar spot in his speech, Bradley and the women mumbled the phrase together:

"I tripled my money in one year."

That created another burst of hilarity among the knowing. Mike and Doug simply sat staring at the rest of them as if they had just stripped naked and run around the room.

Cate silently wished that Derek's case had been about a Ponzi scheme.

DEREK AND CATE

After lunch, Cate, Doug, and Mike went to Derek's cabin. Doug told Cate to wait in the hallway. A few minutes later, Derek appeared. He had given Doug his Glock, just in case, but he was quite sure they had nothing to worry about. It seemed that Joey had had enough of mobster living and wanted out. The only way out was if Benny White vanished.

"Hello, Cate."

"Hello, Derek," she said haltingly.

"Do you want to go out on deck?"

"Okay."

They took the elevator up three floors, then walked in silence down a hallway to the door leading to an outside deck. Derek held the door open for Cate.

"Thank you."

"You're welcome. Are you going to talk to me, Cate?"

"I'm upset, Derek. I thought I could trust you."

"You can trust me, Cate. You can trust me more than anyone else in this world."

"How can you say that, Derek? How?"

"Because I love you, Cate."

Cate hadn't expected that answer. She expected him to make excuses about how he was protecting her and how he didn't want her to worry. She had comebacks for those remarks. Instead, she stood silently in front of him, looking at his bruised face and said nothing. Tears formed in her eyes, and she started to sob. Derek enveloped her completely, holding her tight to his body.

"Cate, I don't ever want to let you go. Don't you understand? I love you with everything I am. I've never loved anyone like I love you."

Cate tried to speak but couldn't find her voice. It abandoned her, forcing her to use her body to accept his assertion. She gave her all to him at that moment. They stood in a fierce embrace for several minutes.

The silence broke when Cate regained her ability to speak.

"I love you, Derek."

He leaned down to kiss her and winced as her nose bumped against his.

She giggled. "You deserved that, you know," she said.

"I know."

"How long do we have?"

"I told Doug and Mike I needed an hour."

"We'd better hurry." Cate pulled out her phone and started tapping.

"What are you doing?"

"Texting Sheila. Follow me."

HOLLY, SHEILA, LYNN, AND BRADLEY

Sheila saw the text from Cate.

Don't come back to the cabin for at least an hour.

That's when Sheila knew that everything would be all right. But she didn't say a word to the others.

Holly, Sheila, and Bradley did everything they could think of to keep Lynn's mind off Doug's whereabouts. Holly and Sheila took her to the casino for some roulette while Bradley watched through the glass window. That lasted all of five minutes.

"How about some yoga?" Sheila asked. Holly gave her a look that silently asked, *Are you serious?*

"Maybe they have a bingo game going in the bingo hall," Holly suggested. Sheila returned the questioning glance.

They rejoined Bradley, and the four of them wandered the deck until Lynn ducked into a doorway. White letters emblazoned the blue sign over the door. It read, Frozen.

Sheila, Holly, and Bradley rolled their eyes. If sitting through a kid's movie is what it took, they would do it for Lynn. But, boy, they hoped she appreciated the sacrifice.

They walked through the door into an ice blue bar. The air conditioning blew extra cold, simulating winter in Norway. Lynn took a seat at the bar.

"Hey, Lynn," the bartender greeted her.

"Hi, Elias," Lynn replied.

"Where's Doug?"

"Busy. Elias, these are my friends Sheila and Holly and my son Bradley. Is it okay if he is in here with us?"

"Sure, as long as he sits at a table. Wouldn't look good to have you belly up to the bar now, would it?" Elias laughed.

Sheila and Holly were stunned. It was barely after one o'clock in the afternoon, and Lynn had led them into a bar. Had Sheila realized that option, they wouldn't have wasted their time in the casino.

"Chilled cider?" he asked.

Again, Sheila and Holly exchanged a glance.

"Yes, please, Elias." She turned to her friends and said, "I highly recommend it."

"Make it three," said Sheila.

"What would you like, Bradley?"

"Would you mind if I went to the activities room, Mom? It's just down at the end of the deck." He pointed to the stern of the ship.

"I know. Sure, that's a great idea, honey. Why don't you go there? But don't leave until I come get you. Or text me when you're ready to leave."

"Okay. See you later."

"Now I get it," Sheila laughed. "You bring Bradley to the activities room and hit the first bar you come to."

"Not quite," Lynn barked. "We've had to wait for Bradley a couple of times in the afternoon. This is just convenient."

"Lynn, I'm sorry. I didn't mean anything by it. I was just joking." Sheila felt bad.

Lynn sighed. "No, Sheila. I'm sorry. I've no right to bite your head off because I'm worried about Doug." Lynn reached for Sheila's hand. "I'm really very sorry."

"I'm sure everything is going to be just fine," Holly said. "My dad can be a scrappy guy when he needs to be." She laughed nervously.

"Well, Doug is a marine. He won't take shit from anyone. That's what has me worried. It doesn't happen often, but when he loses his temper, things can get bad really fast."

"I think we saw a little taste of that downstairs." Sheila remarked.

"Mmm. And that was Doug being nice."

Elias centered a *Perth* coaster under a frosted glass of amber-colored cider in front of each of them. The three clinked glasses and took their first sip.

"Damn. You were right about this cider. It's delicious." Holly smacked her lips.

"Just be careful. It packs a punch. That's why I came in here." Lynn laughed for the first time since lunch.

"And here I thought I was going to have to sit through a kids' movie. Cheers!" said Sheila.

"Cheers!"

THE LAST HURRAH

Only a few minutes late, Cate walked Derek back to his cabin. He kissed her one last time before knocking on the door. Three taps, pause, two taps. Mike opened the door.

"I'll see you in the morning," Derek said to Cate.

"All right. But text me later."

"I will."

"Are you coming in or should we move the party out there?" Mike asked.

Derek laughed. "Okay, okay." He closed the door behind him. "How was our guest?"

"Much more comfortable than we are," Doug said as he motioned over to the bed where Joey slept.

"Thanks, guys, I really appreciate it. I know I owe you big time for a lot of things."

"Derek, is it true you're taking down Frankie Piscelli and Benny White?" Mike asked.

"Yes, tomorrow is a big day."

"Big? That's huge. That's beyond huge," Mike said.

"Oh, that's right. I forgot you are from Massachusetts, so you know their reputation."

"Hell, yeah," Mike said. "This is going to be bigger than Whitey Bulger and the Winter Hill Gang."

"What the hell are you talking about, Mike? What the hell is Whitey Bulger and the Winter Hill Gang? It sounds like the name of a rock band," Doug laughed.

"Come on, Doug. Whitey Bulger? He was on the FBI's most wanted list forever. They finally captured him somewhere in California, I think it was. Of course, it gave the Boston FBI a black eye."

Derek touched his face and winced. "Seems to happen a lot."

"Listen, Derek, I'm sorry I punched you. I . . . ," Doug started.

"No, Doug. You had every right. You didn't know. I'm sorry I had to keep you in the dark."

Doug understood.

"Friends?"

"Friends!" They shook hands.

"I better go find my wife. If I know her, she is nervous as a mouse in a cathouse."

"Thanks again, guys."

"Let us know if you need anything. Just call or text," Mike said.

"You bet."

Doug texted Lynn. Her reply read, **Come get a cider.** Doug smiled.

"How about a drink, Mike?"

"You're on."

Holly had texted Jack to meet her at Frozen, and Cate joined them after dropping Derek off, so when Mike and Doug showed up, they comprised a crew of seven. They enjoyed another round of drinks before they left the coolness of Norway and emerged into the warmth of the sun. Doug and Lynn decided to pick up Bradley and go back to their cabin for a nap. The stress of the morning had taken its toll.

Mike considered a nap himself, but instead changed into his bathing suit and went for a swim before he lounged poolside to drift off for a short time.

Holly and Jack found a quiet spot on the ship's stern. Jack explained his obligation to spend the final night of the cruise with his family. Holly understood. They knew it might be their last chance to be alone. They had formed a close bond. Holly thanked Jack for his part in opening a whole new area of possibilities in her life. She was no longer afraid—maybe nervous, but not afraid.

Sheila and Cate went shopping. Sheila wanted to pick up something for David, and Cate looked for a souvenir piece of clothing for herself, something with the cruise-line logo, something she would never previously have seen herself wear.

The hectic morning slipped quietly into a comfortable and relaxed afternoon for everyone.

Everyone but Derek.

EXECUTION

PLANNING THE ARRESTS

Joey snored as Derek and his associates planned to apprehend Frankie Piscelli, Benny White, and the Websters. Once they had the Websters in custody, they agreed they could probably persuade the couple to turn state's evidence against both Frankie and Benny.

Derek had learned from Joey that Benny White's hidden safe contained items from the jewel heist that scored the sapphire necklace and enough cocaine and heroin to put Benny away for life. When asked if Benny had taken possession of the jewels and drugs or if Joey had planted them there, Joey would not respond.

Derek could only guess that Joey and Patti intended to frame Benny White.

Once the FBI agreed to the deal, Joey contacted Patti. She was already on her way to the safe destination they had chosen.

Derek noticed a change in Joey once he learned that Patti was on the move. The Suit seemed relieved. Derek couldn't help but feel Joey's genuine affection for Patti, and it made him think of Joey in a different light. Had it all gone down before Derek met Cate, he may not have been as empathetic.

Logistics of such an operation verged on monumental. The FBI contacted proper authorities on St. Thomas to plan Benny's capture and the search of his property. Derek learned that Fred Jenkins and George Ross would lead the operation to raid Benny's place at the same time the FBI captured Piscelli in Florida. Derek would contact Fred with the combination of Benny's safe as soon as Joey sent it to Derek.

Derek participated in a conference call with his boss, Fred, George, and four other agents Derek knew from the Boston office.

"Okay, Fred," began the boss, "so once you have Benny in custody, you'll wait for us to send you the safe combination. Anything else to wrap up on Benny's end?"

"Yeah, boss. I was just thinking. Is there any way we can confirm Benny is in the house? I won't have surveillance set up until early morning. Who's to say Benny is even there?"

"Derek, is Joey sure Benny will be there?"

"Hang on."

Derek went over to the bed where Joey napped.

"Hey, Joey," Derek said loudly. Joey didn't budge.

"Hey!" he yelled louder. Still no response.

"Hey, lover boy. Wake up." Derek nudged Joey's shoulder.

As swift as a stotting gazelle, Joey jumped from the bed, twisted Derek around, and placed him in a choke hold.

"What the hell, Joey!" Derek yelled.

Joey cleared his head, opened his eyes wide in alarm, and quickly released his hold on Derek.

"What are ya doin'? I coulda killed ya! Don't ya know not to sneak up on a guy like that?" Joey yelled.

Derek resisted the urge to strike back.

"Are you positive Benny will be in his house tomorrow morning?" Derek asked.

"Yah. He has a routine. He'll be there."

"Would he suspect anything if you called him, you know, to check in?"

"No. He ain't that smart."

Derek turned his attention back to the conference call. "He says Benny will be there, but what if I have Joey check in with Benny just before we enter?"

"Fred? Does that work for you?" the boss asked.

"Perfect. Thanks. Derek."

"Hey, Fred, did you take care of that thing for me?" Derek asked.

"On the way."

"Thanks, buddy."

"Fred, we're done with Benny. You guys can sign off now," the boss said to Fred, George, and the four others. "Check in with me later."

"Okay, boss, will do. Hey, Derek, I like the new look. What shade of purple is that?" Fred chuckled, then turned serious. "You watch your back."

Derek held back a snappy retort. "You too, Fred, George."

An audible ping signified Fred and George signing off.

"All right," Derek's boss said. "Piscelli is going to be more complicated. Where are we with the disembarking process?"

"The ship will dock at seven thirty in the morning," Derek began. "Normal disembarking begins at ten. We're going to make thirty flyers announcing the availability of early departure at nine and slide them under the doors of thirty cabins, including the Websters'. We'll handpick the rest so as not to include children.

"We think the Websters will bite," Derek continued. "We can only hope they can contact Piscelli and let him know they are getting off the ship earlier than planned. If we can get them off the ship, we can hold the rest of the passengers on board until the operation concludes.

"We'll keep the passengers that take advantage of the early offer at customs so they won't be anywhere near the garage," Derek said. "Once the Websters hand over the package to Piscelli's crooked cop, they will go to customs where our guys will pick them up.

"That's the key," Derek summarized. "We've got to make sure we are in a position to see the exchange. We can't lose sight of that package, and the Websters cannot bring it through customs. The exchange is going to happen quickly once they disembark. The fewer people around, the better our advantage."

"What if they don't bite? What if they wait and disembark with the masses?" his boss asked.

"Then our guys better be ready. Either way, I'll be near the gangway and let you know when they leave the ship," Derek said. "It is the best way to handle it."

"Right. We'll have people dressed as dockhands. They will cover every police vehicle on the dock."

"Good."

"Parking attendants will be our guys, too. I want to know exactly where that bastard is parked. Piscelli will be prepared for anything, so we're not going to take him until he gets to the gate to leave the garage. We can box him in better and hopefully avoid a shootout.

"As far as the son-of-a-bitch cop," his boss continued, "if he leaves first, we let him go and pick him up later. If he sticks around, we grab the prick before he gets to the parking garage gate."

"Someone will have to give me the all-clear when you pick Piscelli up. I won't be able to hold the passengers on board too long. If this thing drags out, it could be a problem."

"Don't let them move until you get the word directly from me," said his boss.

"I won't."

DINNER MINUS DEREK

With an empty chair the stark reminder of how close the eight had grown in a week, a somber mood set the tone for dinner. No matter who sat next to whom, they trusted each other with their lives.

"Has it only been a week?" Lynn asked the question that seemed on everyone's mind. "I feel like I've known all of you for such a long time."

She smiled.

"I know. I feel the same way," Cate said. "It doesn't seem possible."

Each nodded in agreement.

"So much has happened," Holly said. "My life will never be the same." She reached for her dad's hand.

"I'm really going to miss you guys," Bradley murmured.

They went silent.

From two tables away they heard the boisterous voice of Edward saying, "Did I tell you I tripled my money in a year?"

The women and Bradley erupted, breaking the lonely silence.

"Okay, that's it," Doug said, throwing his napkin down on the table. "Why do you ladies keep doing that? What's so funny?"

"Hey, I'm no lady!" Bradley took offense.

Everyone chuckled, and Mike said, "Yes, please tell us what we're missing."

The women looked at Bradley as if to say, *You have the floor.* Bradley explained how they originally thought Derek may have been helping the loudmouth guy run a Ponzi scheme. He went through the whole story as only Bradley could and, when he was done, he said, "How could you guys not notice him? He's been everywhere."

Doug and Mike shrugged shoulders. "I guess we're a little more trusting than the rest of you," Doug said.

"Now that's funny," Lynn choked out.

Not once for the rest of the night did they experience another somber moment. After their final dinner, they spent the remainder of the evening drinking champagne or, in Bradley's case, sparkling cider, and dancing under a nearly full moon. Jack surprised Holly after breaking away from his family obligation to spend the later part of the night with her and her friends. Playing their version of musical chairs, they swapped dance partners midstream, with modified rules that left no one standing alone. Mike found Jenny and her sister-in-law in the crowd and invited them to join the celebration.

When Jenny asked what they were celebrating, Mike answered, "Life. We're celebrating life."

They clinked their glasses.

MUFFINS FOR DEREK

Derek didn't sleep well. Between his nose, hand, and Joey's snoring, he was lucky if he got three hours under his belt. But he would need to be at his best. At six thirty, the ship hadn't yet docked. That gave him time to review the plan to make sure everything was in order.

He heard a light knock on the door.

Derek whispered, "Who is it?" He didn't want to wake Joey.

"It's Cate."

"Cate?" Derek opened the door. Cate stood holding two cups of coffee and two pineapple-macadamia nut muffins.

"It's six thirty in the morning," he said, looking surprised.

"Uh-huh."

"Cate, I can't let you in. Joey's . . ."

"Oh, I know. I brought these for you and him. I knew you wouldn't be able to go out and figured you could use some coffee."

Derek smiled. "And muffins!"

Cate returned the smile. "I'm going to learn how to bake them."

Derek chuckled. "I love you, Cate. Now get out of here. I will see you in a little while when I get this gorilla off my hands."

Derek gave her a quick kiss and shut the door.

"Gorilla, huh?" Joey scowled as he woke up.

"Figure of speech."

"Gimme the joe. Keep the fancy-pants muffin."

THE BALCONY

Mike sat on the balcony with his coffee when Holly woke. The sun peeked over the horizon, and the air had a slight chill. Holly wrapped herself in a blanket and joined her dad. He handed her a cup of coffee, still hot.

"This has been an incredible trip," Mike said. "I've been sitting here for the last few minutes replaying the days over in my head."

He went silent for a moment, and Holly heard him clear his throat. She realized he was choking up.

"Holly," he continued. "I'm so proud of you."

"Thank you, Dad. You were right all along. I just had to give myself a chance. But I'm proud of you too, Dad. I guess it's time we both give ourselves a chance."

"I guess you're right."

NOT A KID ANYMORE

Lynn helped Bradley get dressed, although he found ways to do most of it himself. Pretty soon, Lynn thought solemnly, he wouldn't need her help at all.

Doug packed the bathroom items into the case. He had been practicing his so-called speech since he woke up. It was time.

"Bradley, let's have a talk."

Lynn turned to make herself busy folding, packing, and cleaning.

"Yeah, Dad?"

"I want to apologize for my reaction yesterday. I was wrong to yell at you like that."

"It's okay, Dad."

"No, it's not. Look, I need you to understand something. My first instinct since the time you were born and for the rest of my life is to protect you. That's what I am here for, to protect you and your mother because I love you both so very much."

"I know, Dad. I know that."

"The thing is, you're growing up so fast. I wasn't prepared for that. You're a young man now, Bradley. You're not a child. I understand that now more than ever."

"Thanks, Dad."

"But you're not an adult yet, either. Agreed?"

"Yeah."

"So, you have to help me out here, Bradley. There are certain situations that require an adult, and taking down a mobster certainly qualifies as one of those situations."

"I get it, Dad. I'm sorry. I should have told you sooner. Then we could have done it together."

Doug laughed.

"Well, that's true, son. But I'm guessing your mother would prefer if neither one of us messes with the mob."

"Yes, I would," Lynn confirmed.

"What I'm trying to say is, I'll try to remember that you are not a child anymore if you try to remember that you are not an adult yet. Deal?"

"Deal. Hey, Dad?"

"What, son?"

"How old do you have to be to join the FBI?"

SISTERS

Cate tried to sneak back into the cabin without waking Sheila, but as soon as she opened the door she heard, "Who are you and what have you done with my sister?"

Cate laughed. "Funny, ha."

"Really, Cate. The first time in history you've been awake before me and dressed before me. You even have makeup on before me. What gives?"

"I brought Derek some coffee and muffins."

"Now I'm certain you're in love. And I'm so happy for you."

"Sheila, I've never felt this way about anyone. Did you know, I mean really know when you met . . .?"

Sheila couldn't help but laugh. She did not feel offended. More than anyone, she understood her shortcomings. But something had changed. She could feel it.

"You know, Cate, I think I did feel it when I met David. Maybe not quite like you and Derek, but in my way, I think I did. I just thank God I came to my senses before throwing that away. Or maybe I should thank you."

"Me? Why me?"

"You're my standard, Cate. You are the person I strive to be, although it took me a while to figure out how."

"Oh, my God, no, Sheila. You are *my* standard. I've always tried to emulate you—without much luck, I might add."

The sisters laughed.

"I guess if you put us together, we are the person we want to be," Sheila said.

"Or, if we spend more time together, we may each become that person," Cate responded.

"I would love that so much, Cate. But I don't think I could ever get David to move from Hollywood Hills. He loves it so much."

"Well, I'm not grounded in Sacramento. There are a lot of places I could find work. It's worth exploring anyway."

"What about Derek?"

"Well, if he asks me to move to Boston, then I'll see you at Christmas," Cate joked. "I really don't know. We haven't had a chance to think about a future. I guess I am wide open to whatever may happen."

"That's not a bad place to be, Sis."

EIGHT THIRTY

Derek made the final arrangements with the captain and sent a text to everyone. He hoped, in a small way, it would make things up to his friends.

The text read:

Since I have asked you to stay on board until everyone else has departed, I have found a room for you to wait together. The room is available now, including breakfast and a stimulating view. Bring your luggage. The Empire Deck, Skylight Room. See you all soon.

He checked his gun and slipped on the earpiece and microphone that would allow for private radio communication with the team. It was eight o'clock.

"Okay, Joey, let's go."

Derek led Joey to the *Perth's* security office where the ship's security director met him. Once anchored at the dock and the gangway attached, two federal agents dressed as dock workers would board the ship, go to the security office, and take responsibility for Joey. They planned to keep him there, out of sight, so the Websters didn't spot him.

Derek handed Joey the cellphone he had taken from him the day before.

"Okay, Joey. It's time to call your your boss. Keep it simple."

"Hey, I know what I gotta do."

He dialed his cell phone, since he didn't have the number stored. *Smart*, Derek thought.

The phone rang and rang. Joey's face showed signs of panic. He let it ring six more times before hanging up.

"What the fuck, Joey? What's going on?"

"Wait. Maybe I dialed the wrong number." Joey dialed again. It rang again five times before Benny finally answered.

"Yeah!" Benny yelled into the phone.

"Hey, boss, it's me."

"Goddammit, Joey. I was havin' a good shit on the can. What do you want?"

"I'm just checkin' in, boss. I took care of that thing. You want me to come back now?"

"Yeah, you do that!" Benny slammed the phone.

Derek spoke into his microphone.

"We have confirmation, subject number two is in the house. It's a go."

"Roger. Subject number two is in the house. Will pass it on."

With Joey secured, Derek went to the disembarking gate to scout the area. It would be his first good look at the Port Everglade dock and its layout. The terminal, some forty yards across the paved dockyard, was a straight walk from the bottom of the gangway. Fences on either side of the busy dockyard prevented passengers from leaving without processing through customs. Security staffed booths that guarded each entry and exit point to keep unauthorized persons and vehicles from entering the area. Cranes and forklifts loaded and unloaded crates from commercial trucks. Dock workers scurried to their posts to secure the ship to the dock and move the port's gangway into position. The *Perth*'s crew readied to secure the gangway once it moved into place.

The ship moved slowly and settled in easily beside the dock when Derek heard audibles through his earpiece.

"Derek, do you read?" he heard his boss's voice.

Confused, Derek replied, "Yeah, boss. Where are you?"

"I'm just inside the terminal."

"I didn't expect you to be here. How are things developing so far?"

"On schedule. What about your end?"

"Joey is on ice. No movement on board yet. Everything is in place."

"Keep the line open, No unnecessary communication. I'm out."

Derek had never known his boss to attend a takedown. This highly unusual fact emphasized the importance of the operation, and Derek guessed his boss wanted the ability to adjust the plan without delay if needed to avoid casualties.

He glanced up and over his shoulder toward the Skylight Room, but he saw no one.

SKYLIGHT ROOM

A ship's officer led Cate and Sheila into the Skylight Room after checking their names off a list. He opened the door to the private room and left their large pile of luggage for a ship's officer to keep an eye on. The room reminded them both of Sylvester's on the Panorama Deck where they had gone dancing the second night of their trip. Almost a mirror image, its floor-to-ceiling windows permitted people outside to see in. A bartender stood at a small bar in the corner of the room, and he served them a smile. A skillfully arranged buffet of hot and cold breakfast favorites filled a table next to the bar.

Nearly void of furniture, one round table was set for seven near a window that overlooked the dock. Cate approached and peered down at the main deck. She saw Derek standing near the gangway, looking toward the terminal.

"Sheila, come here. Look."

"A stimulating view," Sheila said, repeating the words from Derek's text. "Well, then, we might as well settle in properly and watch the show."

As Sheila ordered two Bloody Marys, the door opened, and Holly and Mike entered.

"We knew it had to be you two. Even the three Whitmans wouldn't have packed that much luggage," Mike laughed as he teased Cate and Sheila.

"Keep it up, and I won't buy you a Bloody Mary," Sheila joked.

"The drinks have already been taken care of, Miss," the bartender announced.

"I'll give him this. Derek sure knows how to apologize," Mike laughed.

"Two more Bloody Marys," Mike called out.

"Bloody Marys? It's not even nine o'clock," Lynn chuckled as the officer held the door for them to walk through.

"Is it getting that late already?" Doug laughed. "You'd better make it two more of those."

Bradley went to the bar to scope out his options for beverages. The bartender offered to make him a Virgin Pina Colada, and Bradley enthusiastically accepted.

One by one, they noticed the view Derek had alluded to in his text. They lined up at the windows, and Derek saw them side by side the next time he looked up. They each raised a glass to him. He gave them a quick two-finger, if broken-finger, salute before turning his attention back to the deck officer.

NINE IN THE MORNING

The first passengers began gathering at the gangway just before nine o'clock. The Websters were not among them.

Derek had instructed the officer attending the gate to wait for his signal before allowing any passengers to disembark. He had moved into the shadows beside a newly painted iron beam jutting from the floor of the deck and continuing up through the deck above. He had an unobstructed view on both sides and looked left and right in anticipation, although he fully expected the subjects to appear from the right.

"The limo has parked, space C14."

"C14."

Frankie Piscelli had shown up. Now they needed the Websters to take the bait or the operation would prove more difficult.

Derek's watch read 9:08, and he noticed the gathered passengers getting restless. He breathed a quick sigh of relief when he saw the Websters walk from his right toward the gangway. Mr. Webster carried two pieces of luggage. Mrs. Webster held a smaller carry-on bag and cradled a book-sized box in her right arm. The decorated package impersonated a gift suited for a golden anniversary.

Derek gave the signal for the gate to the gangway to open. He spoke the words, "Subjects approaching gangway, package in hand."

Derek waited until they were halfway down the ramp and out of earshot before he spoke again. The Websters had emerged in the middle of a pack of about forty-five people.

"The woman is wearing a white blouse and black skirt and is carrying a gold-wrapped package with a white bow. The man has a brown suit and is carrying two pieces of luggage. They are halfway down the ramp now."

Derek waited.

"I've got them." He heard someone in his ear.

Derek could see three Broward sheriff's police officers on the dock. Two spoke with a handful of dock hands at the far-right side of the fenced-in area. The third officer carried a duty bag and walked toward the *Perth*'s gangway. Derek came out of the shadows and watched as the Websters reached the bottom of the ramp, moved a few paces to their left, and stopped. Mr. Webster knelt as if to tie his shoe.

The policeman with the duty bag approached the Websters. Mr. Webster stood and shook the officer's hand as they smiled and chatted. Mrs. Webster nodded her head and smiled as she gestured broadly at the officer while surreptitiously allowing the package to drop into his duty bag. Waving animatedly to the couple, the officer turned and walked to his police vehicle while the Websters fell in line and headed toward the customs area. To bystanders, the drop drew little attention on the busy dock.

"Did you see that?" Derek asked.

"Affirmative. We got this," the voice replied, also implying that Derek should back off. *My job is done*, Derek concluded.

Rightfully so, Derek told himself.

It was out of his hands. Derek felt helpless as all he could do was watch.

The police car drove out the gate followed by a gasoline truck. Once the official vehicle passed through the gate, Derek noticed a man on a motorcycle fall into the line of exiting vehicles. They turned a corner.

Derek could no longer see them. He could only wait. He looked up at his friends watching from the Skylight Room. He tried to appear confident but found it hard to do so.

He began to pace.

Silence.

Derek tried to imagine what was happening outside his view.

He wondered if Fred and George had begun their raid.

He wondered if the Websters were in custody.

He knew it was too early for them to have taken Frankie.

Still silence.

Then . . .

"The Websters are in custody. Repeat. The Websters are in custody."

Derek recognized the voice of his boss and ceased his pacing.

BACK TO THE SKYLIGHT ROOM

"Did you see that?" Bradley asked. "See the cop at the bottom of the ramp? That woman put a package in his bag."

"I wonder what's in there?" Sheila pondered.

"Probably drugs," Bradley supposed.

"Do you think that's it? Do you think Derek is out of danger now?" Cate asked.

Doug put his arm around her. "He's going to be fine, Cate. He's good at his job. I've seen him in action . . . " he glanced toward Lynn, " . . . a little bit anyway. He knows what he's doing."

"It's not his abilities I'm worried about. It's the mob guys."

"Don't worry, Cate. This place is crawling with feds." Bradley said. "See? There and there and there . . ." Bradley pointed to some of the deck hands below.

"How do you know they're feds, Bradley?" Holly asked.

"Look at their shoes. Not one of them is wearing boots. They must have been in a hurry."

"Well, I'll be damned. You're right," Mike said. "I didn't even notice that."

"There goes the cop. Look. They're following him. Aw, man. I can't see them anymore."

"I need another drink," Cate moaned.

FRANKIE'S TAKEDOWN

The Websters in custody is good news, but they are the least of the problem, Derek thought.

Derek had supposed by now the police officer had reached Frankie. He figured it would take time for the transfer. Frankie would want to inspect the goods while he could still intercept the Websters in case of a problem.

Playing the scenario out in his head, Derek tried to time everything as it would happen. He had to do something. The waiting was killing him.

"BSO is on the move."

Damn, Derek thought. They would have to let the Broward Sheriff's officer go for now. He hoped someone had already informed the authorities of the corrupt cop's identity.

"Ready the gate," he heard through the earpiece.

Here we go, Derek thought. This was it. He wished he could be there in the thick of it.

Forgetting that he had seven people staring down at him he paced the deck. He repeatedly checked his watch. *The limo is slowly making its way down to the first floor*, Derek thought as he pictured Frankie's Mercedes limousine making U-turns at each end of the garage as it descended into the clutches of the Federal Bureau of Investigation.

"Drop the outer door!"

Through the earpiece, Derek heard the screeching of tires.

"FBI, FBI. Drop the weapon."

"Out, everybody out, hands high."

"Now, out."

"Drop it. On your knees."

"Open it. Open the door."

"Don't move. Don't move."

Furious screams intermingled.

"Open the door. Now!"

"Hands behind your head. Now!"

"On your knees."

Nothing. Derek heard nothing for what seemed like minutes.

"Frankie Piscelli is in custody."

Derek heard a series of happy hollers and then stumbled. He didn't realize he had been holding his breath. He drew in some air and let it out slowly as he fell back into the ship's railing.

And then he remembered.

He looked up into the expectant faces staring down at him and gave them a left-hand thumbs up.

He even mustered a smile.

CELEBRATION

Hugging and kissing each other, the Skylight Room broke out into a thunderous cheer, followed by raucous laughter. The investment they felt toward the outcome of Derek's assignment surprised each of them.

The bartender did not know what to make of the sudden outburst, and the officer outside the door checked in to make sure everything was all right.

When Cate saw the officer, she ran to him.

"Can I go see him now?" She assumed the officer knew what had transpired, but he did not.

"I'm sorry, miss. I'm supposed to keep you here until Agent Richards comes for you."

"Oh, okay." She gave the officer a hug. "Thank you," she said. "Yes, Agent Richards."

The puzzled officer closed the door.

"Champagne!" Sheila yelled. She looked at the bartender. "Do you have champagne?"

"Yes, miss."

"Champagne for everyone! Even Bradley!" She looked at his parents. They shook their heads *no*.

"Sparkling cider for Bradley," Sheila yelled, and everyone happily laughed.

JOEY

Derek got the all-clear and gave the signal to allow the passengers to disembark on time, at ten o'clock. At 9:45, the two bureau agents dressed as deck hands brought Joey out to Derek.

"We have a car waiting for you on the dock," Derek said to Joey. "It will take you directly to the airport. You will call me with the combination once you are in the air. Right?"

"Yeah. You gonna keep youse guys' deal?"

"Yes. I'll forget you ever existed. Just one question. How did you know we were on to you? How did you know I would be on this ship?"

"I didn't. I seen Duke watchin' ya from a fishin' boat in St. Thomas. Did some diggin'. Found out who you was. We was gonna call the feds in Florida, let them take Frankie. You made it easy on us. Whaddaya do with Duke?"

"Let me put it this way. I look better than he does."

The agents led Joey down the ramp and to a waiting car.

Derek's phone rang. It was his boss.

"Yes?"

"Just got word. We got Benny. Unfortunately, not as cleanly as we took Frankie. Fred took a bullet, but it's only a flesh wound. He asked me to tell you that you owe him a good bottle of bourbon. What's that all about?"

Derek chuckled.

"Well, you know Fred. He'll take a bullet for a good bottle of bourbon any day."

For the first time, Derek heard his boss laugh.

"Finish up on board and come see me when you're done. I've got an office at customs. And, Derek?"

"Yes, boss?"

"Great work."

"Thank you."

DEPARTURE

REUNION

The officer guarding the Skylight Room opened the door, and Derek walked through. He looked tired. They saw that his face had swollen overnight, and the bandage on his hand had unraveled.

Cate ran to him but stopped short of jumping into his arms when she saw how worn he looked. Instead, she wrapped her arms around his waist and sunk her head into his chest.

"I love you. I love you. I love you." She couldn't help herself.

He lifted her chin and kissed her. "I love you, Cate."

The rest of them clapped and cheered. Sheila got a glass of champagne from the bartender and handed it to Derek. She raised her glass and said, "Cheers to Derek."

"Cheers," they repeated together.

They all drank, except for Derek.

"No," he said. "Cheers to all of you. We couldn't have done it without you."

"Hear, hear!" They drank again.

"Is it done, Derek? Is it finally over?" Cate asked.

"Almost, Cate. A few more details to take care of, and it will be over."

"Is everyone all right? I mean, did it go well?"

"A friend got grazed with a bullet in St. Thomas, but he's going to be fine. He says I need to buy him a good bottle of bourbon."

"Well," Cate said, "at least he's got good taste." She laughed.

"Look," Bradley said. "Everyone's leaving."

They moved to the window to watch hordes of passengers leaving the ship. Then they remembered they, too, would leave soon.

"Hey, Holly. Do we have everyone's contact information?" Mike asked.

They exchanged phone numbers, emails, social media addresses, and, of course, lesser used snail mailing addresses.

"So, what are everyone's travel plans? I'm assuming you're going to let us out of this room sometime today," Doug said pointedly to Derek.

"Yes, I'm sorry," he responded. "We just have some small details to wrap up first. You know, paperwork stuff. Once all the passengers are off, my guys will come aboard, and we'll get to it. Is anyone in danger of missing a flight?"

"We have to be at the airport by three o'clock," Lynn said.

"Our plane leaves at five, so we should be there by two thirty or so," Mike said.

"We booked the red-eye. We don't leave until eleven o'clock tonight." Cate winked at Derek.

The next hour and a half went quickly. They chatted like old friends. No matter the plans they made, they knew the likelihood that they'd ever be together again was small, but they knew their friendship would last forever.

Derek's phone buzzed. He looked at his text message.

Patti sends her rigards. L32-R6-L64-R28

Derek smiled at the misspelling. *Joey may not be a top student, but he certainly isn't stupid.* Derek found himself wishing him and Patti well.

Derek forwarded the message to his boss. Just a few more details, and he could begin to think about his future.

A PICTURE TO REMEMBER

Derek put his hand up to his ear. He heard his boss say, "The passengers are off. They're waiting for you on deck."

"Okay, everyone, It's time. Your luggage is already downstairs. We can go down now."

The moment brought home the reality that the *Perth* cruise had come to an end.

They followed Derek to the elevator that brought them to the main deck near the gangway.

A man stood at the top of the ramp. He held a box big enough to hold a football. The man handed it to Derek, and Derek handed it to Holly.

"Here, Holly, this is for you."

She looked at Derek, confused and hesitant.

He nudged his head, as if to say *go ahead.*

Holly opened it. The box held a Nikon camera, just like the one she had lost.

"Derek, you didn't need to buy me a new camera. It wasn't your fault."

"Yes, Holly. It was my fault. And this isn't a new camera. It's your camera. All the pictures are still on it except the one's we needed to lift from it for security purposes. I stole your camera, Holly. I'm sorry I had to put you through that. I hope you can forgive me."

"My pictures? I didn't lose my pictures?"

She giggled and smiled and gave Derek a hug. "Thank you, Derek. There's nothing to forgive."

"Now that you have your camera back, you may want to get ready to use it," Derek said.

"Wait."

Derek heard the familiar voice. He thought it was in his earpiece, but it came from the area of the gangway.

"Ah, boss, I was just . . ."

"I know what you were just going to do. That's why I'm here," Derek's boss stated.

"Oh, all right. Everyone, this is my boss."

"The name's Harrison. Jim Harrison. Nice to meet all of you."

He walked over to Bradley.

"And you must be Bradley. I've heard a lot about you, young man."

Bradley was awestruck. *The boss of the FBI*, he thought.

Someone handed Jim Harrison a thick envelope.

"Bradley Whitman, on behalf of the Federal Bureau of Investigation, I hereby award you the Outstanding Citizen Award for bravery and duty to your country."

He pulled a framed certificate from the envelope and handed it to Bradley. Holly snapped a photo.

Tears welled in Lynn and Doug's eyes. Bradley was speechless, but Sheila, Cate, and Holly were all over him with congratulatory kisses and hugs.

"Congratulations, Bradley. Well done." Mike shook his hand.

Jim Harrison made the rounds and shook everyone's hands before moving Derek aside.

They saw Derek nodding his head in affirmation.

"Can I just get one more picture with everyone?" Holly asked.

"Of course, young lady. Set up the camera and give it to that gentleman right there. That way you can be in the picture too."

They positioned themselves around Bradley, and the fake dock worker took the picture and returned the camera to Holly.

"Just one more thing," Derek said as he put his hand up to his earpiece. "If you guys wouldn't mind stepping away from the gate a few feet. Over there, about six feet away."

The friends moved in a pack as if they were tied at the waist.

A doorway opened at the end of the deck. Two agents, one on either side, led a man by the arms. The friends couldn't make him out from a distance, but they all recognized his voice.

"My lawyer will have me out in three hours. You're making a big mistake. I know people, big people," the man shouted.

Their jaws almost hit the deck. Using his boisterous voice to try to convince the agents how important he was, Edward, the loudmouth, walked toward them in handcuffs. Shocked, they turned to Derek for answers.

Derek took in their stunned faces and laughed. Then he explained.

"When you told me that crazy story about thinking I was part of a Ponzi scheme, I had to check it out. You were right. This guy has been stealing money from retirees and unsuspecting hard-working people for at least five years. Because of all of you, he's going to jail and won't bankrupt anyone else, ever."

Derek looked at his boss.

"Well, I don't have certificates for the rest of you," Harrison said, "but I hope you will accept my sincere thank you."

Stunned, nobody knew what to say. They just stood there in dead silence.

"Well, this is the first time I've had peace and quiet since I got onboard," Derek laughed.

"Thank you, Mr. Harrison. Thank you," Doug finally spoke.

"Derek, meet me in the terminal as soon as you're done. There's news from St. Thomas."

Derek perked up. "I'll be right there." Harrison walked down the ramp.

"I guess this is it," Mike said.

"Yes," Doug replied.

"Your luggage is at the base of the walkway. Unfortunately, you've still got to go through customs." Derek's expression resembled an apology. "I tried."

They descended the gangway together, gathering at the bottom to retrieve their luggage. Derek picked up a *Perth* duffel bag and his briefcase.

A cellphone rang, and they all instinctively reached for their phones. It was Sheila's. She moved away from the group so as not to disturb them when she answered. It didn't matter. Even the dock hands heard Sheila's high-pitched squeal. Like a young girl readying herself for a round of jump rope, she skipped back to the group.

"That was David. He sent a private plane to pick us up, Cate. You and I are flying back to California in style. It's at the airport in the charter area whenever we are ready. Apparently, it belongs to one of the producers of the movie he is backing."

Cate was not enthusiastic. She hoped to spend more time with Derek. The thought of refusing the private jet entered her mind, but she quickly decided that it would hurt Sheila and David's' feelings if she did.

"I don't know how long I'm going to be, Cate. I don't know how long you're going to be here, either. Most everyone has already gone through customs," Derek said.

"I'll wait for you, Derek, on the other side of the customs area. I'll wait," Cate responded.

Sheila nodded in agreement.

Derek hugged and kissed Lynn and Holly and shook hands with Doug, Bradley, and Mike.

"I don't know how I can thank you. I hope we will meet again. You have become like family to me."

"We will meet again. We have to. I'm going to come see you after I graduate. I'm going to join the FBI," Bradley stated.

"I don't doubt it one bit. Goodbye."

Derek walked away before they could see the tear in his eye.

"Okay, let's do this," Doug said, gathering their bags.

Customs went quickly, as none of them had anything to declare. It also helped that they had just left the presence of an FBI agent.

"What do you say, guys? Share a shuttle to the airport?" Mike asked.

"We're with you," said Doug.

"We're going to wait for Derek," Cate whimpered. "God, I'm going to miss you all so much."

She began to cry.

"This was the most wonderful birthday week I've ever had." Sheila sobbed. "I love you all so much. I will be in touch to make plans to get together again. I promise."

Holly couldn't muster any words. Her throat burned with the anguish she felt over saying farewell. She could do nothing but hug and cry.

Doug, Lynn, Bradley, Mike, and Holly disappeared through the front door of the terminal.

Heartbroken about having to say goodbye to the others, Cate and Sheila held each other. Neither of them could fathom how Cate would be able to say goodbye to Derek.

EPILOGUE

A PICTURE OF PROMISE

"Joey was as good as his word," Harrison said. "There was enough in Benny White's safe to put him away for a very long time. You did great work, Derek, under pressure and on short notice. We'll talk about your position when you get back to Boston."

"Thank you. But I had a lot of help."

"They seem like nice people," Harrison replied. "Especially the young woman."

"Yes, Jim, they are. She is."

Derek found himself choked up.

They spoke for another twenty minutes before Derek exited the customs office.

He found Cate and Sheila waiting for him near the front door of the terminal.

Cate didn't speak. She ran to Derek and held him.

"Well, I guess that's it," he said. He held his duffle bag and briefcase.

"When do you leave for Boston?" Sheila asked.

"Oh, I'm not going back to Boston right away. My boss gave me some time off, a couple of weeks. He said I looked like I needed a rest."

Cate looked up at him. "Where are you going to go?"

He looked deep into her emerald green eyes and said, "I heard California is nice."

ACKNOWLEDGMENTS

To my family and friends who are always there to support me, you are my anchor, there for me when my ship needs grounding, and you are my sails when it's time for me to fly.

To Mary-Ann DeVita Palmieri, who copy edited *A Picture of Pretense*, and Richard Bruno, who proofread it, thank you for taking such diligent care of my characters.

And finally to my editor and publisher, Marcia Gagliardi of Haley's Publishing, your constant encouragement gives me the confidence to challenge myself. I thank you for your expertise and your friendship.

About the Author

You can't always plan where life will take you. That is certainly true for Christine Noyes. Growing up in Shrewsbury, Massachusetts, as a tomboy, she spent her youth building forts, playing sports, and enjoying the perceived innocence of the 1960s.

Not having a clear vision of what her life should be, she went where she was most comfortable, to the kitchen. Beginning her work life as a cook at her grandfather's restaurant at the age of eleven, she spent the next several decades re-inventing herself, becoming an accomplished chef, a sales representative, an entrepreneur, and now a writer and illustrator. She never chose her professions. They chose her.

She married her husband and

Christine Noyes

photo by Paula Francis

soulmate, Al, in 1989. They moved to Orange, Massachusetts, where, after Al's passing, Chris remains today with thirty years of wonderful memories to keep her company.

When not at her keyboard, she can be found in her kitchen: back to her roots and love of cooking.

Colophon

MVB Verdigris is a Garalde text family for the digital age. Inspired by work of sixteenth-century punchcutters Robert Granjon, Hendrik van den Keere, and Pierre Haultin, MVB Verdigris celebrates tradition but is not beholden to it. Created to deliver good typographic color as text, Mark van Bronkhorst's design meets the needs of today's designer using today's paper and press. A full-featured OpenType release with an added titling companion, it's optimized for the latest typesetting technologies too.

Garalde: the word itself sounds antique and arcane to anyone who isn't fresh out of design school, but the sort of typeface it describes is actually quite familiar to all of us. Despite its age—born fairly early in printing's history—the style has fared well. Garaldes are the typefaces of choice for books and other long reading. And so we continue to see text set in old favorites—Garamond, Sabon, and their Venetian predecessor, Bembo. Yet many new books don't feel as handsome and readable as older books printed in the original, metal type. The problem is that digital type revivals are typically facsimiles of their metal predecessors, merely duplicating the letterforms rather than capturing the impression—both physical and emotional—that the typefaces once left on the page.

CPSIA information can be obtained
at www.ICGtesting.com
Printed in the USA
JSHW020232150621
15915JS00004B/18